ID

ALSO FROM SHORT STORY DAY AFRICA
AND NEW INTERNATIONALIST
Water: New Short Fiction from Africa (2016)
Migrations: New Short Fiction from Africa (2017)

ID
IDENTITY
NEW SHORT FICTION FROM AFRICA

SHORT STORY DAY AFRICA

2018

NewInternationalist

ID IDENTITY: New Short Fiction from Africa

Published in 2018 by
New Internationalist Publications Ltd
The Old Music Hall
106-108 Cowley Road
Oxford
OX4 1JE, UK
newint.org

First published in South Africa by Short Story Day Africa in 2018
Registered NPO 123-206
shortstorydayafrica.org

This collection © Short Story Day Africa 2018
The copyright of individual stories remains with their authors.

Edited by Helen Moffett, Nebila Abdulmelik and Otieno Owino
Cover design by Megan Ross based on an image by Nick Mulgrew

Typesetting by New Internationalist

Printed by T J International Limited, Cornwall, UK
who hold environmental accreditation ISO 14001.

MIX
Paper from
responsible sources
FSC® C013056

British Library Cataloguing-in-Publication Data.
A catalogue record for this book is available from the British Library.
Library of Congress Cataloging-in-Publication Data.
A catalog record for this book is available from the Library of Congress.

Print ISBN: 978-1-78026-459-2
Ebook ISBN: 978-1-78026-460-8

CONTENTS

INTRODUCTION

*W*hen planning this anthology, its title playing both on the abbreviation for 'identity' and the psychoanalytic construct of the 'Id' – that deep structure that houses our unconscious desires – we called for "innovative short fiction that explores identity, especially (but not limited to) the themes of gender identity and sexuality... In modern Africa, our identities are too often defined for us and not by us... We hope to see work that seeks to break and redefine the strictures put on our identities, as individuals and as peoples; fiction that looks beyond the boundaries of expectation, into the truest definitions of ourselves."

We were impressed as never before by the multiple ways in which writers from all over the continent responded – by the depth, variety and innovation of their interpretations. From Benin to Ethiopia, from Morocco to South Africa, the stories in this collection reveal uncomfortable and fascinating truths about who we are. We have no doubt the reader will share both the delight and enlightenment we experienced compiling this anthology.

Some figures will perhaps give a sense of the quality between these covers: a team of volunteer readers sifted the hundreds of stories received and came up with a 'long' longlist of forty-odd stories – which had to be reduced to twenty-one. The debates that ensued were long, earnest and sometimes heated, and we still think with regret of those discarded stories, as well as the flashes of excellence and intrigue we saw elsewhere in the submissions. We only wish we had the capacity to send feedback along with rejections; the talent, in and from the continent, into which this project allows a glimpse, is prodigious.

Seen here are a variety of explorations of queer sexuality – an extremely important and necessary creative intervention, given the grim march of homophobia, including in legislative forms, across the African continent. Susan Newham-Blake gives voice to the experience of parenting as a lesbian couple in 'The Things They Said'; Michael Agugom charts the challenges of negotiating biracial and sexually complex identities in a small and watchful Nigerian island community in 'Ibinabo'; and Cherrie Kandie provides a powerful and painful portrayal of the silencing (literally) of lesbian love in urban Nairobi in 'Sew My Mouth'. In 'The House on the Corner', Lester Walbrugh presents a moving interpretation of the perhaps ubiquitous 'gay life in Cape Town' narrative; in 'Plums', Kharys Laue tells of the devastating consequences of a collision between childhood sexual exploration and overt racism; and Innocent Chizaram Ilo provides a delightfully unusual and fantastical account of heartbreak as experienced by a lesbian scarecrow in 'Limbo'. In 'Transubstantiation', Genna Gardini playfully tangles a young woman's Catholic roots, drama-student anxieties and attraction to a more sophisticated friend into a witty and vigorous 'coming of age' story; and Adelola Ojutiku tells of young women resorting to a maternal erotic tradition in 'Taba'.

But writers also tackled thresholds and faultlines in the making and unmaking of identities: in 'Unblooming', Alexis Teyie traces the inclusion and exclusions marked by the onset of menstruation; and in 'This Is What Waking Feels Like', by Alithnayn Abdulkareem, a rape survivor from a comfortable urban family takes a brave step towards connection. Chourouq Nasri presents a haunting account of the claustrophobic life of a single woman professional in a modern Moroccan city in 'Anna', with the protagonist hearkening back to a friendship from her 'lost' years as a student in France. Nadu Ologoudou takes up a similar theme in 'Who We Were There, Who We Are Now', looking at the delicate negotiation of identity, especially in terms of sexuality and independence, when caught between home country and colonial country. And in 'Per Annum', a fast-paced piece of speculative fiction, Mpho Phalwane explores the notion that we root our identity in our memories.

Interestingly, the two stories that chart heteronormative love set their characters' experiences in the framework of madness. Éric Essono Tsimi's 'One Brief Eruption of Madness' is a dark and painfully funny account of the gap between a writer's self-perception and that reflected by the beloved he has won from an apparently mentally afflicted friend. Michelle Angwenyi's lyrical and hallucinatory 'The Geography of Sunflowers' presents love and loss as experiences that both heighten and blur identity.

Harriet Anena explores a different element of sexuality; in 'Waiting', her protagonist experiences an absence of desire that runs counter to the expectations of courtship in Uganda.

Identity is also formed through friendships and family bonds, and in Farai Mudzingwa's delicate and moving 'South of Samora', a young man whose social standing is dependent on where he lives, forms a friendship with an ailing child that forces him to define himself. Likewise, in 'What We Could Have Been', Heran Abate gives us an account of a young woman doggedly pursuing her goal to become a musician against the backdrop of the Ethiopian civil war – while her brother is increasingly defined by the violence of that conflict.

Although, as this shows, the interpretations of the theme were varied, if there is one quality all the stories in this collection have in common, it is their complexity. Interestingly, none of the stories engage with nationalism or ethnic identity. The contributors chose counterpoints to crude and over-determined aspects of identity – to the warmongering seen in the media, to the increasingly simplistic constructs found online, which fuel antisemitism and Islamophobia, and sharpen the teeth of racism and sexism, with lethal results. This collection is a bracing corrective: it celebrates difference, nuance, intimacy and insight.

Once editing (more about this process below) was completed, the debates began all over again. This year, for the first time, we opted for a broad spread of volunteer judges, ably assisted by *The Johannesburg Review of Books*, rendering the evaluation process flatter, more consultative and democratic. The combination of the new scoring system and the extremely high standard of the stories meant that for the first time, we produced a shortlist of nine stories, instead of the usual six.

Although, in terms of critical attention and excellence, the

SSDA anthologies have punched well above their weight since their inception, this platform is indeed only six years old, and the learning curve still slants upwards. The decision to edit the stories and to engage with the authors before judging (this is the second year we have done things in this order) has proven to be invaluable in enabling novice writers and raw talent to compete on an equal footing with their more established and experienced peers. The final stories and indeed the shortlisted stories are more evenly balanced between those already making their mark in terms of publication and awards, and extremely talented writers who are new to the adventure of publishing or only just venturing into the terrain of short fiction.

Although it was a close-run thing, democracy worked smoothly (not something to be taken for granted) in throwing up Tochukwu Emmanuel Okafor's 'All Our Lives' as the clear winner. We have published this gifted writer before, and were enchanted by his wry, clear-eyed, humorous and characteristically compassionate account of the identity (multiple identities, in fact) of a much-maligned community – young and disaffected men who drift into Nigerian cities in pursuit of a 'better life'. Two stories – 'The Piano Player' and 'God Skin', by Agazit Abate and Michael Yee respectively – tied as runners-up. The former is a brilliant inversion of the 'African abroad' narrative as it presents snapshots of life in Addis Ababa through the eyes and ears of a pianist in a luxury hotel bar. 'God Skin' weaves together alienation, forbidden love and intimate violence against a subtle backdrop of the scars of Liberia's civil war in 'God Skin'. We heartily congratulate these worthy winners.

A final word about the SSDA Editing Mentorship programme, now in its second year; not only do we offer intensive editing to the contributors, we also use the platform to provide mentoring and training to young editors or would-be editors. The hope is to strengthen and enrich African publishing structures, which, while lively, energetic and far-sighted, face significant financial, geopolitical and practical challenges. It is not enough to support

African writers; those who edit and publish them also deserve attention. This year's Editing Fellows were Kenya's Otieno Owino and Ethiopia's Nebila Abdulmelik; it was a pleasure and a privilege to work with and learn from them. I thank them for their cheerfulness and conscientious application as we worked thousands of miles apart, negotiating day jobs, travel, and interrupted internet connections.

Be prepared for amazement and insight as you read on.

Helen Moffett
Editing Mentor

All Our Lives

Tochukwu Emmanuel Okafor

$\mathcal{W}$e are city people. We live in wooden shacks alongside lagoons that smell of decaying fish and shit. We live in rented apartments with flush toilets and airy bedrooms. We live under bridges, with torn tarpaulins to cover us, feet pounding and vehicles speeding above our heads. The air in this city is rancid with sweat, gas flares, and sun-warmed garbage. Some of us live in face-me-I-face-yous. We are tired of the daily bickering with our neighbours. Of the lack of privacy. Of infections contracted from pit latrines. We wish we had our own homes. Homes full of servants and pets, with pretty gardens, and fences to shield us from the foulness of this city.

We are Chikamneleanya, Ogheneakporobo, Abdulrasheed, Olarenwaju, Alamieyeseigha, Tamunodiepriye, Onuekwuchema, Toritsemugbone, or Oritshetimeyin. We are twenty-five, twenty-six, twenty-seven years old. We are from the North, South, South-east. Some of us do not know where we come from. We are tall, plump, lanky, short. We speak Igbo, Yoruba, Kalabari, Hausa, Itshekiri, Ijaw, pidgin English, or a mix of them all. We are Catholics, Pentecostals, Muslims, Adventists. We do not believe in any god. We are single, we have wives and children that we have left behind in our villages. We come from families of five, eight, ten. Or we come from polygamous homes. Or we do not know if we have families at all. We like to eat akpu and ofe ogbonno, eba and gbegiri, amala, tuwo, beans, rice. We do not eat salad or chicken or pizza because they are expensive.

Each morning before leaving for our workplaces and each evening before bedtime, we gaze into the mirror and touch our faces, thinking of ourselves as ugly, pimply, handsome, beautiful. Our noses are like those of our ancestors – bulbous, pinched in the corners, fat, aquiline, straight, or scarred. We braid our hair into dreadlocks or in neat cornrows, or we leave our hair to grow into afros. We are bald. We crop our hair low, or our hair is unkempt, tufts of foam with lice nesting in them. We are black. We are not black. We bleach our skin. We refuse to bleach our skin since we toil under the sun – we do not want the heat to scald us, leaving patches of red here and streaks of black there.

We are newspaper vendors, taxi drivers, waiters, housekeepers. In this city where the buildings breathe into each other, and the power lines are thin black criss-crosses in the skies, we hustle, threading our paths in a busy crowd. We look for customers. Some days, when we make good sales, we are happy. We buy drinks. We invite our friends to join us. We eat salad, chicken, or pizza. We thank God in many languages. Other days, we endure insults from customers. We curse the day we were born. We do not thank God. We survive for long stretches without food. We fold our arms and watch the government take down trees to erect mega city halls. Yet we have no proper homes. We have no light. We have no water.

At four, five, six, we were running naked around the dusty grounds of our villages. We attended schools that had no blackboards or desks or libraries. We never went to school. The lucky ones among us were taken away to live with a rich uncle or an oga and madam, who turned us into slaves and made us sell wares on the street. We raced each other to see who was the fastest. We shot down birds with our catapults and planted traps for antelope. Later, we presented the game to our mothers who praised us and then carried it into their kitchens, to cook meat soup. We sat around small fires, opening our mouths to chew the scents escaping our mothers' pots, hearing our bellies groan as we swallowed. We told one another stories. We were happy, comfortable. We were enough.

At fifteen, sixteen, seventeen, we were chasing girls. We attacked them at streams, or in dark corners where they gathered in fours and fives to gossip. We squeezed their breasts and ran away. They pursued us, hurling curses at our grandfathers and great-grandfathers. At home, we refused to wash the hands that had touched them. We smelled our palms and imagined things. By night, we played with our manhoods with those hands, shutting our eyes tight. Not once, not twice, our mothers caught us. They laughed and said: Obere nwoke. Keremin mutum. Small man. *You don't even know how to catch a woman.* But we knew we were champions. After all, there were other boys who shied away from girls, who had never come close enough to touch a breast. We were different. We were men. We knew how to hunt, farm, fight, kill, grab breasts. The girls enjoyed it, but they pretended not to. They strutted around the place, ululating praises to their gods as their feet slap-slapped past us, thanking them for the gift of sun, rain, and future responsible husbands. We knew they would be ours one day, or not. Or we knew better, classier women awaited us in the depths beyond our villages.

At nineteen, twenty, twenty-one, this was how we dreamt. We found ourselves walking down an expanse of gold-carpeted road. On both sides of the road, trees climbed into the skies. They bore bananas, apples, mangoes, avocados, all the fruits we could imagine. As we walked down the road, animals – monkeys, goats, tortoises, rabbits, lions – bowed, waving at us after we had stepped further away. At the end of the road, a neem tree whistled, twisting towards us. Its branches swayed in the breeze, and it lowered itself before us, urging us to climb its trunk. We obeyed. We held on tight. The neem tree straightened and grew and grew. Eventually we climbed off onto the clouds. We shielded our eyes; it was bright all around. A gate creaked open. We saw people lying flat on their bellies, singing, *All Hail the King*. We marched on their bare backs and walked on into glass mansions that were ours and ours alone. House servants fell on their knees, welcoming us. We walked past great fleets of cars, past gardens square and verdant, past pools clearer than the skies, and on into enormous palaces. We sat on thrones. In this dream, we owned the city. We owned the people. We owned power.

At twenty, twenty-one, twenty-two, we were leaving our homes in the villages. Our mothers cried their hearts out. They said, *Who will bury us when we leave this world?*

Us, we answered.

Who will take care of us when we are old, guiding our paths when our eyes grow tired?

We kept silent.

Who will look after the wives and children you have left behind?

Silence.

Who will marry our girls?

No reply.

When will you return?

When we are rich and famous and own people and power, we said.

Fools, they called us. *You cannot even weed your fathers' farms properly. What makes you think you will make it in the city? The city is full of night women who will steal your senses. The city will devour you.*

Still, we packed our few clothes, wrapped them in raffia baskets, wide linen wrappers, polythene bags. We left. Our mothers cried. Our fathers gazed into the night.

We are now city people. We can be Matt, Jason, Alex, Garth, Arthur. We can be twenty, twenty-one, twenty-two. We can come from London, New York, Paris, or any other exotic place our fingers can never locate on a map. We can be tall, athletic, broad, sinewy, thick. Our hair is auburn, rooty blond, steel grey. We can speak American English, garnishing our sentences with "wanna" and "gonna"; flecks of "fuck," "holy fuck," "shit," "damn" or "nigger". We act like we own stretches and stretches of land, stately homes, estates, penthouses. We say we are cousins to the President of the United States, grandsons of the Queen of England, close friends with the Prime Minister of France. We carry ourselves like people who don't shit.

This is the year the internet arrives in our city.

The cybercafés are our second homes. They are tight spaces on ground floors in one- or two-storey buildings. Because the government never provides us with regular power, you can hear generators, chained outside to metal rails to stave off thieving boys, bleating into the day and night. All night, mosquitoes sing into our ears, their songs louder than the clacks of our fingers on the keyboards. We rub insect repellent onto ourselves until our skin is waxen.

By night, the internet is so fast that the drowsiness in our eyes flees. We download photos from websites we cannot recall. A wiry-built white man baring his chest. An African-American, grinning, his hair tousled, both ears studded in a full semi-circle. Hunks. Perfect jaws. Perfect cheekbones. Glorious bodies. By night, we glow in these bodies that are not our own.

Do not think we are searching for love. Love does not exist in this city. We are men of the night. Our reward is money.

In the beginning, we fill in lengthy forms on dating sites. We keep a note of the sites we have signed up for: Matchmake.org. CupidHearts.net. DateMe.com. We begin with our sisters who live in the more comfortable African cities: Johannesburg, Cape Town, Douala, Windhoek, Accra. They are foolish, these sisters. See how they bare their breasts on screen, as though they are a thing for sale, raw meat displayed at a marketplace, flies and dust licking at them. *Whores*, we call them. *Darlings*, they call us.

Will you take us to America? they ask.

Yeah, baby, we say.

Do we get to fly first class?

Yeah, baby. And you're gonna roll in my jet and watch the world beneath you fade to nothing.

Darling, you are so sweet, you make me wet.

Yeah, baby. You are sweeter.

The sisters loyal to their families ask if they can bring along sick parents and younger siblings who have been sent off as apprentices. They ask if they can bring their favourite aunts and uncles. *Do they make masala chai in Texas? Can a decent meal of bobotie be bought in the streets of London? Baby, I hear there are tall tall buildings and many Rocky Mountains and the weather is always freezing cold in Canada, will there be gardens at least to plant ukazi?* We tell them, *Yes, yes, yes.*

It is upon their eagerness that we feed. But this eagerness dies all too quickly when we ask them to send money.

Darling, they say, *you are rich. What do you need my money for?*

Baby, we begin, *issues with the bank. The fucking account is frozen.*

And this is how we watch them delete us from their lives. Sometimes, they ignore our online presence. Other times, they ask, *Baby, have you sorted out the problem with your bank account?* We do not reply. We pay heavily for the internet. Time is a luxury. We cannot waste it on them.

The city is a fat, dark aunt with a tight-lipped smile, who embraces her prodigal sons. Yet, she cares little for them. She churns and churns us until we are millet chaff that the strong breeze sloughs off. And we drift deeper and deeper into the pitch-dark corners of her home. We lose our jobs. We lose the shelters where we once lived. We roam the streets.

By day, we climb into molues – those rickety peeling buses, whose insides smell of all things foul and rotten, compressing us, sticks in a matchbox. We pick pockets. Sometimes, we are lucky. We swindle fine leather wallets and purses, and, in them, wads and wads of crisp notes. We celebrate festive seasons like everyone else in this city, with chickens and beer and cheap, russet-haired women we coax off the streets. Other times, we are unlucky. Some of us get caught, dragged off the molues, and beaten with clubs and machetes, until our bodies are bloodied canvasses. Some of us have our fingers chopped off. Some of us sleep in tight cells where older inmates sink cigarette ends into our bare backs. We scream and scream. The city does not hear us.

We return to the internet, to our second homes. Now we

choose to be women online. Black women flaunting bodies with an oily sheen. We visit websites that we cannot recall, downloading photos of the women we are pretending to be. At first, we are shocked by what we have become – our sisters, who have cast aside the dignity of their bodies. Now we are them, parading our *assets*, toying with ourselves, laughing in our borrowed nakedness. Still, we glower. We wonder if there are still good girls we can marry and take home to our dream mansions. In our hearts, we are angry with our sisters for their cheapness. We hope they come back to themselves from this place in which they are lost. But who says we are not lost too?

In our stolen bodies, we create new profiles on new dating sites. The sites seem to multiply every day as though they are birthing children and grandchildren who can no longer recognise their ancestry. Each one struggles to outperform the other with its new features: voice chat, live cam, a "viewed profile" check-box, location filtering, custom avatars. We meet men who are gullible enough to buy anything – a bra, a necklace, a handbag – if we tell them it has touched our skin.

Perverts, we call them. Old white men, with streaks of greying hair and lined skin. We detest them, but they promise us the whole of the States. First, they send postcards. We never look at them. Then they send pictures of their burly selves in thickly wooded hills. *Me going camping, hun*, the handwritten caption says. Then they send half-naked pictures of themselves, beer in hand, sitting on a patio. A patio we long to sit on, breathing in American air and watching cars and flimsily dressed skinny white women amble by, white wafers from the skies landing and melting down our parched throats. We tell these old men that we wish to come to the States, to Paris, to London. We beg them. We say we will be their slaves. We say we will let them have us any way they know how to. We say we are dying to bring their children into the world.

They send money. Chunks of foreign currencies. We rush to the banks, smiling. We convert the money into our local currency. We feast. We jam the city with loud music. We close off streets, invite the world to our celebrations and have the best of young women. Sometimes we remember home. We send money and gifts, imagining our mothers dancing around the villages, eulogising us, our fathers gazing skyward, thanking their gods for the generous blessings. The foreigners ask if we have received the money. We don't answer. We shut down our accounts on the dating sites and set up new ones elsewhere.

Or.

Some of us are unlucky; they do not send money. They say they are going through a divorce and are heavily in debt. They curse their ex-wives. They tell us to get a loan from a bank or a family member. They promise to pay back the loan when we arrive in their foreign lands. When we tell them that we are incapable of obtaining loans, they rail at us. They threaten to stop loving us. Soon our chats dwindle, and we become strangers. We part ways.

We are tired of our fake lives. We are bored. We become ourselves again, or we become partly ourselves, or we give up on cyberlove for a while. We take pictures of slums and send them to foreign organisations, and foreign men and women to whom we profess our love. We beg for their pity. We say we are poor Africans who sniff glue, or poor Africans who exhume freshly buried people and roast their flesh for food, or poor Africans fleeing tribal wars.

Or we do not say we are poor Africans. We act like normal people who wish to love and be loved. We are humans, after all. Our own needs are valid, too. We send pictures that show us garbed in our Sunday best – in clothes that are tailored from kaftan, brocade, kente or akwa-oche. We long to marry our online dates, to be absorbed into another world so different from this city, but we cannot afford to cross the city's border. We do anything to get our lovers to send money. We take nude photos of ourselves. We film scenes of self-pleasuring. We record ourselves dancing naked. They get excited. They mail us tickets. We leave, or we do not leave.

Some of us encounter a different kind of love, and the city

tries to lynch us. A cybercafé manager has caught us visiting sites where men seek love from their fellow men. Men kissing men, one sucking the other's manhood, each taking turns to ply themselves from behind. At first, we are disgusted. Our minds scream abomination. We wonder how a man can find joy in another man's body. How unnatural it is that the love between them is consummated through the small hole where shit exits the body. We don't understand this kind of love. We are confused when our bodies begin to respond to such passions, longing to be explored by men. We imagine men's lips crushing against ours. We imagine being held at night. We yearn for this different kind of love.

But the city is spitting us out. It has had enough of us. The police want to take us off to cells that smell of shit and never see daylight. The people are burning our homes and demanding our heads. We are fleeing. We are placeless. The city no longer recognises us. The skies burst open, drenching the littleness that is left of us. We leave our dreams behind. We cross the city's border. We take up new lives.

The Piano Player

Agazit Abate

*D*on't walk too fast. Look straight ahead. Nobody is watching you. Nod to the waiter who doesn't know your name. Focus on the destination. Think about the routine. No eye contact with any of the guests. When you start playing, the music will be a surprise if they hear it. You're almost there. Two more steps. Now, take your seat.

Fifteen people in the lobby today. I saw shadows, of course, not actual faces. To see their faces, I would have to look at them. I see silhouettes, the safest way to view people. More will come, some will leave. Fifteen people is good for a Monday night. For the hotel, not for me. It doesn't matter to me how many people show up. Seven songs before the break and seven songs after. It's always the same. Well, no, that's not true. Sometimes it's eight songs before, six after. Five songs before, seven songs after, six songs before, and five songs after.

It's easy to change your routine when nobody is paying attention. The waiters and waitresses are too busy thinking about their tips and how much of their service charge management will take from their pay. Management is focused on the number of people in the lobby, who's ordering food and who's ordering tea, who's here to eat and who's here for the WiFi. Mostly, they're all thinking about the guests in the hotel who give them extra money and how to service their needs. If they ever ask me about the arrangements of the songs or the timing of my break, I'll tell them that I test the energy of the crowd. It's a lie, of course. I am facing a wall; the room could be filled with people and I wouldn't know. Besides, I have never been able to feel an audience's energy. Audience, in this respect, is used loosely; nobody comes to this hotel for the piano player. They won't ask because they'll never notice, but if they do, I can tell them that there are times when people need to hear tizita and other times when they need 'Banana Boat'. I'll also tell them that some songs are longer than others, which is true.

Breathe in, G sharp, C sharp, E, G sharp, C sharp, E, G sharp, C sharp, E, G sharp, C sharp, E, breathe out, G sharp, C sharp, E, G sharp, C sharp, E, G sharp, C sharp, E, G sharp, C sharp, E. A girl I knew in primary school used to bite her fingernails. Lots of kids bite their fingernails, but her biting was more pronounced; she bit her nails with the urgency of an acute habit driven by severe anxiety. In class, she tapped her right heel on the ground so fast and for such an extended period of time that if I looked at it for too long, I would get dizzy. I could relate to her, even before I began counting the keys to control my breath.

I wonder what it feels like to be someone whose breathing is automatic. Doctor Tesfaye says that my airways are chronically inflamed, which at times makes it hard for me to breathe. Three hundred million people on this earth have asthma. Quarter of a million people die from asthma every year, mostly from the developing world, all preventable deaths. That's what it says on Wikipedia. I'm not scared of dying, and my asthma isn't as bad as it used to be. Still I think it's good to know how many people on this earth have died of the same affliction that ails me. Of course, this is only the official number. I'm sure many more people have lost their breath without a proper diagnosis. I wonder what the world would be like if everybody was forced to pay attention to their breath. Sometimes I think that there's nothing wrong with my lungs. Sometimes I think that it's perfectly natural, at times, to lose your breath.

I stopped breathing when Ayne left to go to America with her family. Eleven is a hard age for a girl to lose her best friend. "I'll write you every Sunday so I can tell you what happened during the week," she said to me the day she left. I told her that I would write her every Monday to tell her what I hoped would happen during the week. I begged Gash Gezahegn and Eteye Maaza to stay. I told them that we would be good and get good grades and always come home right after school. They didn't say anything. Eteye Maaza grabbed me, kissed my forehead, and told me to go play outside with Ayne. I was so upset, I told Ayne that it wasn't fair, and then I called Gash Gezahegn a fascist. It was a word that I heard our neighbour Fasil use. I didn't know what it meant, but he was speaking about Mengistu, so I knew it was an insult. Gash Gezahegn heard me and started laughing. He told Eteye Maaza, "In this country, everybody is a fascist except for the fascists."

We began writing to each other right away. Our parents wouldn't let us send a letter every week, so we would send four letters at once at the end of each month. In Ayne's first letter to me, she told me about the day she arrived in Dallas, Texas. She said that it was cold, that the streets were big, and that all of the cars drove in straight lines. She said people only honked if something was wrong, and things were very rarely wrong. She wrote about all the family members she had met for the first time. She was in awe of her cool older cousin Nardos, who had a nose ring, big curly hair, and wore black lipstick. She had told Ayne, "When you turn eighteen, I'll take you to get your nose pierced." She said that Nardos's said it out loud, like it wasn't a secret. Ayne thought it should have been whispered, since Gash Gezahegn was in the next room. She lived with Nardos' family for a few months until they got their own two-bedroom apartment, where she shared a room with her brother. They slept in what she called bunk beds. She was on the bottom and he was on the top. I was probably as nervous for her first day of school as she was. Luckily, it was painless, and she made friends right away. A girl named Julie asked her if she wanted to sit next to her at lunch. She became friends with her and her friends.

I was happy for Ayne, but missed her deeply. My stories to her always felt less interesting; everything was new in her life, everything had remained the same in mine. I told her about all the kids at school who asked about her. I told her that Mahelet said that she would probably forget Amharic, and if she came back, she wouldn't be able to communicate with us. I told Mahelet that she was wrong, that Ayne could never forget Amharic. I wrote about Dawit kissing me on the lips in the yard in front of our home. How it was wet, and how I thought that people were making a mistake by kissing on the lips. How I thought that we should just stick to kissing on the cheeks. I told her about the first time I played the piano, and how Wezero Etaynesh played like an angel. I told her that I didn't think that I could be good at it, but that I wanted to try. Our letters went from once every week to once every month, to every few months, until they stopped completely. Five years after she left, we stopped writing to each other.

Ayne is my Facebook friend now. She is married with two kids and lives in Houston, Texas. It's not obvious from her posts what she does for work, but her husband is black American, their kids are smart, funny and well-behaved, and she has tena adam, along with red and white flowers growing on her patio. From my Facebook posts, you can tell that I play the piano and that I once went to Abu Dhabi to perform in a concert. Sometimes I think that I got my first asthma attack the moment that Ayne's plane took off.

"Hello, my name is Simon. The waiter told me about you?"
    "Yes, I know."
  "Can I get you a drink?"
  "Coca-Cola, please."
  "Oh OK, ummm, two Cokes please."

"Two Coca-Cola, yes."

"So, it's my first time here in Addis Ababa. It's an interesting country."

"When did you come here?"

"I've been here three days."

"You like it?"

"I work in finance, I never thought I would come here. But really, you know, Africa is so underrated. I mean, this city will be completely different in five years. So many Chinese, though. The Chinese know how to invest. They don't bother with the details; they pay attention to the big picture. But we have our eyes on this country, too. We're gonna put some money into this economy. The Chinese have a head start, but they open the door and we come in too, you know what I mean? I mean, we want to do some good here, help the country out of poverty. It's a win–win situation, you know what I mean?"

"Yes, I know."

"Crazy, all this construction, but so much poverty. There is poverty in America too, in, you know, the ghetto. You know, the Coke here is sweeter than the Coke back home."

"It's sweeter in America, no?"

"No no, the Coke is definitely sweeter here."

"It tastes good with red wine."

"With wine? I've never heard of that. Excuse me, can I have a glass of red wine?"

"Yes, sir."

"Don't fill it too high. I'm gonna put some Coke in it!"

"Yes."

"Hmmm, interesting. It's like carbonated wine. It's not bad, really sweet, though. Drink some."

"No, thank you."

"Come on, you have to try it. You made me drink it."

"OK."

"Hey! That's Celine Dion!"

"Yes?"

"The piano player is playing Celine Dion! You guys know Celine Dion here?"

"Yes, she is very popular."

"Amazing. Celine Dion in Africa. They put me up in a nice hotel!"

"Yes."

"I'm on the fourth floor, really nice view. I mean it's all construction, but it's cool. I mean, it's like I'll be able to say that I was here when the change happened. You know? This country is just beginning."

"Fourth floor?"

"Yeah, really nice view."

"You are ready?"

"Yeah yeah, I'm ready. Let's go."

Not tonight. It doesn't feel right tonight. But one night, soon, I will play it. If nothing happens, then that means I can do anything here and still have a job the next day, as long as I show up and play. Also, it means that nobody is paying attention to the music. I think people will hear it, but it will be so quick that it will mean nothing. The funeral march for ten seconds, and then back to the regular schedule of songs. I won't be able to see them and they will only have a view of my back. I'll reveal nothing in my body language. If there is no eye contact confirming that it happened, then you can't be sure that it happened.

Maybe I'll compose my own funeral march. How can I create a song from the cries of hazen using piano keys? Maybe I should do some research. Meseret's brother died yesterday. I was going to visit them anyway. I'll go tomorrow and I'll pay close attention to the sounds. Maybe I'll record them on my phone. I can listen to it when I get home for inspiration. Would that be morbid? Yes, of course it would be. But I'm an artist. I'm supposed to do strange things. Lady Gaga wore a dress made of meat to an award show. Of course, that's in America and they do those kinds of things there. It doesn't have to be morbid. Gash Mulatu went to the south to study the music of some of the people there. He called them "scientists in sound", and compared them to Debussy and Charlie Parker because they play diminished scales and create their own version of jazz. He wasn't researching the sounds of hazen, but still he did research, just as I would do research.

Yes, I'll compose an original Ethiopian funeral march. It won't be used at funerals because nobody hires a piano player for funerals here. Maybe that can change, like everything else is changing. The rich are always looking for ways that they can be different. If death is the great equaliser, their resistance can certainly create hierarchies of mourning. I could compose a death song for high-class funerals in Addis. An elegy for the rich. I'll test it out in this lobby. I won't do it the same way that I would have done the funeral march. I'll play the full song and then take a break. I'll walk to the break room the same way that I always walk to the break room, straight lines and no eye contact. But I'll try to check the pulse of the people, the vibrations of their energy. I wonder if people will feel fear or know to cry.

∽

"Look at that table. Three of them, and they haven't talked to each other in the past fifteen minutes."

"You've been watching them for fifteen minutes?"

"They haven't looked up from their phones. What's the point of even being here together?"

"WiFi."

"Look at her. How much closer can her face be to the phone before her glasses touch the screen? Look at her posture. It's not good for her back."

"Abiye, these are the times that we live in. This is what people do."

"We are supposed to socialise. They are going against nature. When you are alone, you must commit to being alone. When you choose to be around people, you should be present with those people. They came here together; they should follow through on the plan to be together. It's a big problem. Young people today are never genuinely social, and they are never truly alone."

"Eshi Abiye, so, where are they?"

"They don't even know where they are, how can I know?"

"Abiye, I mean the stories. Tell me about the stories."

"Yes, yes. I didn't bring anything with me, but as I told you over the phone, I've been writing for years now. I am in my eighties, you know. I don't want to forget anything. I'm telling you this because you are the one who appreciates stories in our family. You know, I always thought that you would be a writer. It's not too late."

"You are right, it's not too late."

"Even today is not promised. You must start immediately."

"Eshi Abiye."

"I've written down all of my memories. Your grandfather and grandmother's stories about the Italians. The poison in the river, weapons in coffins, the woman who invited five Italians to dinner and how their friends spent the following weeks looking for them in vain. I tried to write it the way that I heard it. The way the woman spent the previous day preparing a feast. They said that she was tall, teyem, beautiful and wore dresses with a thin belt around her waist. I wrote about your father, and how he used to imitate John Wayne before he became a socialist. The day Alem's father gave me permission to marry her, and the way Robel looked when he was first born. I wrote about our neighbours. Wezero Alganesh and the time she tried to take her husband to court for selling her gold necklace. It's all there, and I'm still writing."

"I didn't know you were writing, Abiye."

"Yes, I've been remembering all my life, I've been writing for three years now."

"My father used to imitate John Wayne?"

"He went to Cinema Empire to watch *Stagecoach* at least five times."

"Tell me more."

"It's all there, written down. Ask me questions after you read it."

"When can I read it?"

"I need your help organising it and typing it on a computer."

"You want to publish it?"

"I want it to be complete and saved. I want one printed copy for myself and one copy for each person in our family."

"It will be a treasure for us."

"It is the story of our lives. It is your inheritance…"

"Abiye, what did the woman do to the Italians?"

"You will read everything I know soon."

"But what happened to her?"

"She lived. She had nine children and died at ninety-six years old, a face full of history and perfect posture. You will read it all… You know, it really is bad for their backs. They are destroying their bodies, for the sake of what? Why does the phone demand that level of concentration? Look at that piano player. She has to sit straight in order to play. Good posture is important."

"You are right."

"I asked you to meet me here because I wanted to speak with you in private. But your aunt knows everything. She helped me remember. Next time we will meet at my house."

"Tomorrow?"

"Yes, tomorrow."

*W*alking to my seat has always been my favourite part of the performance. Still, I am anxious in those moments. I'm the most at ease on the chair, playing. My second favourite part is walking away.

The first time that I played here facing the audience, I thought that I would quit. I love playing, but I hated playing to them. Perhaps the most forceful I have ever been in my life is the day that I asked the manager to move the piano so that it faced the wall. I told him that it would be more intimate for the hotel guests, live music without the expectation of having to pay attention to the performer. He agreed immediately, and had two of the waiters move the piano. It was fast and easy, the piano was on wheels. I would like to think that he agreed because he knew that I was good, and wanted to appease me. But, most likely, it's because managing the piano entertainment is such a small part of his job that he didn't care enough to argue about it. Either way, I get to play free from their eyes and compulsory stares.

"What song is that?"
"The one the piano player is playing?"
"I know that song. What is it?"
"I don't know. I don't recognise it."
"I hate this feeling. I know this song. I wish there was a way to Google an audio recording."
"I think there is a way to do that."
"How?"
"I don't know, Google it."
"Are you almost finished?"
"Yeah, I just wrote the last line. 'With inspiration like this, the Kerkasa Collective is sure to draw long lines at next week's art exhibit.' I'm sending it now."
"Gobez. This is going to make me crazy. I know this song."
"Close your eyes and it will come to you."

When Nina says that the sun is coming, I believe her. When I play it, I believe me.

"Beniyam and Meski are getting a divorce."
"What? I don't believe it."
"Meski told me herself."
"They just got married. It hasn't even been a year."
"I know. I thought that she was going to tell me that she was pregnant."
"What happened?"
"She said that they are too different, that he drinks, and that she doesn't like his friends."

"She didn't know all of this before?"

"She said that she hoped that he would change once they got married."

"Hope."

"She was so upset. I feel so bad for her."

"Is she sure?"

"She said, enquan shimagele, danyam aymelesewom."

"She must not love him."

"I'm going to see her tomorrow. Let's go together."

"OK. What did Gash Berhane and Adiye say?"

"I don't know. I didn't ask her, and she didn't say. I'm sure they're upset."

"I can't believe it."

"I know. Life doesn't always work out the way we plan. After I saw her, Eleni called me to tell me about Henok."

"How is Henok? I keep forgetting to ask you."

"He's OK. The house is gone."

"When?"

"Last week. I don't think that he believed that it would be demolished until they gave notice the day before. Even then, not until the trucks came in. He took down most of the tin to sell and put all of their things in plastic bags. They're living with my uncle now."

"What are they going to do?"

"I don't know. He's trying to get a second job. His wife is saying she wants to go to an Arab country. Her sister is in Jeddah. When he told me the story, he said it in a whisper, like it was too heavy to speak out loud. We told him not to build there, but he was hoping it would work out. He thought it was his only chance of having a place of his own. Now he says that this world has no room for poor people."

"He's right. Hope is dangerous."

"They say hope is the currency of poverty."

"Who says that?"

"I don't know, but I've heard it before."

"What about Meski?"

"There are different kinds of poverties."

"I can't believe they're getting a divorce."

"It was a big wedding."

"It was a very big wedding."

*I*said it out loud and made it appear. That's what Emaye said. She said that when I called its name, I invited it into the house. Instead of saying its name, she said I should have said that I think I saw my in-laws. Calling it an in-law would have made it stay away. I'm sure that the rat was in the house when I said rat, because I heard it and that's why I said rat. It's hard though, to compete with my mothers' logic.

"*L*et's hold hands under the table like forbidden lovers."

"We've been married for six years."

"Let's do it anyway."

*W*hat would I call into existence if I had that power? Tiramisu? Enrico's millefoni. I wouldn't have to go to Piassa in the morning or wait in line. I could just say "Enrico's millefoni" and it would appear. It's almost too good to imagine. Enrico's millefoni anytime I want. I wonder if I would get tired of it. I would probably get tired of it. Human beings have no loyalty. Kebe cake. I really love Kebe cake. The crème tastes just like Enrico's. I heard that the person who owns Kebe used to work for Enrico's. My mother's dufo dabo. I could never get tired of my mother's dufo dabo. It would be strange, though, to get the dabo without my mother giving it to me. A bowl of the seeds of cardamom. Actually, the pods of cardamom. I enjoy opening them myself. Maybe calling out good pods of cardamom. Too many times, the seeds are dry and brown, not black, sticky and sweet as they should be. Sometimes the pods are even empty.

*A*yne? But I would only do that if she could come back as a seven-year-old and if I could also be seven years old again. We could play akukulu and make predictions about the moon. *What will the moon say tonight? The moon will be smiling tonight. It will say that all of the children of the world will have good dreams tonight. The moon will look like a full bowl of qinche. Tomorrow, we'll drink warm milk and get desta ceremela. The moon will be in the image of your face tonight. You will look up and see your reflection tonight.*

I would call for Ayne, but I would really be calling out for my childhood. Seven was a noble age. I knew love only from the people who were meant to love me, I still believed in the story of the girl who falls in love with the half-man half-horse, and I liked my grade one teacher.

Money? Why not? It's not the first thing that I thought of, which means that I am a moral human being. I would call out for it, though, which means that I see the world as it is. I am a realistic adult with some of my soul intact.

I got the visa."
"I don't believe it!"
"Medhanealem, I just picked it up this morning. Look."
"It's beautiful."
"I couldn't believe it when I saw it. I thought they would give me back my passport the same way I gave it to them. Empty. I couldn't believe it."
"Let me touch it, maybe I can share some of your luck."
"Touch it, hold it, talk to it, kiss it. Just leave it in the passport."
"When are you leaving?"
"Next week."
"It will be a long goodbye."
"I'm coming back; it's just for a gig."
"Don't joke around with me. People are leaving on foot, on boats, in dreams. You're going first class. The next time I see you, you'll have changed your citizenship."
"I still can't believe that I got it."

"The organisers will be surprised when you don't come back."
"Not if they're paying attention."

*M*y second favourite part of the performance. Reach for
my purse and stand up. Turn around and look straight
ahead. My dress moves with me, like there is wind in the room.
That's why I bought it, the function, the movement. It was a good
purchase. Keep walking. Black shadows. Keep walking. They are
paying attention. Somebody is paying attention. I can feel eyes on
me. Keep walking. The corners of my lips betray me. I am happy.
Keep walking. Applause. They never applaud. Who is it? Don't
look. Keep walking. You have to look. Her eyes burn through
me, her hands proudly meeting each other. My feet begin walking
to the sounds of her praise. I lose my breath. She smiles, and she
ruins the routine.

God Skin

Michael Yee

*T*he last of the customers leave the restaurant, as I smoke my cigarette I can hear the ghost of the sea, surf and sky distilled to photographic negative, as the earth slows its orbit, as she turns the sign from *Open* to *Closed*, as I open the door.

I walk into the Golden Phoenix.

She sits by the front desk in reception, by the cash register, the menus, napkins, and a crystal bowl of peppermints by the tips jar. A family of West African masks hangs on the wine-red wall behind her, but all I can see is her reflection, staring back at me as I lock the glass door.

I turn. Face her. She disappears into the restaurant. Glances over her shoulder as she slips through the curtain of beads and into the restrooms.

I feel beautiful until I catch my reflection in the door. God, look at me still covered in sunscreen. I spit on a napkin and wipe my face. Good news: I don't look like a ghost any more. Bad news: I've become even darker than that summer I spent hunting river crabs as a girl back in Chengdu.

C'mon, think. I'm always in the restaurant. How am I getting sunburnt? Granted, it's a different animal out here, but what sun can penetrate brick walls? And why am I the only one getting darker?

I'll work it out later.

I can't be late.

I pass through the archway and enter the restaurant. Six round tables with white tablecloths stand empty. I go to one with the chopsticks and the bowls turned upside down on the saucers.

Here she comes, Vannette Okanta.

I haven't breathed since she walked through the bead curtains. Out of all the empty seats, she sits next to me. I can smell the soap on her skin. Blood's high in my cheeks, down in my thighs. Under the table, my foot has become a needle pointing to true north. Where do I put my eyes as she studies my face?

"I like it."

"Huh?" I say in my best English.

"The tan." She tilts her head. "It suits you."

The kitchen doors swing open. I whip my head back.

"Come and get it." Yelling in Mandarin, my sister-in-law charges in with a tray of fish-stomach soup, steamed rice, deep-fried youtiao, tofu pork and bak choi. She flings the dishes onto the Lazy Susan and levels her gaze at me.

On my feet. To the restroom. Lock the stall. I'm standing over the squat toilet, still shaking.

But have I ever felt so alive?

Vannette Okanta. Okanta. Okanta. How she wears her hair free. Her skin, her temperature, how she stops to find the right words, how she slouches when she's thinking but never when she walks. The dignity she gives to a pashmina. How the other day, solving an inventory problem, it felt like we were running side-by-side, leaving the world behind. How she rearranges my chemistry from across the room, the friction of our genes – I've never been in love, is this it?

I pass water. Hike up my skirt. Light up a Chunghwa. Dissolve into nicotine, fingertips tingling as I take a second drag.

Who's banging on the door?

"Hey, what the hell you doing?" It's my sister-in-law. "Everyone's waiting for you, moron!"

"I'm coming." I unlock the stall. Push open the door.

"What are you doing in there?"

"I was taking a shit."

She barges past me, checks in the bowl for turds. "So you say."

I pull the chain. Go to the basin. Wash my hands. She's glaring into the back of my head. I sneer at her bitter melon body. Blow smoke in her face and slam the door behind me. Oh god, oh god, oh god.

My husband and brother-in-law are already sitting with Vannette at the table, tracking me as I part the curtain of beads.

"Ah, the guest of honour." My husband slowly applauds. I sit down as fast as I can. Once he's done glaring at me, he reaches for the Johnnie Walker. Fills everyone's glass but mine. "A toast," he says.

I sit with my empty glass.

Vannette's shoulder brushes mine as she rises, she smiles out of the corner of her eye. I'm out of control, I should stop looking at her.

My husband raises his glass. "To the Golden Phoenix."

I smile at her. Does he catch that? Does he see?

"Ganbei," he roars.

I sit down. Thank god, everyone's too hungry to give a damn about me any more.

Clinking of chopsticks, slurping of soup. While they stuff their faces, I roll the tofu pork on my tongue. Bland. Bland like all her food. A fact she covers up with MSG. *That's* why customers have stopped coming since that new restaurant opened. But will he listen? Pfft. The sun shines out his sister's ass.

My brother-in-law sees me leering at her and winks, that shark; they're all the same.

"Vannette, business so bad lately? Why? Why?" My husband throws up his hands while his eyes crawl down her cleavage.

"Times are hard, Mr Li." Vannette straightens her blouse.

He laces his fingers behind his head, red-faced, slurring. I can smell his sweat turning sour.

"New restaurah, Lucky Dragon… you know?"

Vannette takes a sip from the doll-sized teacup and nods.

"She go spy on them other day." He points to his sister. "Tell them."

She shakes her head and pours him another whisky.

"She say Lucky Dragon more customah because prettier waitresses there. I say we no in the restaurah business. You know what business we in?"

Vannette shakes her head. "No, Mr Li, what business are we in?"

"Tits and ass."

My in-laws laugh like it's the funniest thing they've heard, while my husband growls at me in Mandarin. "So when you insist on staying out in the sun all day, insist on getting this fucking monkey tan," he waves his finger in my face, "you jeopardise us all."

Vannette doesn't speak Mandarin. She doesn't have to.

"Sweetie, you think my wife pretty?"

Vannette bristles. "She is so pretty."

He drains his glass, switches back to Mandarin. "Pretty little monkey."

My in-laws hoot.

Later – after Vannette has left – with the whisky bottles drained, his sister will fry up a plate of greasy plantains. She'll make monkey sounds as I eat them.

"Unfortunately, some girls can end up with men who are… shall we say… in need of a woman's touch? But your daughter is so fair, such lovely skin, don't worry, we'll find a good match for her." What the marriage broker told my mother echoes as I open my eyes in bed, my saliva thick with plantains.

While I wait for the kettle on the windowsill to boil my drinking water, I place a mirror on the floor and stand over it.

Even the pasty skin on my thighs has tanned brown. But now, as I squat down I see that my labia, always the darkest part of me, has turned black. These are not my genitals. This is not my skin.

My knees are shaking. This cannot be from the sun. What

sun can burn here? His sister has cursed me. Colluded with witchdoctors. Circlets of hair. Amulets of fingernails. Hidden in my mattress. Sewn into my clothes. The room spins. My lungs shrink. My mouth is ash. Everyone is a foreigner somewhere, none more so than here, so what am I so afraid of?

Was that girl from Chengdu so perfect before?

My knees have stopped shaking.

Roots grow from the soles of my feet, through carpet, through floorboards, through concrete, through earth, through bedrock, through water, through fire.

Vannette flashes before my eyes all skin and touch and tenderness as I stare at my wet sex below. I piss on my shame. I pull up my pyjama bottoms. Go to the bathroom sink. Run the tap. Bring my mouth down to the stream; the water on my lips is lukewarm, tasteless. I wash my mask off. And watch it spiral down the drain. We abandon so many faces to discover who we are, what is one more? I soak the sponge. Wipe the wells of my clavicles, my umami armpits, between my legs, rinse and wash and rinse.

I've been hating myself since I opened my eyes. But enough now, I should get dressed. Vannette is downstairs.

I leave the bedroom. At the end of the long corridor, I open the door to the stairwell. My pencil skirt takes a ride up my legs as I go down two flights of stairs, surprise, everything's shorter since that new restaurant opened. It's so quiet in here, nothing but concrete and metal rails. I can hear my heart as I open the door and step into reception.

Vannette is waiting by the entrance, backlit by the morning; I could stand here for eternity.

But why isn't she behind the front desk? And why is there a box filled with her West African masks, Beyoncé mug, and the little cactus I gave to her last week?

"She said they don't need me any more."

What the hell?

"I had to say goodbye."

Has she been crying?

She keeps searching my face like maybe I know something. I'm shit in these situations. I get paralysed.

Oh god, she's taking it the wrong way. She's picking up the box. My face is a goddamned mask. I look like a goddamned robot. I should open my goddamned mouth. Tell her how I feel. But I can't, even now as she opens the door.

Love is an act of war. Love is older than reason. Love is choosing sides.

My breath stinks of fear, but somehow I take the box from her arms and shut the door. The way she's looking at me now, my heart stops. My eyes well up. My world is salt water. Reflected in the glass door, I see her body dissolving into my body, her edges melting into my edges, we are liquid now, colourless, as love, as suffering, as right, as wrong.

Who the fuck is breathing down my neck?

Spin round.

Hands on hips, lips pursed. How long has my sister-in-law been standing there?

"You! We pay you! Go! Go!" She waves Vannette away like she does the feral cats outside of the kitchen.

Vannette unfurls her shoulders and grows before my eyes.

My sister-in-law blinks. How many times have I lost face to her? What does it matter what she thinks any more?

Vannette is by my side. The woman I was without her is becoming unstitched, unhemmed as I lean over the front desk, open the cash register, grab the money, pick up the box.

Love makes fools and gods of us all.

Elegant fingers slip between my fat ones as I take her hand, as we walk into the sun, as we leave the restaurant behind, this is what I hold on to, this can keep me alive.

Vannette drinks me in as my high-heels-her-sneakers crunch across the courtyard, as we make our way to the giant metal gates, peppered with bullet holes from the war.

Can she hear me? Has this love that grew during ordinary days made telepaths of ordinary people?

We stand by the gates wide open. There is only the wind kicking up dust and the things I must say, things that have stayed secret so long, even as they nourish, they poison me.

"I never planned for any of this to happen. I only admitted last week how I felt about you. I couldn't sleep, my skin itched terribly, so I went outside. I saw the sun rising. It's been the strangest season. One smile from you and I was rearranged. Oceans of feeling surged and swelled, as if being so stretched and alive were normal."

"I'll get us a ride. You can stay with me if you like," she smiles.

Everything I said in Mandarin has been lost on her, already it withers, killed by the noise of this world. Motorbikes, cars and tuk-tuks rush in all directions. She hails down a taxi, hooting now for the traffic to give way. It pulls over. She opens the back door, drops the box on the seat, waves for me to get in.

He starts yelling something at Vannette, but a flurry of traffic steals the words before they can reach me.

I put my head inside the taxi. It sounds like they're arguing about the fare.

"He wants to rip us off," Vannette says.

What am I doing? I barely know her. This is insane.

"I wasn't born yesterday," she tells the driver.

New skin says go; old skin says stay.

"No, what are you doing?"

They are enemies; this is civil war.

"I don't want it."

I take the money from the cash register out of my pocket and put it into Vannette's hand.

I walk back to the gates.

I shut them behind me.

*D*ays, once light as air, now oil spill; fortune shines elsewhere. Weeks have passed.

Night has fallen.

He's expecting me. Hates waiting. I leave the bedroom. Walk

the leylines women like me must follow, on tiptoes, on eggshells, husband awaits at the end of the dark corridor, in the master bathroom, knock on the door.

He grunts.

I say his name and pray he had a good day.

"Come."

I creak open the door to a humid, steamy world. His arm dangles over the bathtub while his finger points to the door. "Shut it."

Air still, bathwater still, only his eyes stir as I unbutton my blouse, as I step out of my skirt, as my underwear falls to my ankles, as I climb into the warm water and slip between his handsome thighs.

"Where have you been?" He pinches my nipple. Water sloshes over the sides, onto the floor. I don't struggle. He will break me.

"Sorry I was late, my love," I say and turn around. I go down on him. Choke on him. It's OK to struggle now. This struggle he likes.

He is done.

I twist open the tap. I break open. Sorrow spills like the bathwater over the sides, onto the tiles. Worse to come.

His legs coil around me. Fingers trace down my chest. Nipples harden.

"You like that?"

I nod. Sigh. Sell it. I can hate myself all I want, but at least I'll wake up with my teeth tomorrow morning.

Hot water soothes him. His legs loosen their grip on me. Spidery hands crawls down my small breasts, down between my thighs – goosebumps of pleasure break out on my skin, how awful – as expert hands work me from the inside out. My breath is connected to him now. My back arcs against his chest. Sparks shoot from his fingertips, explode in my womb, limbs, chest, toes, nerve endings awaken like a coral reef. I tremble in his arms. He licks the tears from my cheek.

"You know, it's growing on me, your new colour."

I say: "I'm so glad."

"No, I like it a lot."

I smile, at least the worst is over.

"Speak to me like Vannette."

I spin round. Hot water sloshes over the sides.

"C'mon, I've heard you practicing English with her."

I look him in the eye.

"Speak like Vannette."

Have I ever hated him more?

His hand flies out the water, grabs onto my ponytail, my neck yanks backwards like the lid of a tin can.

"Speak like Vannette."

"Go fuck yourself."

*T*here's a slit where the maroon drapes meet each other at the bedroom window; where sunlight charges through, hammering my eyes. What's this caked on my lips? I lick it. Dry flakes dissolve on my tongue. Why can't I taste what it is? Why am I mouth-breathing? It comes rushing back now. Don't touch my nose. Only lifting my head from the pillow hurts more. It's not the first time. Keep it together. There's blood on the sheets turning dark brown. Better get rid of it before he decides to break something else. But easy does it. My balance is shot.

I take my time putting my sunnies, hoodie and slippers on. I shuffle my way to the stairwell and go down the two flights of stairs. I push on the steel door and emerge in the rear of the compound. They keep the dumpsters and industrial generators in this courtyard.

*E*arly morning, but the sun is a beast already. Through my swollen eyes I see William by the generator opening one of those glass jars everyone uses to transport petrol in over here. His Nissan pick-up is parked a few metres away, all rusty from the sea air. For years, William's been refuelling generators for businesses up and down the boulevard. Seems to enjoy telling me stories about President Tolbert (good), President Taylor (complicated), President Sirleaf (useless), the displacement camps in Guinea that sheltered him during the war (c'est la vie), but mostly about his retirement if the government ever builds that grid that will put him out of a job (happy days).

"Well, hey girl," he sees me coming.

I keep walking to the dumpster and toss the sheets. I'm grinding my teeth. I want to crawl back into bed and die, but I'm done with the old me. The new me goes back to William.

"How you been keeping now?"

It hurts to speak, so I just stand there. It's fine, William's a talker. Like many Liberians, he throws away the ends of his words to confuse outsiders, but I like it, it soothes me. Only William's not saying much today.

His eyes keep wandering to the swelling under my sunnies.

Before I can ask him about the petrol, he blurts out, "Hey, I ever tell you about the dogs in the camps?"

I shake my broken clock of a head.

"Ah, well now, they were these street dogs, mangy old things, always trying to sneak into camp. One day they go and steal a baby. Got in through a hole in the fence."

I wonder how many jars of petrol William has left in his pick-up truck.

"By the time the mother knew they were gnawing on the bones."

What will it take to burn this all to the ground?

"Now some people said they was just dogs being hungry, but uh-uh, I always said they were bad to the bone."

He starts pouring petrol into the generator through a funnel. "You know any dogs like that, darling?"

"How much?" I point to the empty jars by the generator.

William leans away from the fumes as he looks at me.

"How much?" I rub my fingers together.

"How many you need?"

"All."

"All?"

He catches me looking at my husband's office on the first floor of the compound. When I stare at him, he twists the cap back onto the tank and restarts the generator. The noise punches me in the nose. I want to vomit, but there's no time. William's carrying the empty jars to his vehicle. I stagger over there and brace myself on the side of the truck. Everything's blurry, but I can see jars of petrol inside.

"How much?"

William scratches his head. "Hey now, where's Vannette at? I ain't seen her all morning." He stares down the length of the dirty compound towards reception.

"Wait, William."

I cross the courtyard as fast I can. Push against the steel door. Crawl up the stairs. I'm in my bedroom. Where did I hide the shoebox with all the cash that I made? As I kneel to look under the bed, my stomach tips over. I puke down the front of my pink hoodie, but there's no time to change. I hurry down the stairs. I open the door to the courtyard, but I already know.

William's gone.

My kneecaps turn to cartilage. I hit the ground so hard I throw up again. I'm lying in the gravel, staring at the deserted parking lot sideways.

The sun climbs in the cloudless sky, making everything itch.

I start scratching my sides, but it's no use. It itches like skin growing under a bad burn, like skin still blistered from when my heart was an oil rig and my blood was gasoline.

But it itches less when I'm moving.

I get up slowly on my iffy knees. I go to the front gates and roll them shut. I take the key tied to the string around my neck and snap it off in the padlock.

I go back to the restaurant. I scratch around in the ashtray on the silver pedestal outside. While I smoke the end of somebody's stale cigarette, I press my face against the front door.

I imagine seeing Vannette working the till behind the front desk as I push open the door now and step inside. That look on her face. That light in her eyes. It is mine. I have earned it.

I walk away from her for the last time. I do not falter. I march into the restaurant, go past the round tables. When I reach the back, I shove open the swing doors and enter the hot and smoky kitchen. Stride past the roaring gas burners, two of them side by side.

My sister-in-law is scrubbing a pot in the sink, singing her gaudy love songs, too drunk to see me coming.

My new lips whisper new truths: There is no one left to be. Nowhere left to go. Nothing left to burn.

My new ears hear the ghosts of those who fought on Tubman Boulevard, distilled to tooth and nail.

Yesterday I knew how to be deaf, how to be blind, how to be somebody else's. Today I know why bullet holes still riddle the walls outside. Why war soaked this wind, these skies, these rivers, this soil.

I pick up the cleaver.

Plums

Kharys Laue

*T*his is not my first act of disobedience, nor my last. It is never for no reason that I disobey the rules.

I have brought the child who gave me the dream. It must be him, for on the night he came, the dream came and would not stop coming. In it, I am back on the farm, standing in the orchard. Rotten plum-flesh squeezes between my toes, pips cut my feet. I lurch forward and leave a track of crimson behind. Plums hang all around me. Every one of them is imperfect, their skins broken by the beaks of birds, pockmarked by the toothless mouths of worms. Still, they are pungent and sweet. I am searching for Gloria. I know she is behind me, but every time I spin around she is behind me again. I turn and turn and turn. Finally, I pick a plum and lift it to my lips. Its skin splits under my teeth and my tongue catches the first of its juice. Then I wake. I wake to the taste of sunlight and hay.

I have waited a long time. I watched the seasons change from my bedroom window. The lean trees grew fat and green on the warmth and the abundant showerstorms. The spring buds, sheathed like new feathers, broke and effloresced along the bony branches, until the trees seemed like fledglings on the brink of flight. I waited still longer, and the flowers came. They shed their petals. Their fruits swelled, day by day, and grew plump. Then I knew the time was right. I took the child and the car and drove to Pick n Pay.

I have come for plums.

A woman is bending over the crate when I arrive. As she picks through the plums, dropping them into a plastic packet held open with her free hand, she dips her neck and her fine wingbone dances under the thin blouse. In the elegant, clear shape of her, I feel the full weight of my own body.

۵

*I*t is while she is knotting the package that I realise. Inside the vault of me, something changes and I know. I imagine a cataract of moths nosing, blind-faced, through a slit and falling into my belly. Winging upwards. Beating against the pale glow of my heart and my heart beating back.

I am taken back to the day of our secret and what came after.

That day – the day I took Gloria up into the loft – the sun hung yellow and swollen and heavy in the sky. Ripe as plum, Gloria said. Kneeling in the orchard among the debris of our afternoon plunder, I saw in the lengthened shadows of the afternoon my approaching solitude.

I rose and said, I got a secret, Glo.

She left off snapping twigs and looked up. What you got? She searched me over. Wherezit?

I turned and pointed. Up in the house.

OK, she said. She stood up in the low lazy sunlight. Her knees, pimpled with things of the earth, jutted out below the hem of her dirty beige dress. I gotta be back before the sun gets vrot, though, hey.

I nodded. I took a quick step towards her and caught her fingers. Our hands were sticky from the soft insides of plums we'd stolen from the trees and eaten in the shade, and as we ran, I felt the stubble of sand and grass pressed into my palm. The wind heaved hot against my face and the cicada-song thrilled my ears. She laughed. When I glanced over my shoulder, I saw her little tongue pushed out between her teeth, and then I too was laughing.

I follow her from aisle to aisle. She has a list on a scrap of paper, which she grasps, crumpled, over the handlebar of her trolley. Every now and then she lifts the list, looks at it absentmindedly and pushes the trolley along with one hand. She is fastidious and methodical. She scans shelves, running an index finger along price tags, picking out items and reading their contents. Sometimes she puts an article into her trolley.

I imagine taking her hand in mine and turning my face to hers and saying something.

I was still holding Gloria's hand when we entered the house through the back door. We paused in the kitchen and stood silent, waiting for our eyes to adjust and inhaling the cool, luxuriant fragrance of baking. Flies bickered on the windowsill and hurled their bodies angrily against the glass. All around us a solemn drone rose and fell. No one was about. The sticky fly-trap, accumulating black bodies, lolled from the ceiling like a decayed yellow tongue. On the table below it lay a plate of oat biscuits so fresh that when I pressed one, the crust buckled and my forefinger sunk into the warmth below. I cast a glance at Gloria, grinning, and took up the plate. She shook her head.

Ma will get in trouble. Let's just take two.

I stared at her and at the plate in my hand. Then I fetched another, took two biscuits off the top, put them on the second plate, and rearranged the pile on the first plate. Gloria nodded.

I led her to the spare room where my father used to sleep, and, crossing to where a ladder leaned against the wall, pointed up at the roof.

See?

She looked up at the faint outline of the trapdoor. Then, spiderlike, she climbed the ladder. When she was high enough to touch the roof, she reached with the tips of her fingers, lifted the trapdoor, and set it aside. She hauled herself up into the loft, and I followed with the biscuits. In the dim light, I located the extension cord and threaded it through my fingers until I felt the switch and snapped it on. A low hanging bulb flared yellow. I replaced the trapdoor and turned to Gloria.

Thisisit? She gazed about. This the secret?

Her scapula, drawn up tight and restless behind her like the wings of a readying bird, shifted and strained against the thin cotton dress.

By the time she comes to a standstill in the last aisle and holds out the scrap of paper, I can't say how long I've been following her around. She runs a finger over the list, mouthing each item, pausing once or twice to peer into her trolley. Satisfied, stuffing the list into her bag with one hand and pushing the trolley before her with the other, she retraces her way through Pick n Pay and replaces everything except the plums. Then she chooses a teller and waits.

*A*s a makeshift tent, we pushed together a semicircle of hay bales and threw over them a red sheet fetched from the room below. When we had crawled into the embryonic light, sheathed snug in an envelope of heat, and settled cross-legged with the biscuits between us, Gloria whispered, tilting towards me, This is *our* place. I picked up a handful of straw and, watching her, let it slip through my fingers. Ja, she said. Looking skywards, her lips parted, she touched the flat of her hand against the sheet, gently, as if it were a soft skin stretched over us.

When, with hot fingers, we ate the biscuits, she closed her eyes and jogged her shoulders with pleasure. Afterwards we lay down on the straw and slept. I don't know how long I slept. When I woke, I kept my eyes closed. Air rested between my finger blades as if it had a weight of its own. I listened. The tiny swell and ebb of Gloria's breath was the only sound that stirred the liquid stillness. By degrees, I opened my eyes and raised myself onto my elbow to gaze at the sleeping form beside me, the rich hues of her skin luminous and unreal in the red light. As I touched the feverish centre of her palm, lying open in the straw beside me like a tossed flower, it gave a slight contraction against my fingertips. Glo, I whispered. Her eyelids, fleshy from sleep and spanned by tight black lashes, flickered, and the tempo of her breathing changed. Though her eyes remained closed, I knew she was awake.

I stand waiting behind her in the queue. Her warmth is palpable, coming off her like a fine mist. A series of tight delicate curls cling to the nape of her neck and a film of perspiration glistens along her shoulders. Her breath, like the shoreline lap of water, is steady and small.

If I were to reach out and touch her, to embrace her, to press my lips to hers, to lie down with her, she would slip through my knowing like mercury. I know this and so I stand verystill veryclose nottouching.

I close my eyes and wait.

*W*hen Gloria sat up, she inclined her head and rubbed her ear with the bones of her bare shoulder. Then she looked across at me and smiled, the tip of her tongue held like a pink sweet between her teeth. With her eyes still on me, she pulled off her dress, her panties; I, my shorts and shirt. Each of our movements seemed slow, prolonged, like a subaqueous dance. We lay down facing one another, so close I could smell the round nutty scent of her breath, the sharp fragrance of her sweat. I put my arms around her neck and drew her to me, so that our bodies touched all the way down. The heat of her little hand against my abdomen. The dogpant of our breath. And then suddenly, in that centre place like a half-closed bud over which I had bent time-and-time-again and with my fingers opened and pulled apart, something broke open and burst into life. We each took the other's leg in between, scissor-wise, and opened like sunned fruit one another's glowing groins, inhaling the inside-scent of urine, unwashed skin, sweat. With blind intent I searched the lineaments of her and discovered the tip of her hot between and stroked it, smooth and soft and wet as her tongue, and the roof of my mouth ached as if I had tasted something too sweet. I pressed my cheek into the curve of her neck and touched her arched spinal bones, straining my feet against the floor. Between my toes I felt the broken spines of straw.

To find a way into her, shrug on her flesh, breathe her air, live the pulse of her blood. To know her perfect heatbeat as my own. This is what I wanted.

Perhaps I come too close and she feels my breath on her shoulders, for she turns. I open my eyes to hers. I am conscious enough to understand that this is not Gloria. That this is the face of a stranger. That the sound inside of me is louder than the sound outside of me. That something ghastly has turned in the pit of my stomach. And then

*B*y the sudden change in light and temperature, I knew that my mother had found us. With the sheet torn away, we cringed naked under the glare of light and the cool rush of air. Swathes of goosebumps puckered my thighs and shoulders, and we curled closer into one another. Save for the throb of blood in my ears, a starched silence stretched over everything. I knew I must get up. I raised myself on my elbows and tried to rise, but I could not. My mother moved, and, eclipsing the light, threw a shadow over us. I squinted but she would not take shape. Her arms jerked in the air, and it was a long time before I realised that sound went with those movements. When the sound came, it rattled against my ears like gravel, sharp and painful, but without the curvature of sense. Again I tried to rise, and again I fell. I twisted and saw that Gloria had her thin arms around my ankles. The whites of her eyes gleamed pale. The light flickered and I felt my legs come free. I gathered up my clothes and stood to dress myself.

*B*rendan must have undressed me and helped me into a T-shirt and tracksuit pants. My breasts loll huge and strange under the baggy cotton fabric. Through it, I feel my hands resting on my enormous belly. I am weighed down by all this surplus flesh, all these fat layers in which the child has swaddled me. I long for the slender strong limbs of my childhood, the tight knitted belly, the unencumbered flat chest. Brendan sits nearby. His eyes are closed and he holds his head in his hand. When I say his name, he opens his eyes, but does not look up; nor does he move his hand. His voice, when he speaks, is unfamiliar.

What happened, Chris.

I look out the window. Beyond the trees, the skyscrapers glint like knives in the late afternoon light. I look at Brendan again.

I don't know.

Silence. I shift the blanket from my ankles and wait. He, too, waits, and for a time we submit to that awful stillness. Then he looks up at me.

You knew you weren't ready, Chris. It was irresponsible. You took the baby. You should have told me and we could have gone together. I'm trying

I was ready.

He makes a gesture with his hand and looks out the window. I wonder what he sees there. When he looks at me again, something seems to release in him and he falls back into the chair. In long slow strokes he rubs his lips with his fingers, watching me.

Chris. Do you know that you dropped the baby?

I gaze at him. I let my eyes rest in his until I grow tired, and then I look away towards the inflamed horizon. There the sun lies. As if it were not a sun nor a plum but a human body impaled on the bladed city, its inside-colours driven out. How far away that morning in this bedroom, the midwife holding out the bloodied child like one of the animal trophies my father used to raise up between his fists. What Brendan does not understand is that in the child's beginning I saw my own end. In him I felt the coming of night.

I turn back to Brendan.

The child

He's OK. You let go after you'd fallen. But

Let me lie down a bit. Then we can talk.

*G*loria and I stood side by side in the living room, looking out through the glass sliding doors. In the west the sun had grown vrot and dropped from its foliage of blue and plunged through the burning air and broken and burst on the ground of that far off horizon. It was hours past Gloria's curfew, but that was the least of our transgressions.

In silence we watched as my mother stalked across the veld and entered, without knocking, the little one-roomed place where Gloria and her mother lived. A moment later two figures emerged and came quickly across the dry grass, the one in front striding, the other running a short distance behind.

I struggle up in bed suddenly and look towards Brendan. He is in the same chair, gazing out the window, but he looks around at the movement.

I forgot the shopping.

He stares at me. No. Not all of it. You bought plums.

He rises and leaves the room and comes back holding a packet of plums. I look at them a long time. When he comes over and puts them down on my bedside table, I ask him to take them back to the kitchen. In silence he picks them up and leaves the room and returns and sits in his chair. Then he looks at me. The skin around his eyes is puffy and red. It is I who has put my mouth around the hole in him and blown and inflated those pockets below his eyes and reddened his lids.

*W*hen they entered the room, Gloria made a small guttural sound and began shaking her wrists as if she had hurt herself. Gloria's mother shrieked and headed for her.

You! Sies!

She grasped one of Gloria's jerking wrists and, averting her eyes from me and my mother, started towards the door. We watched. As her mother marched her across the veld, Gloria ran alongside and kept looking up as if to say something, but every time she looked up she would lose her balance and stumble, and she would have to look down again to steady herself. Halfway, she fell. As her knees collided with the ground, her free arm flailed in the air and she kicked out, unable to regain her footing. Her mother kept on going, dragging Gloria behind her.

They were far out across the veld before Gloria's mother stopped. Gloria clambered to her feet. Her mother squatted and looked at her knees and then looked up into Gloria's face. She touched her cheek and said something, but Gloria would not look at her. Then she rose and hefted her up on her hip, and they went on like this, much slower.

*W*hen I open my eyes Brendan is very close to me, sitting on the edge of the bed. I sit up against the headboard. My face is itchy, wet. I press the heels of my hands against my eyes and wait. After a while I take them away and look at Brendan.

Do you want me to call your mother? She could help with the baby.

I keep my eyes on him a while longer. Then I look off towards the serrated horizon from which the last light is draining.

I don't want to see her again, I say.

*W*ithout looking at me, my mother turned and crossed the room. I followed her with my eyes. She picked up the remote from the coffee table, switched the TV on, and, putting up her foot on the couch behind her, sank down. She sat very still for some time. Then she leaned and, from a side pocket of her jeans, eased out a box of cigarettes and a lighter, shook one out and lit it.

Ma?

She smoked, holding the cigarette up near her cheek, and stared at the TV. After a while she leaned forward and with her forefinger pulled the cut-glass ashtray across the table towards her. She put it on the couch next to her and ashed. When she ashed, she looked at her cigarette very closely. Then she turned back to the TV.

Ma?

I waited while she smoked. I crossed the dusty zebra-skin carpet and stood waiting by the couch. She took a final drag of her cigarette and crushed it into the centre of the ashtray. Then she picked up the box and lit another.

I close my eyes, matching my breath to the deep, even churn of Brendan's. In the place below my lids I rise and skirt the bed and pass down the passageway into the kitchen. I stand motionless in the fragrant light. Wind swells through the trees, pressing out a subtle outline against the clear tissue of sound that hangs about the night. The call and answer of dogs, the ceaseless traffic, the intermittent flash of a human voice. My feet slap the linoleum as I cross to the window. I rest my hand on the sink and look out. A bloodless sickle moon is pressed, like the impression of a fingernail, into the navy skin of sky above.

M y mother smoked on. At last I grew tired of waiting and, fixing my eyes on her, sunk my nails into her forearm. I felt the give of her skin and her pulse underneath. She extinguished her cigarette. Then in one movement she wheeled around, wrenched my fingers from her arm and dragging me up against the couch, slapped me across the face three times. Blood sounded in my cheeks. To keep from crying out, I fixed my eyes on the four red sickle moons pressed into my mother's forearm.

Who do you think you are, she murmured. Hm? Hey? What were you doing up there? I averted my face, but she shook me and craned her neck to look into my eyes. You think you can just go around rubbing fannies with a little kaffir girl, hey? You think you can do that? She paused, as if waiting for me to reply, and then, without warning, her voice flew up. Sies! What are you? A homosexual! That's what you are. Did you know that? She laughed hysterically. Jissus. What would your Pa say. You think that just because he's run off with some Barbie, you can do whatever you want? Hey? Not under my roof.

*W*hen I turn, Gloria is standing by the table. I watch her behind my closed lids. She unknots the package of plums on the table, reaches inside, draws one out. As she bites into it, the juice spills from her mouth and she passes her tongue along her lips to catch it up. A giddy sensation of sunlight and hay passes through me.

I wake in the kitchen, gripping the sink. The cool colour of silver under one hand, the weight of a plum, smooth and slippery and firm, in the other. I turn from the moonless night towards the child's room: for the first time in many months, I know what I must do.

I was forbidden to see Gloria again, but I sought her out nonetheless. I found her behind their one-roomed house, squatting next to a bucket and massaging kitchen towels with her bare hands. The smell of Jik was thick on the hot noon air. I stood and watched her; she had not seen me yet. Every now and then, she would lift out a towel with both hands and twist it and rub it together. Then she would put it back in the bucket again.

When she sensed my presence, she looked up so suddenly that I stepped back. She looked around and looked at me, but her face did not change, and she made not a sound. In slow sweeping movements, as if she were painting, she wiped her hands on her dress and watched me. Once her hands were dry, she dropped them to her sides and was utterly still. She wore the same beige dress, though it was dirtier, and for the first time I noticed her knees below its hem. They were swollen, even bigger than before. The crowns, where she had been caught by sharp rocks and thorns, were torn and scabless. She saw the direction of my gaze and, without taking her eyes off me, tried to tug down the hem of her dress. I looked into her face and she into mine.

I had come to ask her a question.

*T*he child lies sprawled in his cot among the blankets, straddle-legged, his arms flung above his head, his tiny hands half-clenched. Every part of him is filled out, plump with health. Where his eyelids meet, caterpillar lashes slumber. His lips, red and fleshy as something candied, are parted as if he is about to speak, and his skin is a fearful shade of pink. Though he does not know it and perhaps never will, these colours will serve him well in life, as will, one day, the tiny shaft nestled inside his nappy.

He can't yet speak, but when he does, what will he say? What words will he pick up and fling like stones, and pick up again to fling again?

I took a step towards Gloria and looked her in the eyes and asked her the question I had come to ask.

She stopped tugging at the hem of her dress. While the cicadas knitted their shroud of sound all around us, something changed in her eyes. She did not answer. As if her voice had dried up. As if, without a voice, she had rolled back her tongue deep inside her like a useless pipe.

I grew impatient and kicked the red earth. She glanced down at the small mushroom of dust, and looked back up at me. Then she squatted in front of the washtub and began on the dishcloths again. For a while, I watched the quick movements of her wing-bone under her dress, and then I uttered the last thing I would ever say to her.

Ma says so.

I watched, waiting to see the effect of my words. She remained squatting on the ground, washing the dishcloths. She said nothing. Perhaps she was thinking of the things my father once said to her father. How he did not smile when my father said those things. How she longed to see his smile now, with the two incomplete rows of teeth as black as pomegranate pips which looked like they might spill down his chin if he clamped his jaws too hard. How, in those weeks before, no one saw his pomegranate smile. And how he had looked on that day my father had cut him down and put him over his shoulder and thrust him onto the mattress inside their one-roomed house.

I carry the child to the chair by the window and sit down, lifting my feet on tip-toe to level out my knees. When I lay him out on my lap his eyes murmur open and he stares up at me. He watches, astonished, as I lift the plum to my mouth and eat. It is hard, tasteless, pale, but it will do.

I feed him little scoops of the plum and watch how, with each taste, his limbs burst into cataclysms of movement. He flails his arms and opens his mouth for more, his tongue pulsing inside its dark cavity. I feed him until he refuses my finger and turns his head away. Then I look into his small face and nod.

It seems to me that I do not blink that whole night and it is only by the steady sensation of life under my hands that I know the passing of time.

*A*nd then something miraculous happened: Gloria's shadow, squatting at her heels, began to bleed. The red earth turned redder. She continued mashing up the clothes, hauling them up, twisting them, but not a drop fell to the earth. Still, something spread, slow and uneven, in little rivulets around her, gathering and breaking apart, until it made her its centre. As if she were the stamen of some unearthly flower. As if her shadow had fallen from some great height. Then, all at once, it stopped.

I stood watching and waiting. At last it came to me. I turned, careful not to upset my balance, and began walking back the way I had come. Behind me the water sounds stopped. I knew that Gloria had paused her work to watch me go, but I did not look back. Faster and faster I walked, until I was running. Running, I passed through the rotting orchard, and running, I reached the house and entered it. Only once I was in my room did I stop and look around. I crossed to my cupboard and opened the wooden doors and climbed in and closed the doors. I sat in the dark among the clothes without moving. Then I began to heave. When nothing would come up, I raised both feet and, blow upon blow, beat the cupboard's side.

A little before dawn, I hear movement at the door. I do not need to turn and look to know that Brendan is standing there, immobilised by what he sees. His voice when he speaks is like a drowning thing.

Chris Chris what are you doing

It's OK. Everything is OK.

I hear the release in his breath as he stumbles into the room. When he reaches me, he puts his hand to the child's neck to make sure, and then gets down onto the floor beside me. He has seen the child's face, sticky with plum flesh, and the circle of wet on the babygrow where I have held the fruit the whole night.

He sits and presses the heels of his hands against his eyes.

Chris

He falls silent and drops his hands. Together we watch the dawn come. The sky blanches a sulphurous grey. The trees, cowed and dripping in the watery light, house birds that brace themselves and raise their voices to the air. The rattle of morning traffic. The weight and warmth of the child on my knees. The sticky yield of the plum in my fingers.

He speaks.

Chris. You know that you leave me no choice. After what happened yesterday. After this.

As day dawns outside, dusk gathers inside. I close my eyes. I nod. I take myself back to another time and another place when things were not like this.

Ibinabo

Michael Agugom

He who awaits his lover hears the footsteps of spirits.
— Igbo proverb

She's there. At the seashore. Sitting on a broken refrigerator with no door, her bare feet inches above the sandy shore.

Now and then she swings her legs, back and forth, to kill the cramp collecting at her feet. When that doesn't help, she climbs down from the fridge and crouches on the sand, never taking her eyes off the sea. Ibinabo is waiting for her mother. There. At the shore.

She threw Gov'ment's back to the ground, half-a-dozen days back. She had come out to the school's sports field and found Gov'ment at it. Six-toes! Six-toes! He was jeering and yanking the hair of a girl while classmates formed a moon around him and the girl, watching, torn between amusement and disapproval. The girl was sobbing, struggling to free herself from his grip. The girl had a sixth short toe on both her feet; they made her feet look awkward in her sandals. Breaking into the circle, Ibinabo yelled, Let her go!

Who's talking? Gov'ment jested. Oh, it's oyinbo mami wata! He knows calling her that will infuriate her, he knows she doesn't understand why she's called mami wata.

Haven't I warned you to not call me that?

I just did, so what—

Her blow caught Gov'ment's face before he saw her hand coming. It didn't take her any effort, in that dazed instant, to tackle him to the ground and hold him there to the cheering of the other students. Her knees astride him, pinning his hands to the ground, she held his jaws open with one hand; with the other, she fed him sand. And they went berserk: the spectators. For a girl to have done this to a boy was unthinkable, a Guinness-Book-of-Records-level humiliation. When she got off him, he coughed in shame.

She's let her shoulder-length hair down, for her mother; she's wearing a white flowery mary-amaka gown to please her mother when she comes ashore. Last year's birthday, she got it as a gift from her mother; she's never worn it until now.

Her mother had often harangued her for always wearing shirts and shorts, like a Boy Scout; she sighs, recalling one episode. She has anxiety the size of a boulder on her back, crushing her fragile bones. She can't put it down.

At home, she had expected her mother to draw her into her arms and say, "Oh my daughter, I'm very proud of you!" Isn't that the least a mother could do to encourage her daughter for standing up for herself and for a bullied mate? But her mother did differently: Why can't you just be a girl?

Gov'ment called me mami wata!

An' so what if he did? Must you go fighting? Who do you think you are, Rosa Parks abi Dora Akunyeli? Don't I have enough headache feeding you that you have to add to my—

I hate you!

Ibinabo didn't mean it. She hated that her mother didn't understand her. Her mother took her words for what they meant, and a dagger stabbed into her chest would have been less painful. She raised her hand and slapped Ibinabo, leaving a shade of her hand on Ibinabo's face, and stormed out of the bacha.

She hit her, not because she hated her daughter. Far from it. Her hand had acted before her mind could counsel against it. She hated that she couldn't understand her daughter. In her heydays, when she was still sisi – before she had Ibinabo – she was called Ebony-Stainless on account of her beauty. It made her proud, then; it was who she was then, what she was then. But now she's called Mama Ibinabo, she's become Mama Ibinabo, all her daughter's fault: her daughter snatched all her ebony-stainlessness from her the moment she gave birth to her. She had never asked herself, *who am I now?* until she had Ibinabo. And the answer, *Mama Ibinabo not Ebony Stainless*, saddened her. Now, her daughter wasn't just beautiful, she was even likened to their graceful sea goddess, the protector of their clan. *Why can't she just take a compliment like every other girl, ehn?*

In the days that followed, Ibinabo started a loud protest by shutting her mouth to her mother – not even to acknowledge her mother's "Good-morning, dear." And for five days she kept up her protest.

The second day, her mother bellowed: You think you can hold a grudge! Hold it! Hold it close to your chest-o! A bird with a tender head does not attend the funeral of the woodpecker!

Ibinabo didn't respond.

The third day, her mother bawled: How much longer will you keep me quiet? No one on this island gives trophies for the longest grudge kept! If there were any, this bacha could not contain all the trophies I would have garnered for resenting all the thoughtless gossips on this island who think they're better than me!

Ibinabo didn't respond.

The fourth day, her mother said: Sorry-o, Miss Grudge.

Ibinabo didn't respond: to her, *sorry-o* was a mock apology.

The fifth day, her mother snapped: A child strapped to the back doesn't know that trekking is weary! What have I not done for you! I have fed you, given you shelter, clothed you! You took my youth from me!

Her mother stormed out of the bacha, sobbing, breasts jostling, feet stomping the ground. She grabbed a yellow jerrycan and trudged off to the pipeline site. That day, another oil pipeline that ran through the island had broken, and was spilling crude. Like many others on the island, she was going to scoop the black gold. It was an opportunity many wouldn't let slip: what other way to make quick and easy money than from scooping and selling the crude on the black market? She was three poles away from the site when a loud BOOM reverberated all over the island. Thick black smoke and orange balls of fire in the sky could be seen miles away from the site.

The fire caught her mother.

The only hospital on the island was a gigantic colonial relic, with the total number of doctors and nurses as many as the fingers on a man's hands, and as efficient as the trembling hands of a drunken painter: Ibinabo's mother and other victims of the explosion were left at corners of its overcrowded ward.

When Ibinabo dashed into the ward and saw her mother, she didn't weep, she didn't sob. She shrieked so loud her voice scratched the walls of every eardrum there; the two relatives closest to her held her to prevent her from collapsing on her mother. The tears and the wailing came afterward. She wanted to carry her mother's head on her thighs and comfort her, tell her she no longer bore her any grudge. But the fire had spared no part of her mother's body for her to touch. She could only kneel beside her and wail... and wail.

When, much later, her mother attempted to talk, it was with strain. Ibinabo brought her ears to her mother's mouth; all she heard her say was Ibi-na-bo, you're—

And what her mother's last words to her might have been haunted her.

She's scratching her wrist – the way she does it, you'd think she wanted to peel the whiteness off her skin, to reveal black skin like her mother's. Were it possible, she would have done it: her skin, alongside her other physical features, reminds her of how different she is from everyone else on the island.

Her hair is the colour of gold, curly, and long; everyone else's is tar, kinky, and short; her eyes are blue pearls; theirs, brown pearls; her skin, milk; theirs, coffee. But she's only scratching the itchy ringworm on her wrist. She stops: her skin has turned red, bleeding.

How much longer will you keep me quiet, you ungrateful child! Her mother's words bellow in her head again.

The words and images of her mother have become wood splinters piercing her.

She can't go on living like this: with these splinters, with the boulder; she wearily gets off the fridge.

She shakes her head, holding back tears. She recalls that yesterday Peoples promised her he'd find a way she could see and talk to her mother. But he hasn't showed up today. *He's not coming: he never found one.* She's left with one last option that makes her heart begin thumping: she's never swam the sea, unlike her age-mates on the island who are already praised as fishes. She'll need guts to walk into the sea, to the horizon – and go.

And the pain and the guilt will also go.

*P*eoples is sprinting through Colonial Road, through Independent Layout, into Market Road; he cuts through the heart of One Market. Slow down! an elderly woman shouts at him from her stall, but he keeps running, panting. He comes to a bend into Democracy Street and he brushes against a buxom woman as he jets past her. Have you gone crazy? the woman barks behind him, Where're you running to, your grave? You want to...

He's running to fatten the distance between him and the jetty, to shrink the distance between him and the shore. He has to take hope to Ibinabo, to tell her he's found a way she can talk to her late mother. In his left hand is a sachet of water, in his right pocket, a wrapped doughnut.

He can't forget the day Mr Iginiwari, the Social Studies teacher and most dreaded teacher in their school, pointed to him in class and said, boi-girl, come forward and define democracy for the class. Peoples could define democracy, no doubt, but the unexpected mockery of being called a Boi-girl in front of his classmates turned his face into a dark cloud, made his shoulders droop, and turned his thoughts into shattered china plates. He stood before the class, speechless. Mr Iginiwari prodded him with a finger, *like I'm some stain he wouldn't want on his hands*, and said, go on, boi-girl! And the class burst into wild laughter – except Ibinabo.

Peoples' heart somersaulted as he mumbled: Democracy is government from the peoples, on the peoples, and at the peoples!

And the class, including Mr Iginiwari, fell over themselves laughing – except Ibinabo.

Raindrops fell from Peoples' eyes.

Gov'ment stood up and jested: Maybe boi-girl has defined our own democracy for us!

And everyone laughed some more – except Ibinabo.

She could no longer take it. She sprang up and thundered: Sah, even if everyone makes fun of him, you, our teacher, are you supposed to join them and show us your teeth as if you're acting in TV commercial for Close-Up toothpaste? You should know better!

And the class went silent; a graveyard couldn't have been more silent at that moment. Mr Iginiwari's face was a bullet-riddled wall. Few days back and in a similar situation he would have flogged daylight out of her for this, but now he couldn't: there was a ripe rumour that he had touched the school's principal's yet-to-be-touched-by-a-man fourteen-year-old daughter. For this, he was under investigation; his career as a teacher and his prospect of running for electoral position as a House member were in jeopardy – he wouldn't drop salt on an open wound by flogging Ibinabo. He simply nudged Peoples to return to his seat, and walked out of the class. And that was the last time Mr Iginiwari was seen in their school.

From that day on, everyone called Tonworio Peoples – as a reminder of the priceless look on Mr Iginiwari's face that day. Peoples preferred it to being called boi-girl; and it reminded him of the day Ibinabo removed shame from his face and daubed it on Mr Iginiwari's – his debt to her.

*I*binabo starts trudging to the sea. She shuts her eyes and summons guts by chanting, under her breath, words she'd heard from Ol'Bard:

The sea has a voice;
you must have ears to hear it!
I have ears!
The sea sings;
you must love rhythms to hear it!
I love rhythms!

She pictures a happy reunion with her mother: reasons that when she meets her on the other side, she'll explain to her, and reconcile with her, and hug her, and this will be over, and...

*S*he used to be the tender wings of a butterfly, but the loud whispers – about her birth, about her father – among the women on the island made her self-conscious... and she became the hard, edgy teeth of a cub. Other than knowing her physical features come from her father, she knows nothing about him. All her mother had told her, when she pressed her for details of her father and her birth, was: He was a good man. He-was-a-good-man didn't reveal to her who she was; so she went to the school library hoping to find herself there. From *Soul of Lilith*, to *Weep Not Child*, to *The Palmwine Drinkard*, to *The Gods Are Not To Blame*, to *Oliver Twist*, to *Animal Farm*... to everything in print the small library could brag of in its collection, she devoured. But she didn't find herself. Two other things she found there, though: solace and mami wata.

She found solace amidst the bookshelves, the different worlds they held; she found mami wata in the unsolicited verbal narratives of the young, zealous, born-again librarian. In the librarian's peppered yarns, mami wata is the evil sea goddess that drags handsome men into the belly of the sea and holds them there as her slave-lovers; the one that gives with her right hand and takes back with her left; the one that gives barren women children, only for those children to grow up and kill their mothers; the one that makes the sea rumble and flood islands where the people don't offer her sacrifice; the one that demands human sacrifices before a bridge can be built over a sea; the one that put the crude oil under the sea so that one day their people would fight and kill each other over it.

I shouldn't be likened to such a cruel sea goddess, Ibinabo raged. It brought bile to her gullet whenever she was called mami wata.

*A*ll she hears now is the brokenness of her voice against her drumming heart. She seems to float as she shuffles to the sea on bare feet.

She reaches the mouth of the sea and ventures beyond its lips. She flinches as the water envelops her right foot.

She opens her eyes and folds her arms tightly across her chest. The fear of the sea she'd harboured over the years raises its hands to strangle her courage. She adds volume to her chanting, and puts in her left foot.

Her hair flutters behind her ears in the cool assaulting sea breeze; the hem of her gown slithers behind her on the water; the water is crawling up her ankles. On the other side, *I'll again find my feet…*

*W*hat her mother didn't tell her was that she was an undergrad at UNIPORT – poised to become an anatomist – when she met her dashing Scottish lover, an oil worker with Shell. After she lost her parents in the ethnic clash between the Ijaws and the Itsekiris, he became her lifeline: footed her bills, catered for her emotional needs, and planned to take her with him to Scotland. He started talking about having a child, a symbol of the love between them. She never wanted to have a child; she wanted to remain an individual and not lose her identity to motherhood. But she had to adjust her wish to accommodate his. He made it clear: When we arrive in Scotland, you can take a year off and have the baby; there's no need to rush your studies. I have enough money for you not to lift a finger to ever work even after graduation. It sounded good to her.

She was halfway through pregnancy, halfway through organising their court wedding, halfway to securing her visa... halfway into everything when he was abducted by the militant boys. Some said he died of malaria; some said he died in a capsized boat along with a few militants; some said he was mistakenly shot in crossfire between the militants and the rescuing federal soldiers – *which version is true is irrelevant.* Fact, she was left with no money, no certificate, no parents, no government support, nothing but a hungry child. She had to return to the island to fend for her infant daughter. Nothing any more was about her, everything was now about her daughter's welfare; that was when she broke, succumbed to the small dreams and ways of the island women. And the thought of what she had succumbed to made her a bottled storm, ready and eager to burst at every chance.

*T*he calm sea has swallowed Ibinabo to her waist. Peoples arrives at the shore and calls out to her, Ibinabo, stop! But she's too lost in thoughts of her own to hear him. He adds speed to his feet, wades through the water, and grabs her hand. What are you trying to do? he pants.

She stares blankly, allowing the tears to fall.

It's OK, I'm here now. He leads her out of the water – her palm in his feels as tender as Ofoma Bread, his favourite. He leads her beyond the fridge, into the bacha, glad that he could care for her.

When he is with Ibinabo he feels at home, human, alive, and free. He needs her to return to her old self so they'd grow up together to fight the many Mr Iginiwaris and Gov'ments on this island – this their island.

*B*ullying the six-toe girl and calling Ibinabo mami wata were the second and the third reasons Ibinabo's hands were forced to feed Gov'ment sand – the first was born the day Gov'ment became Gov'ment.

That day. She had gone to Peoples' grandmother's tavern, as always, to help Peoples with his homework; Gov'ment had come to buy a bottle of burukutu for his father. A year or thereabouts, it was, since she'd humiliated Mr Iginiwari. Mr Iginiwari had been elected into the State House. He was an Honourable now; living in faraway Port Harcourt, in a mansion; no longer spent hours on a speed boat from the capital to the island like other islanders, but flew into the island in a helicopter; and there was even a rumour he'd soon own an oil-well.

Mr Iginiwari and the principal were in the bar; the principal had confronted Mr Iginiwari for defiling his daughter – a matter whose investigation had gone blind and deaf – and a skirmish ensued.

I'm gov'ment! Mr Iginiwari barked, I make laws, I am the law! You can't do more than a dead rat! Who are you to open your mouth and challenge me? If you ever bring up that matter, I'll make you realise you're just a school principal and nothing more. Once I win my appeal at the Supreme Court, I'll show bad-beles like you what it means to be gov'ment.

The principal didn't utter another word. And Gov'ment saw the principal's silence as proof of his powerlessness; Ibinabo saw the silence as proof of government oppression of the masses.

Shuu! Gov'ment exclaimed. I swear, there's nothing like government power, he muttered to Peoples and Ibinabo.

Ibinabo didn't honour him with a response: she wished she was old enough to punch Mr Iginiwari in the face and dare him to use his *government power* to lock her in prison; as for Gov'ment, she waited for him to fall into her trap for being in awe of Mr Iginiwari.

From that day onwards, Tari insisted he be called Gov'ment: he intended to grow up to be as powerful and intimidating as the Hon Iginiwari.

*I*nside the bacha, Peoples allows her to half the doughnut and sip some water, then announces: I've found a way you can see and talk to your mother – if you still want to.

Her eyes light up: How?

Peoples had gone to the island's jetty, Ol'Bard's hangout, and pressed Ol'Bard for knowledge on how he could see and speak to a dead loved one.

Two ways, Ol'Bard – already tipsy – had said, but each one I tell you will cost you a bottle of burukutu.

Peoples ran home, stole a bottle from his grandmother's wine crate and brought it back to Ol'Bard. Ol'Bard grabbed the bottle, guffawed, and said, Here's one: find any one of the street dogs on the island – in the morning, get the rheum from its eyes and rub it into yours, and you'll begin to see things as dogs do—

Just like that?

My late mother was known for seeing things, how do you think she acquired the ability? It's a secret amongst—

Peoples took off.

You don't want the second option? Ol'Bard called behind him, chuckling.

It's impossible, Ibinabo laments.

We can try. I'll get the rheum for you. I can try it on myself first.

I don't know... I just want to tell her I'm sorry...

*L*ater at night. She's hardly slept for two hours when she jerks awake from a dream, soaked in sweat and urine. In the dream, she was at the shore; her mother appeared before her on the waves as a shark-size catfish; only her head human. Her mother was crying: Ibinabo, mami wata! Ibinabo, mami wata! Is this how you thank me for all the nights I stayed up to keep mosquitoes away from your back? Is this how you pay me back, mami wata?

Then a vortex formed around her mother, and she clutched a faceless boy with her fins. She would submerge to drown the boy, and re-emerge again. Every time she re-emerged, the boy would scream, Ibinabo, help me! And Ibinabo cried, Please, Mother, stop! Mother, I'm sorry!

Recalling the dream makes her flinch. Ibinabo crouches on the bed and hugs her knees to her chest. She scratches her wrist, stops, and drops her head on her knees. The stench of her urine is choking. Shivering, she sobs. Somewhere behind the bacha, Presido is barking persistently.

Presido eats excrement and used to be nameless – not different from other dogs on the island. Peoples' grandmother set it free after poisoning it: realising it might die of hunger under her leash, she thought it better for the poor old, half-sane, half-blind dog to die free. So Presido roams the island having defied death but with a myriad wounds and infections; makes home wherever nightfall meets it. Ol'Bard drunkenly named the dog Presido, the pidgin version of President, because it carries more hungry houseflies with it than a honeycomb would boast of bees.

She sobs herself to sleep. And she doesn't see her mother again.

*D*aybreak offers Ibinabo a fresh feeling, as news of a cure for an incurable disease. The sun is half awake; Ibinabo is fully awake. She doesn't feel eager to see her mother again; she half-heartedly goes through with Peoples' plans mostly not to appear to have grown cold feet.

Peoples has the plan; it's simple. Find a dog, win its attention with a bone, and while it gnaws at it, stoop and caress its forehead, then swipe a finger across the edge of its eye for rheum. The first step is successful, then, as Peoples stretches his hand to Presido's forehead, Presido raises his head, growls, and grabs Peoples' right ankle between his jaws. Peoples topples to the ground and shrieks for help; Ibinabo cries; and Presido lets go of his ankle and trots off, leaving teeth-cuts on Peoples' ankle.

*T*here aren't any anti-rabies drugs at the island hospital. The nurse is willing to look at Peoples' wound, but the best she can do is to dress it and send him home to his grandmother.

*F*our days pass. After consuming various herbal concoctions, Peoples' wound continues to itch and swell; the swelling gradually climbs to his knee. The administrat of the concoction swears the swelling is part of the healing process: he's too proud and greedy to admit the ineffectiveness of his concoctions. Ibinabo and Peoples' grandmother accept the herbalist's profuse assurances – *what other option do we have in the face of despair?* Ibinabo remains by Peoples' side day and night.

*T*he sixth day. Seven of her classmates stop by, including Gov'ment. They file into the sitting room where Peoples is lying asleep on a mattress. Some pull out chairs, some stand, some crouch: all gather around Peoples. The silence in the room is oppressive: they hadn't seen Ibinabo in school since her fight with Gov'ment; she hadn't expected them to come, much less with Gov'ment. She doesn't know how to react to their visit; they don't know what reception to expect.

Ibinabo is sitting at the head of the mattress; the six-toe-girl sits next to her and attempts to lift the silence: Efe and Ebiye also lost their parents in the explosion, she says.

We opened a condolence register for your mother and others, Gov'ment says.

We asked the principal to help get anti-rabies drugs from P-Town, a boy says.

Ibinabo feels grateful for their concern, but remains unsure what to say. Another bout of silence drags; they all keep their eyes on Peoples – he's sweating profusely.

In the bar outside, Peoples' grandmother's radio is on; they catch the tail of a news update:

Hon Iginiwari Douglass lost his appeal at the Supreme Court today. The Appellate Court consequently nullified his election victory into the House of Representatives and ordered the Independent National Electoral Commission to conduct a fresh election in his ward. Meanwhile, Hon Iginiwari has been arrested today by members of the Nigerian Police Force on multiple charges, including child abuse and election racketeering. It is unclear...

Gov'ment springs up and begins to mimic Mr Iginiwari: Listen all of you! I'm the law! Once I win my appeal at the Supreme

Court, I'll stop all of you from going to school and turn all of you into my house-helps!

They all burst into raucous laughter. To Ibinabo, the laughter has the taste of water on a many-days-parched tongue, a cold bath after a many-days-trek under a scorching sun. She relishes it. The laughter lifts the tense air in the room, and the six-toe-girl taps into it. We call you mami wata because you're very beautiful, she blurts out to Ibinabo.

And intelligent, Gov'ment says.

And fearless, a boy says.

You're my mami wata, the six-toe-girl coos to Ibinabo, and leans her head on Ibinabo's shoulder.

Our mami wata! Gov'ment corrects.

As though on cue, another voice from the radio says:

Now to close today's show, I give you Sir Victor Uwaifo's 1966 hit song for your afternoon listening pleasure. And remember…

And Sir Uwaifo's voice rises from the background and soaks up the announcer's voice, crooning his mami wata song.

The song seizes their attention. The surprise on their faces is expressed in wild grins: they hadn't heard a song on mami wata until now. The six-toe-girl gets up and begins a dance move; others join in. Ibinabo feels the boulder lifted off her back, but she still has a scar on her that she needs to clear. As the song closes, she says to them, I appreciate your reasons for calling me mami wata, but I really don't want to be called that. Just call me Ibinabo.

They shrug and grin at her.

Ibinabo scratches her wrist and says, I'm serious! But I promise to still be your mami wata.

They register their agreement.

The six-toe-girl raises her chin to Ibinabo's ear and whispers, I brought strong ointment for that stubborn ringworm — it'll clear it, fiam!

Ibinabo turns to her and chuckles in appreciation.

Their laughter and chatter is cut short by Peoples – he begins to talk in his sleep, drenched in his sweat. He punches the air in fits, seeming to be in a fight. Gov'ment-is-our-enemy, Ibinabo, he babbles, Ibinabo, we'll-force-Presido-down-cripple-Gov'ment. We'll set everyone free! Gov'ment-na-monster...

They regroup around Peoples. To keep him steady on the mattress, Ibinabo grabs his hands; Gov'ment and a boy hold his legs, avoiding the wound. But their effort does little. Peoples screams, Ibinabo, I care for you! Ibinabo, you're—

Anna

Chourouq Nasri

Something is depressing me. I keep thinking of the dream.

Anna, I thought of you the other day. It's nice to think back every now and then. You were kind and generous; people often thought that we were sisters. What I liked most about us were the exchanges, the conversations, the mutual understanding. I had many friends in France, but none matched you.

Yesterday, I stumbled upon an old photo album. You'd be impressed by the quantity of photos it has... photos of us, of our trips. We were young and attractive; we had lovely hair; mine was dark, yours brown. If you were here, we would go through it together; we would put names to the faces; you might even see a face reminding you of my own... of what I once was.

Did this time ever exist? It's gone.

> *Memories take me to unspeakable places*
> *Still unstoried.*

Anna, I thought of you the other day... I was driving to Saidia; just for the sake of driving, thinking, daydreaming. God, I hate Saidia! I remembered how eagerly you longed to come to my home town, to explore the Eastern region: Tafoughalt, Zagzal, Ain Almou, Ras Alma, Saidia. Well, you never did.

But don't worry; Saidia is an ugly town filled with unfinished concrete buildings, and bereft of its natural resources. The sea is almost invisible. Its soul was erased when they removed its huge ancient forest and started the Marina project. Yet its roads swell with tourists from all over Morocco, and even from some foreign countries, in the blazing summer months. People don't seem to have noticed the huge sabotage that transformed a town that was so sparkly, so filled with energy, into a nonsense, soulless place.

I decided to forget you, to forget me... Anna. It's been a very long time. I haven't forgotten you, but I have forgotten me. My God, it's been years! When did we last meet? How did we part?

You had a nice open face. You looked like someone ready to do good to others. When I first saw you at Paris 3 University, I could see immediately that you were someone to trust. I was a complete stranger, and there you were, ready to save me from the loneliness of my long years of graduate studies. You introduced me to Picasso. We took les bateaux mouches to explore the city and watch the fast-running waters that changed colours as the wind pushed the clouds across the sky. You were the best friend I've ever had. But what does 'best friend' mean?

I am tired: the work, the unimaginable stress, the weather, the people... pills are my new friends. I forgot the secret ingredient– that thing that helps people to be happy or at least satisfied with their existence. I searched for it for years. But like a swimmer searching for her jewel in the sea, I was looking for a part of me that I could not see.

Some things in this world are beyond value, like the years I spent in France. Books, images and music console me. There's something magical about music. Music brings colour into my head; it shelters me from the uneasy things that crowd my life. My problem is that I get bored so quickly, and I have to figure out how to break free from this hideous feeling. I move from project to project, hoping to occupy my mind and to escape from the misery of ordinariness.

I returned to Morocco; you stayed in France. I don't know if

I was happy in France. I never felt that Paris was my home; it felt more like a refuge, an escape. I never really had that feeling that binds the inhabitants of a city together. But I was captivated by the museums, the galleries, the libraries, bewitched by the paintings and the sculptures.

I don't feel I belong to Oujda either. I can't stand the female stereotypes, the male traditional culture, the social violence against women. You used to say, a young woman must travel, suffer and explore. The years I spent in France changed the way I saw the world. I spent ten years in France and I'm not sure I ever understood the place.

Back in Oujda, I am confused by Moroccans. I find it difficult to decipher the riddles of Moroccan society. I came to understand that the Doctorate I worked so hard to obtain had no part in answering life's profound questions.

Anna, I still think of you. I am comfortable. I have a car, a job, a salary. I live in my parents' villa in a chic neighborhood. The weather is warm. You used to say, it must be wonderful to be a young woman university professor; to have admirers and to be a poet. I am none of this! I am like a princess locked in her tower, except that I am not a princess, but am locked up anyway.

I don't really miss you. I just need to talk to you.

Oh, that dream! Someone was drowning in the dream!

My colleagues are charming people; yes, they are… I like them… very much. I met a colleague the other day in the supermarket. He talked about his son, saying how brilliant he was. How all his teachers are happy to have him in their classes and think that they will never again have a kid as smart and brilliant. Then he talked about the trip he had just made to Spain with his wife and children. He described how they visited all the important monuments, went to the best restaurants, bought the most expensive clothes. A family man who truly loves his family. Then his phone rang, and I was finally liberated from the burden of pretension and vanity.

I am happy I have come back to Oujda. I like being here. I like walking in the tortuous roads of the medina. I don't really feel tempted to talk to people; but it's fun watching them.

My dreams keep me company, as always. You know me, such a dreamer! I do things loosely, carelessly, recklessly... it's so pleasant to daydream; I feel safe from fear. Sometimes, when we were walking in Park Montsouris, you would say, "You're dreaming, come on, don't do that when I am with you!" You would put your hands in your coat pockets and liked to walk very fast.

What I love about Oujda is its massive medieval walls, the medina's labyrinth of narrow alleys, the disorder of its souks... I love the old city; this part of the city is ablaze with vitality, history and culture. At first, I was perturbed by the poverty-stricken backstreets of Assania. How do we put a city into words? How do we reconcile our love for the city and all it stands for with the pain with which our life is crowded? I was intrigued by the huddled ruined old houses and the wretched lives that must hide within their walls. But then I realised that my life was as rich as the medina, as sad as its gloomy walls. The melancholy of the poor neighborhoods of the medina fuels my own melancholy. I take to the streets of the old city whenever the sadness sits heavily on me.

It's dawn; a new day, but I'll sleep through half of it...

Anna, where are you? I searched for you online, but found nothing. I went to an exhibition the other day at Galerie Moulay Alhassan. Yes; we do have exhibitions... I wish you were with me. How are you? Did you get your PhD? Are you still married to Laurent? Are you happy? Do you have children? Do you remember when I first invited you to my campus room? I was happy to cook for you. I prepared chicken tagine with potatoes and green olives. That was the first time I had ever cooked for anyone. You then invited me for a surprise meal; choucroute. I'd never heard of it before, and you didn't know I couldn't eat pork.

Yesterday, I taught my students the poem by Sylvia Plath, 'The Mirror'. I like this poem; it's as if Plath wrote it for me. The years slip fast through my hands... can we defy death and ageing? Can we defy the passage of time?

In the bewilderment of my first years as a teacher at the university, I had very little free time for me. I spent the first years after coming to Morocco with all my nostalgias intact.

I force myself to go to work everyday. I am not sure that I like my job, teaching... my colleagues lack curiosity – I mean, intellectual curiosity.

That dream! That person drowning! For seven nights in a row, I've had the same dream...

I like the quiet hours of the night. But I also fear the silence, when the world appears in its unbearable nakedness ... that's why I have to fill it with words.

But when the day comes, I am too tired to remember my night-time plans. The fog fills my head. A sharp headache becomes my only world. So, I spend interminable hours watching Egyptian soap operas, as if I have no life at all. Inactivity makes me more anxious ... the anxiety becomes more intense at night. A confused mix of passion and sadness tears me apart. I hate to feel that the world, my world, is repeating itself.

Amina, a colleague, has become a friend. She invited me to her house. It is elegantly designed; much bigger than I thought, with many living rooms, TV sets, bookshelves. That's how our jolly comradeship was born. That's how I was freed from academic solitude. I try to be frank and cheerful, as a good friend should.

Do you remember when we went to La Brioche Dorée, sipped our coffee, ate our tartes aux framboises, and talked about our childhood dreams? I said I wanted to be an acrobat when I was a kid; you said you wanted to be a painter...

Anna, where are you? Are you alive? The person drowning in my dream resembles you. But it cannot be you. Your absence and silence are unbearable.

While I was lying in my bed yesterday morning, trying to figure out a motivation strong enough to make me get out of bed, the phone rang. I thought I had turned it off. It was a private number. I hesitated, then answered. I could hear someone breathing, then a strange voice...

I am living at home, with my family. My parents are good… sometimes they chatter with each other like a loving couple.

I might as well be living in the Sahara desert. Little did I ever think I would spend the rest of my life in Oujda with my now elderly parents. I never cry, except when my heart is full. I pray, I pray, I pray… I am not alone when I pray. This is my only solace. I take comfort in the idea that God is listening to me. Do you remember when you told me that it was good to feel the company of God? We were walking in Park Montsouri. I didn't know it then, but I was happy. I tried to convert you to Islam; I loved you so much I didn't want you to go to hell! How silly.

Sometimes I wake up in the middle of the night with my head splitting with pain.

> *There's a stone in my head –*
> *It's invisible*
> *Yet it hurts.*

I went to a birthday party at a colleague's house. A table was piled with platters of pastilla, roasted meat, cornes de gazelles, and a large variety of fruits. The guests talked: of life, of kids, of husbands and wives. I joined the conversation, but a part of my soul was silent and isolated in the heart of the crowd.

Some of my colleagues are deeply religious, but their only claim to religion is silence. They have no decisiveness, they are compliant with the shifting winds.

There are too many men at university, that's the trouble; and most of the women keep to themselves.

My passion and enthusiasm are unimaginably violent; they cause me many problems. I am anxious, confused, uncertain and afraid… I pray, I yearn for a different life. I am not totally dead! What pains me most is that love is dragging me towards death, and not towards a new life. I spent half my life dreaming of finding love and the other half suffering from unrequited love. I have fallen in love hundreds of times, but I know nothing of the mechanics of love. For years, I found ways to fall in love without ever having

real relationships with my imaginary lovers...
> *The brain, wild, runs,*
> *the heart is continually drunk*
> *the water suspended —*

I never got a chance to live love; I always did all to hide it. Love is just a lonely habit.

Oh, that dream!

I struggle to give shape to my unchosen life! My house does not really have a warm atmosphere – but I rarely leave it, except to go to work, or to the supermarket.

Anna, I think I saw you drowning in my dream! I want to write you a letter. I have so much to say, but what I have to say will never be heard. Queuing in the rain to watch *Jane Eyre* at the Odeon, do you remember? That was the first time I'd been to a movie theatre. My God, I loved that movie. I'd never seen anything so beautiful! I felt I was somehow like Jane Eyre, defiant, stubborn and tender. What did you say about it? You said "I've had my dose of romance for one night," and then we walked back to Le Crous, giggling and chattering... we were so young. I was so young.

To be young and a girl in Paris... we were so lively, so animated, we used to laugh. We were not dead. I was not dead. I was a graduate student juggling with my future.

Do you remember our days at Le Louvre? How we explored Paris and all the museums and the city's old corners? I miss those days. Oujda is not like that.

Is it raining? It often rains in late September in Oujda. I love the sight of the dead leaves floating on the water, I love the flooding rains in autumn; the rain blurs the lights from the cars, blurs the eyes...

Would you recognise me if you saw me? I don't recognise the stranger that looks back at me in the mirror. I am still shy and as stubbornly private as Charlotte Brontë. Nothing has happened to me, I've been nowhere. People think I am strong, but I am just persuasive. I am a good actress. I fake strength; half the time it works. It takes perception to discern the layers that hide my vulnerability. I realise now that you exerted on me a unique influence, without any desire to influence me.

We shared something.

There's a gap in me I can't fill.

The dream was distressing! I think the person who was drowning was me… but I'm not drowned. Or maybe I am.

Why was it we saw so little of each other after I moved to Antony? Were we still close? What a funny thing, we were such close friends, weren't we? And here I am, unable to reach you. I don't know your family name, that's the funny thing!

I'm still searching in my heart for the meaning of my life. Some people search their entire lives and never find it. I'm on a journey, looking for something invisible, of great value… otherwise, I'll never become whole. I want to step outside myself. I want to get rid of this stranger who lives inside me and pretends to be me. I lost the ability to be pleased with anything. When I returned to Oujda, I realised that the world was more confusing and inaccessible than I could ever have imagined. When I was in France, a good film, a play, an exhibition, a trip or an encounter with friends could make me happy. Back in Oujda, I can now only be diverted. Happiness is a world that grows more distant with each new year.

One frequent subject of our conversations was the future. You would say: "Salma, you'll finish your grad studies, find a teaching position in France, and start a family with a French Muslim."

It did not cross my mind to get in touch with you when I first returned from France. The courses I was preparing, the projects I was busy running, my new life at home, made me forget you for a while. Although my waking life is crowded with my books, my classes; my research … I am many things, but some of the things I am are missing. Anna, how can one 'be' in an unhappy, crowded life? Dreams! Nothing in my world makes sense without them. Is there any possibility of a different destiny?

The House on the Corner

Lester Walbrugh

*L*ike his mother, Emile Oliphant has always collected men. His mother called them her lovers. Emile calls them his life.

*T*he couple sits against the granite boulders, their toes burrowing into the sand.

"You think it's the Xhosa boys?" Emile asks.

"What is?" Faizal scoops up a handful of sand and lets it trickle through his fingers.

"The fires on the mountains. To keep warm at night. I was thinking: we don't have anything like their initiation, where we become men, do we?"

"I don't know," Faizal says. The surf fizzes up. Their knees touch. "Emile, here. It's for you." Faizal draws a rectangular box from the inner pocket of his jacket.

Emile rubs his arms and looks out to sea, pretending not to have heard.

"Take it," Faizal says. He prods Emile's shoulder with the box.

Emile takes it and picks at the sticky tape.

"Come on. Just tear it open."

Emile pulls the wrapping from the box and lifts its lid. He feels a hollow mass in his chest, but instead of letting it well up, he pushes back, fearing what it holds.

"I saw it and thought it was so you. Go on. Try it on."

"This is unnecessary," Emile says, and as he runs the golden necklace through his fingers it catches the setting sun. "I love it though."

Faizal folds his hands over Emile's, retrieves the necklace and clasps it around Emile's neck. Emile winces. "It's beautiful against your skin."

"Thank you."

"What do you say? Dinner at mine?"

"I told my mother I'd be back tonight."

"You'll do no such thing. Tonight, you're staying over. Come on. I'll make dinner."

They pull off at a garage. Faizal swerves around the petrol tanks to park in front of the shop.

"Just getting a few things," he says, slamming the car door.

Emile watches as cars pull up. They are fuzzy and dull in the leftover light of the day. A young couple in a GTi sit staring in front of them while a petrol jockey cleans their windscreen.

They have been together for two years. Emile has met Faizal's mother once, the only woman in a house of men. She flew down to Cape Town for the day. At the lunch she was impeccably dressed. She ate her salad in small bites. Emile had expected a woman softened by the boisterous presence of four men in the house but her stare raised the hairs on the back of his neck. Faizal introduced him as a friend from his running club.

The car door opens and Faizal gets into the driver's seat with a grin on his face and two servings of blueberry cheesecake.

The curry is delicious. Faizal has even washed the rice. It tastes clean and fresh.

"How was the interview?" Faizal asks.

Emile picks at the chunks of spiced lamb. "I won't get the job." His fork clinking against the plate, he scrapes the last of the rice into a little heap.

After dinner, they clear the kitchen in routine silence and with the cheesecake forgotten in the fridge, retreat to the dark living room. A muscular Table Mountain seems pressed up against the wide windows of the eleventh-floor apartment. Emile peers out, and spots a flickering dab of orange on its summit. As he pictures the Xhosa boys trying to find a way down the crags, their loins on fire, Faizal steals up and grabs Emile around the waist. His free hand pushes Emile's cheek against the window. "You did it again," he says.

"I'm sorry."

"You don't listen," Faizal says, punctuating each word with a sharp jab.

Emile visualises the glass pane shattering – sending them plummeting to the street below – and says, "Faizal. Please."

Trembling, Faizal releases his grip. And he slips back as if into an old pair of shoes, the soles of which had long lost any tread. Emile takes the brunt of the punch. He raises a hand to his cut lip, then with each word spraying blood, says, "You will leave me, won't you?" Forgoing the remorse – the tremble of lines on Faizal's brow, the curl of his lip that might be mistaken for a smirk – Emile turns to the bathroom, and in the white cabinet above the basin, he finds the little orange box. From it he slides a sliver of steel.

"You should get it done. It's just more hygienic," Faizal had once said, tugging at his foreskin.

He pulls his trousers and briefs down to his ankles, closes the lid of the toilet and sits down, fumbling with his penis, dark against the white rim. He swallows the blood from his nose. Between thumb and forefinger Emile Oliphant pinches his foreskin, stretches it over the glans of his penis and brings the razor down in a single slice.

— *Do you have a place?*

— *I do, babe.*

— *Address?*

— *Sea Point Main Road. Taronga Mansions, No. 20.*

— *On my way. Give me ten minutes.*

*I*t had all started one afternoon as Emile came home from school. In their backyard, under a peach tree that never bore any fruit, he found his father in yellowed underwear, sitting in the dust, legs drawn up, his knuckles bloodied and swollen. He saw Emile, flung a handful of dry, dark earth aside and said, "Your mother."

His mother was in the kitchen slicing green beans, her hair a black veil over her face. "It's because he can't find a job. Takes a toll on men. Plus, he's a wild spirit. People like that, good luck with them," she said.

Emile shared a nose with his mother. Had he been a girl, he would have moved with the same swing of the hips. With her long, straight hair, green eyes, her full figure, and her free laugh his mother captivated all sorts of men to a silly degree.

In the years after his father left, the men kept flocking. After sex, invigorated and their masculinity restored, her lovers would sometimes enter the bathroom and upon finding Emile in the tub would make a big show of pissing into the toilet bowl. Up and down, left to right they would aim, their half-turgid members on display for Emile to see. Their raw exhibitionism thrilled the young Emile to no end. Few minded staying behind with Emile, after his mother had left for work. Emile was an easy boy, and they were all too keen to satisfy his endless curiosity.

As his mother grew older and her gait became laboured, the parade of men dwindled. It prompted her to say, "It's because of you, you know." For a while Emile lamented the situation, but he was a resourceful boy and soon started gathering his own men. At a precocious fifteen, he would find them in online chatrooms and invite them to the house when his mother was out. Never would the same man visit twice. Emile would block all contact once they had satisfied him. Tall and short, married and single, young and old, they all loved him.

— *Sexy.*

— *Gimme some of that.*

— *Up for a meet?*

— *Can't now. Busy. Maybe later?*

— *OK.*
— *More pics?*

*U*nlike the others, Faizal stayed. His online profile suggested something beyond wet, sticky sheets and morning regrets. "Are you man enough?" its introduction read. Emile sent him a message. When Faizal eschewed the usual conversation openers of "top or bottom?" or "dick size?" and asked Emile if he would like to join him for a coffee, Emile, phone in hand, felt the stirrings of something new and settled deeper into the cushions on his bed.

For all his physical attributes, Faizal baulked at mirrors. He hardly noticed the virility of his reset nose, his angular jaw or dark plummy lips that curled upward at the ends. He was a handsome man, but Faizal saw little that distinguished him from other coloured men. Dress him in a blue overall, squeeze him in between the other overalls on the back of a bakkie on the N2, and he would disappear.

The tendency to downplay his looks might suggest a lack of confidence, or hint at hubris, but to the keen observer, it imparted an attractive insouciance. Emile sometimes thought, had they been raised in the same village, that Faizal would have found him indistinct from his friends: all ash-brown limbs, mini afros and knobbly knees. Faizal was five years older than him; at thirteen, he would have already tasted a cigarette; would have known the appropriate dash of Coke to brandy; would have French-kissed a girl. In summer, he would have been the one in the group of friends to cordon off the patch of white sand on the banks of the farm dam, where they would laugh and gambol and throw one another into the rooibos-tea water, cackling and screaming, while on the far side Emile would be leaning on a branch dipping into the cool dam, dreaming of being noticed.

Faizal was sturdy by design. He lacked superfluous elements. The simple building-blocks that made him were pleasing to the eye and comforting to the heart. However, Faizal only gave as much as he received, and since Emile rarely relented his emotions, for a long while they would meet each other as strangers.

They spent long, lazy days in bed. Emile once loved to run his hands along the ridges of Faizal's torso. He learned to read with his fingertips, like braille, the trio of moles on Faizal's back, imagining it a code for 'I love you'. With fresh eyes and curious hands, Emile explored his new lover as he had countless others before.

Then they grew close.

In a rare instance of intimacy, Faizal confessed how in Johannesburg he had felt adrift, a helium-filled balloon in the aftermath of a birthday party. In Cape Town, he said, despite the physical resemblance to the locals, he felt no more at home – his speech, a Highveld staccato cut from summer thunderstorms and rubbed dry by the winters, still betrayed his roots. Yet he preferred Cape Town. He reasoned that it was far better to feel like a stranger in an unfamiliar city than in your own home.

In the same limited breath, he mentioned his family. He let slip how his father loved women, and told Emile that he supported the blows his mother rained on his father's head. Up until the present day, his father had never stopped loving women, and his mother had never stopped dealing out the blows. But despite all this, they were still together. "My father provides for her, you see," Faizal said. "In return, my mother gives meaning to his role as the provider, the man of the house."

They need each other, Faizal said.

Emile nodded at this, switched off the bedside lamp, turned, and went to sleep.

*D*iscreet older guy new to Cape Town. Looking for fun or more. Faceless profiles will be ignored. So will racists, ageists, homophobes and all other 'ists' and 'phobes'. Moneyboys go find your luck elsewhere. Kind and gentle soul.

*A*round Emile's hometown, the sun is struggling to pierce through the thick, dirt-yellow smoke from the burning mountains. It is the seventh consecutive day of fires, and the wind is showing no sign of abating. Soot is whirling about their house while his mother roams the kitchen. She is frying eggs, mumbling about the fires being the work of vagrants, or maybe the Xhosa boys keeping warm. "This time of the year mos where they go to the mountain. Should have sent your father that way, too. Would've done him a world of good. But anyway, I wonder how many of the poor boys will survive this time. Some die mos because of that thing they do, cutting off their foreskins and smearing the wound with spit and wrapping it up in leaves. No medicine, nothing. Now how can you do that in this day and age?" She fidgets in the fridge. "Mustn't forget to bring in the washing." Her hair has greyed. It looks as if she has stood outside, collecting flecks of ash from the fire.

*W*ith a finger, Emile dabs at the yolk in the corner of his mouth, then traces the raised skin of the cut on his lip.

"Will you see Faizal today?" his mother asks as she slices green beans. Watching the flicker of the blade gripped between her thumb and forefinger, Emile sinks into a daze.

It needed to rain. Emile concluded he and Faizal needed to stand outside until they were soaked. Wind and sun would bring rust and a comfort with the familiar. If they were to be men, both would have to whisper, "I'm cold". But Emile recognises the wall inside him. He feels its hard surface underneath his skin, and imagines if he scratched his arm, it would release a fragrance redolent of wet cement.

"Yes," he says, snapping out of his reverie. He grabs his car keys.

"Tell him he must come visit again. And good luck with the interview!" she shouts after him.

On Nelson Mandela Boulevard, just past Groote Schuur Hospital, Emile plunges his car headlong into the city bowl. As in his village, the air in the city suggests burning bush.

In a coffee shop, Emile finds a seat at the counter running the length of the street-facing windows, and fishes his phone from his bag. He checks his email and scrolls through Instagram. A message from Faizal pops up. He will join Emile, briefly, for a coffee. Then, with some resignation and more out of boredom than lewd intention, Emile logs onto the dating site for the first time in days. Messages have piled up. They like him. They like his profile picture, his carefully worded introduction, and have taken the time to send a brief message. At first, he replies to a nice smile, to a witty remark, to a photo showing off a work of abs. His replies soon grow indiscriminate, and when Emile lifts his head to catch his breath, he finds he has chatted with over twenty men. Some of the more risqué exchanges have given him a hard-on. In his last visit, the doctor had said to wait one more week, but everything seems fine. There is little discomfort. The burn on his penis has been curbing his desire, and has given him a legitimate excuse to dodge Faizal's advances, but somehow Emile has never failed to get excited by the thought of being with one more stranger.

— *Meet now?*

— *Do you have a place?*

— *No. Any ideas? I'm open.*

— *Bloubergstrand. The parking lot there?*

— *Give me twenty minutes. I'm in a blue Opel.*

— *White Golf.*

— *OK.*

They met at the crepuscular beachfront. The stranger's hand fell on his shoulder, and the frisson drew a gasp from Emile.

*E*mile slips the phone back into his bag. Faizal, in his singular presence that sucks all the air from a room, will soon arrive.

"Could I have a glass of water, please? Just tap water is OK. No ice, thank you." Emile catches the eye of a bearded, slightly older man to his left, and smiles at him just as Faizal strides through the ornate doors of the coffee shop.

Faizal sits down, orders a flat white and mentions the fire on Signal Hill. "We need rain," he says.

Emile looks at his boyfriend, at the slight bulge where his eyebrows meet and he wonders, not for the first time: if the mark of a free soul is to become tangible, how would he be able to tell? How much easier would it be if there was a sign, he laments inwardly: the lift of an eyebrow, a glint in the eye that said, "Listen here, you're my man. This is important. This matters." But there is no such thing as a real man. No amount of cut foreskins can replace a limp character, or fortify a fragile self. Emile knows. This is his life.

"What time's your interview?" Faizal asks.

"Eleven. I'm still debating going. Don't think I'll get the job."

"What will you do, then?"

Emile sips from the glass of water, surveying the coffee shop. The waiter is scribbling on his pad and his customer, a woman, nods vehemently, as if she wants to get the order over and done with. Emile empathises. "I'm not going. I'll go to a bookshop. Read. Browse. Whatever. I'll wait for you."

Faizal knows better than to try to reason. "You sure? Can we meet at five, then? Let's go out for dinner."

Emile nods. Faizal rises and kisses him on his cheek. "See you later," he says. He pays their bill and leaves, throwing a last, hopeful glance at Emile.

As Emile watches his boyfriend drive off, the bearded man slides into the seat undoubtedly still warm from Faizal's buttocks. "Hi, I've seen you here before."

"Oh, uhm. Yes. That's very observant. I usually come here. Best coffee."

"Hard to miss a handsome man like you. Your boyfriend?" The man raises his chin in the direction of the door.

"Yes." But on his cheek, Emile feels Faizal's kiss fading. He pauses for a second, then adds, "Oh, I mean, no. I mean, he's just some ... a friend."

"I see. Good." The man smiles. "I was wondering. If you have time and if you're free for the next couple of hours, I live just here, on the corner. How about it? Let's get acquainted there? My coffee is better anyways."

Emile glances at his watch, a perfunctory gesture. He shifts, and his open shirt exposes his necklace. It catches the light from an overhead lamp, throwing a golden twinkle onto the man's face.

"Sounds good," Emile says.

While back in his home village his mother is collecting his briefs from the washing line before they turn yellow from the smoke, the men leave the coffee shop, and slip past the line of cars collecting ash from the Signal Hill fire to the house on the corner.

This Is What Waking Feels Like

Alithnayn Abdulkareem

I wish Ismailah would return my body the way it was before he left himself inside me. I wear a false skin now, underneath jagged pieces of meat, blood and electricity. All he's left me with are dreams and fractured memories. Every night I close my eyes and the same story plays out.

I am in a corner looking at myself on a prayer mat in supplication, kneeling in a yellow scarf with eyes lined with kohl. An animal leaps towards my form, baring white fangs in a black mouth. It hovers over my head for a second before biting it off, clean. The rest of my body flops onto the mat and red spurts from the hole between my shoulders, spreading in the direction of Mecca. I scream and the animal turns toward me. It opens its mouth and Ismailah's voice emerges from it, saying "assalamu alaykum waramatullahi wabarakatu". Then it roars. I turn and run towards the stairs. My throat hurts as Surah's trip over themselves to reach my lips. Ayatul Kursiyu singes my bottom lip as I recite it over and over. The stairs are never-ending, and desperate verses pump energy from my chest to my legs. I reach for my tingling ears, but my traitorous hands refuse to move. A wind blows past, and I look at the corridor. Something soft touches my back. I turn to look, but I am blinded by a surge of light and fall back into my bed where everything is dark again. My eyelids won't open, my body will not move.

"Wriggle your toes," I chant as I brace myself for the surge of memories.

My nose picks up the scent of cognac and sandalwood. I can hear the sound of Ismailah's laugh. My skin starts leaking sweat and spit trickles from the sides of my mouth. My cheeks remember the feel of his bristles and the heat of his breath on my pores.

"Wriggle your toes."

My body remains defiant as the rest of the night rushes at me in high definition. My skin, burning at the points where the carpet hit my elbow and ass. The slap of Ismailah's balls against said ass. The sound of air escaping as my head was pushed into a futon. More sweat and spit and nerves and skin.

"Wriggle your toes, Alif!"

My legs jerk under the final command and my lids snap open. I sit up, wet.

In the bathroom, I soap my panties and hold them under the water until my juice stains are replaced by lather. Then I stand under the showerhead, letting water run over me for at least twenty minutes, as I have been doing every day since the incident. I spend another five holding the shower head under my crotch, feeling hot water on me until I prune.

Back in my room, there is a text from my brother. "Breakfast." I pick the day's pretence. Yellow abaya to bring out my golden eyes. I pack my braids into a bun and cover them with a black scarf.

Lion texts me on my way downstairs. "In your area."

"Pick me up in twenty," I text back.

Downstairs, my brother Isa is pouring out coffee while his wife Huddah is scooping eggs onto three plates. They are a picturesque couple. Their wedding pictures were so adorable they went viral. Everyone in Abuja considers them couple goals. Isa is six foot and earns seven figures as an engineer. Huddah, former consultant, now runs a small centre for the arts and writes poetry. The whites of her eyes stand out against her skin, which is as fresh as just-ripe bananas.

Isa has chased normal all his life. Now living in a three-bedroom bungalow expecting a first child, he has the perfect family, at least on paper. He might have the same in life, if God hadn't saddled him with a sad sack of a sister. I sit at the table, and they look at me. Huddah's eyes rest on my hijab and her lips tilt up a little. Isa scans me until he reaches my arms. He blinks twice at my long sleeves before sitting down and putting his cup to his lips. I take one bite of toast and use my fork to turn my poached egg into a scrambled one.

"How was your night?" he asks.

The "night" is never just a word from him. Every time he corners me with concern, he stuffs the question mark with extra air that leaves his mouth to enter under my skin and heat it up. I can't cool down until I give him a satisfactory answer. After a year with them, I have practiced enough so that when I say "fine", my voice betrays no slips. I never want it to break in front of Isa or Huddah again. If I hadn't told them about Ismailah, maybe by now I would have my own place. Somewhere near Maitama or Wuse Two.

Don't ever tell your brother another man raped you. He will keep you in a well-meaning box with gilded gold bars that burn if you touch them. He will forget about who you used to be. Who you still are. Witty and easy to false outrage. He will forget that you can laugh. All he will remember is the sound of water slapping stone because the blood from his heart is pumping too fast against his chest and sloshing about his ears. He will remember you bleeding from your eyes as you tell him in a calm voice that a boy took your body, and you are only telling him now because last night you found yourself researching ways to cut yourself.

He will shiver and his legs will lose their strength, and he and Huddah will whisper behind you and order you to see a doctor for six months. Even after the doctor gives them encouraging feedback, the image of you breaking will never leave them. They will feed the image poached eggs and perfect toast, crisp jollof and spicy èfọ́ riro. They will bristle when you wear anything above the ankles or short sleeved. They never tell you you have a curfew but the day you got home at 10pm, Huddah was crying in the corner and Isa had already called the police.

So I practice my tone and movements to match theirs. Isa favours greys and blues. Huddah likes purple and black. They don't shake hands with people of the opposite gender, they smile and wave, they both cross their legs, they sip not gulp, they always say please and thank you. They never try to jump queues. I copy them until their concern over me slackens. It is why after taking two more bites of toast and two spoons of egg, I can say, "I'm going out."

"OK, where?" Huddah asks. Isa is drinking, but his sips have paused.

I don't know where Lion is headed. Still I reply, "Jabi Lake Mall. Movie."

My phone vibrates. "I'm outside," Lion texts. I stand and move to hug them both.

Isa makes to stand up, but Huddah holds his hand. They chorus "Bye" as I leave.

Outside, Lion holds the passenger door open. I climb in and she closes the door, then gets into the driver's seat. I don't realise I've been holding my breath until she closes her door and starts the car.

"You look pretty," she says.

"Thank you."

I don't know that I would normally be friends with Lion. She is skinny and taller than me, with long straight hair and round glasses. She has more than one idea for a perfect day: "Some days I want to eat ice cream and play guitar all day; some days I want breakfast, lunch and dinner in different countries."

"Mine would be drinking the finest wine and reading the best books in the world."

"That's unimaginative," Lion laughed.

"And ice cream is the stuff of fantasy."

She laughed again and ran a hand through her hair before

swatting the air near my ear. That night, we were drinking rum and pineapple juice, walking around Asokoro.

I kicked a stone. "I think my perfect day would be one without any men in it. In a great museum, dancing barefoot and alone to music."

"Art has never really done it for me."

"Nothing does it for you, Lion."

She smiled. "You just have too many feelings about too many things." Then she leaned towards me and stopped, her little finger just shy of mine.

Lion has never touched me, not even by accident. Whenever we're together, I can take the space between us, and load it with all my disgust and fear. And it can stay there until it is time for me to go home.

"You don't have enough feelings about enough things," I sighed.

"I have one more. Some days I'd want to spend just fucking."

Inside Lion's BMW, Apo brushes past us in a trail of mountains and makeshift shops. I fasten my seatbelt and bob my head to the pop track playing from the car's speakers. I turn to her.

"I like this song. Makes me feel like anything can happen today."

"Well, I have to help PK set up for an event at Aromire place."

"Oh. The art fashion thing. I saw it on Insta. Do you need help?"

"Not really, thanks."

I turn my head away and pick up her phone to scan through her songs. I make a playlist, selecting the songs slowly to keep my hands busy. I never quite know how to be around Lion. She is like white ink on blank paper. I don't know if she's inviting me to the event, or if I have to head back home soon. I start the playlist.

She coughs. "PK asked about you a few times."

"I've missed him."

"Good. Because we're picking him up before going to the space."

She leaves the offer in the middle of the car between us. I pick it up and fold it over my lips, which curve up. "I guess I'm seeing him."

PK is waiting in front of Orange Bank, holding bags. He is wearing a lime-green bomber jacket and black pants that stop at the ankle, with leather sandals. A red bead bracelet on one wrist, and a white one on the other.

Lion gets out and collects the bags from PK, who sees me and screams. I run towards him, and he spins me. I inhale; he smells like vanilla, beautiful and non-threatening.

PK holds my shoulders and pushes me back to look at me fully. His eyes narrow. "Is this what you're wearing to my event?" he piques.

"Green bomber jacket under Abuja sun? OK, Rihanna," I retort.

He laughs and I follow when Lion closes the boot and opens the back door. PK gets in front. I lean forward and tap PK before pointing at my abaya: "I didn't know we would be going out today."

"It's OK. I can lend you a kimono."

"Thanks. Love your jacket. It's a proper baby-boy uniform."

PK laughs. Then he turns to Lion. "I finally saw Shogugekinashoma."

They slip into anime talk, and I lean back until I am lying on the seat with my legs folded up. PK and I used to be close. We spent many late nights dancing, laughing and splitting bills for alcohol when we both lived in Lagos. I don't know why he kept me around. I kept him because his eyes never landed on my lips or cleavage, his hands never grazed my butt, and he was always kind.

I asked him once if he liked men or women. At an after-hour's event, when we were soaked in live music and menthol cigarettes. He smiled. "I don't know. I'm still young and finding out."

When I told Huddah, she laughed and told me, "Honey, that's code for gay."

Another time, I heard PK tell someone he was asexual. Since then, I've never asked who he's fucking. I heard not too long ago that he's become the possession of Chike Onaokwu, who owns

Aromire place. They spend a lot of time together. PK calls him his mentor. His running line is "Chike wants to set up something in Lagos and I'm helping him with my subculture connects."

Since when did a millionaire need connects from a twenty something up-and-coming curator? I've never asked him, it's not my business. It is also why I ignore the fact that the baby-boy jacket is an original Black Culture, something beyond the salary of a small-time curator.

I close my eyes to try to let the music sink in. I like and respect PK. And sometimes I pity his poor hiding skills, but who am I to speculate? If a gun was put to my head and my only way out was to fuck another man, I might take the gun.

"Babe, are you still celibate?" PK chirps from the front. Lion accelerates and PK bangs his head on the car door before she hits the brakes.

"Ouch, Lion," PK chirps.

"Sorry," she responds as she gets out to open the door for me. I blink a thank-you to her for not making me answer. She shrugs. We get the bags from the boot and walk inside.

"I'm getting you laid tonight," PK chuckles.

Aromire is a studio-size space. Chike, who had artistic ambitions, initially used it as a space to experiment with oil and acrylic. He ditched them for photography when he realised he didn't have the patience or skill to be a painter. Photography also failed him, and the place had become an ironic spot for types who were dissatisfied with what the television and radio stations deemed appropriate. Like some reverse rebellion fuelled by youth and too many Red Bulls and Red Labels, young people from the fringes flocked to Chike's studio to drink and mock his works. He became an icon of the so-bad-its-almost-good movement, which he termed Fuck Art. He recruited his curators: PK, and a video guy who made minute-long Instagram highlights that barraged society. He had excellent taste in films, so screenings started there. This art and fashion fusion event was his first foray into respectability. Now the whole studio had been repainted white with gallery lights hung above the canvasses. PK had sourced the best talent from Kano and Kaduna. No Lagosians, PK had insisted; this victory could do without their stink of superiority.

The space was filled with a din; the screech of wood dragging on cement, the bang of nail on plaster, the tear-slip of tape being removed, and a babble of inflections and words.

"Call them again."

"No, this won't fit here. Move it to the right?"

"The beers are more than the ciders."

I lean on the balls of my feet and rock myself forward, then backwards. I'm not sure if I fit into this puzzle. I go behind a table and watch Lion. She puts on a blue elastic headband to stop her hair getting in her face. She is allocating space to designers circled around her. When they dissipate, she marks out marks out areas with tape, pointing them to their respective places.

The space transforms in the next few hours. By the time dusk approaches, a DJ is testing out his turntables, and a line is forming in the bathroom for people to change. The pieces have been hung and the studio is filling up with people who aren't dressed up in black T-shirts that say "Aromire Presents".

PK is directing men who are lugging paintings around. "Try it there, a little to the left. Put this one on top. We need to adjust the light."

"Have the catalogues arrived?"

Occasionally, his arms slacken and his head tilts towards me, then towards a new guy who has entered. I haven't been out in public in weeks, but all the men seem to look alike. Monotone shades, pants that end at their ankles and glasses that probably contain no prescription. I shake my head at all of them. One of them approaches Lion. They exchange some words, he smiles at her, and she smiles back. He reaches for her arm, but she turns at the last second and his fingers clasp air. She signals to a carpenter and pushes him at the boy. She smiles at him, and turns to walk towards me. She looks good in white.

"Water. Carton behind you."

I hand it to her, and watch how she tilts her head to drink, observing the journey from lips to belly as the water pushes her skin forward and goes down her throat. I'm surprised by how much I want to lick some of the sweat away from her neck.

It's not the first time I've thought about Lion. Not often, but sometimes in the middle of a book or writing a story, details of her flash and I find myself crafting characters that are based on her. I've never asked who she likes. She has exes she refers to as "they". Once, I thought she wanted to kiss me. She had said something in the car and I'd unwittingly blurted out, "Damn, that just turned me on". She smiled and her eyes lingered. I swallowed and sneezed when I saw her pupils dilate.

"Thanks." She smiles and palms my wrist, and I inhale sharply. Lion was holding cold water, but my wrist bears the imprint of heat.

A boy approaches me smiling, "Hello".

"I have a girlfriend," I blurt.

His brows furrow, and I point to Lion. "She's a jealous type. Or did you just want water?"

He turns and walks past Lion to PK, says something in his ear. PK walks over to me. "Am I missing something?"

"No."

He smirks. "Let's go. Your kimono is upstairs, and I need help bringing the wine down."

We climb upstairs to Chike's office. PK locks the door before turning to me with pursed lips and raised brows. "Hmhmmn."

"I was just trying to fend the guy off, I swear."

He walks over to some cartons and starts rummaging. "Alif, I see how you look at Lion." He brings out a pink shirt. "Are you bi or something? Because I know girls who are less complex and down."

"It's not like that."

He takes off his jacket and slips on the pink shirt. "It's not like that with Lion, or it's not like that with other girls?"

"It's not like…" I help him with the buttons. "I don't know. I'm still young and finding out?" I raise one brow.

He smiles and turns back to the cartons. He brings out a black kimono.

"PK. It's OK if you're gay, you know that, right?"

I remove my abaya and stand in my bandeau and trousers.

His response sands over my skin "Oh, thank you for your permission."

"I didn't mean it like—"

He raises one hand, "Mainstream people and heteronormative labels. I exist on the spectrum, Alif." He holds out the kimono and I slip into it.

"Keep the trousers."

"Maybe I do too."

Someone knocks. PK goes to open the door.

Lion enters. "PK, you're needed."

PK nods and slings a scarf around his neck. He picks up a carton. "Lion, Alif likes you. Alif, I think Lion likes you back. Deal with your shit and come downstairs." He closes the door.

I start twisting my fingers.

Lion stares at me. "I need help with the buttons at the back," she says.

"Lion, I—"

She turns around and I unbutton. She has a birth mark in the middle of her spine and two dimples on her lower back. I flex my fingers and run them over her back. This is a new language, and I am eager for context. I want to take Lion's hand, open her palms and rest them where I am warmest. To have her lift a finger and press my nub until I scream. I finish undoing the buttons and watch her put on another white dress. I zip it up and she turns to me.

"What do you want, Alif?"

I open my mouth, but air pumps into my tongue and it swells up. I bite down on it, but the air stays locked in. Lion looks at me, sighs and walks out.

I don't go down for thirty minutes. I find some cartons of beer, and I guzzle one and a half cans before washing my face. The crop top I had worn under the abaya goes well with my pants. The kimono covers my broad shoulders nicely. The hair is a plus. I trudge downstairs to a party almost in full swing. People are milling about holding cold drinks and leaning their heads towards each other. I spot the newcomers, busy eyes scanning the venue looking for familiar faces, or someone famous to cajole into a selfie. PK and Chike move around together, talking to bloggers and posing for pictures with rich people. I don't see Lion.

I stop in front of a Dami Ajayi. His series, *Power and Potential*, sees him painting society's elite with society's lowest. On the left is Zainab, the actress who starred in the highest grossing film this year and is tapped to be the lead in a TV series in America. Beside her is Mama George, with bleached pink lips and blue eyebrows, an alabaaru who carries loads for people shopping in the market. Both women have brown eyes and clear irises. I lean in to sniff the painting before turning. The real Zainab is standing in front of the painting. She's smiling and talking to her date, and they both turn to walk towards the painting of her, the one I'm in front of. I am shifting to make space for them when I realise her date is Ismailah.

My bottle slips and I grab the neck before it drops. Ismailah reaches for it, then looks up at me. His eyes widen and he smiles. I move past him, but his hand grazes my shoulder before I can escape. I hear "Alif" before my feet carry me towards PK. I pinch the corner of PK's shirt with my thumb and index finger, holding and moving with him as he works the crowd. I sneak glimpses, and Ismailah is there between folds of cloth and flutes of wine, with furrowed brows, running hands through his hair as his head follows PK, who drifts until he gets to Zainab. They air kiss and I look down, ignoring Ismailah's "Hello."

His voice sounds the way I remember it. Like stones skipping over water. He repeats his greeting and tacks my name at the end of it.

I say "Hi," and he reaches for a handshake. "Long time." He turns to Zainab: "A friend I haven't seen in a while."

"Well, you guys catch up then," PK says and takes Zainab aside.

Ismailah leans down until his face is near mine. "Why are you dodging me?"

He looks genuinely concerned, like we are friends. The way PK would ask why I've been avoiding him, or Mummy when we haven't called her in three days. Even as his hand leaves mine, leaving behind dead skin where his palm has touched me, I think about his soft grasp, never too firm. He never pushes. Only that night.

"You're not still mad about that thing, are you? I said I was sorry. I am sorry."

I look down again, willing my body to take the heat out of me and scald the air surrounding him. If it does, he is not showing it. He just keeps staring. I see Lion heading for the exit.

"I have to go," I say and I run towards the exit, ignoring the last "Alif" until the air conditioning is replaced by a warm breeze. I run to Lion's car and lean on it before I exhale. I open the door and sit beside Lion. She's put on makeup. She has beautiful long lashes and her bottom lip sticks out, pink. The humidity lines my collarbone and Lion's neck with sweat. We open the car doors to let in more air. She turns to me, and I look away from her.

"Alif, look at me."

I turn to her.

"Say it," she whispers.

"Lion—"

"Say it."

"You have to help me. I'm not good at this."

She leans until her nose almost touches mine. She's moved more than halfway. A few feet from us, Aromire is lit in green, some feet away from me. The building shoots pricks of light across the floor and pushes bass out from its concrete. The road is nearly empty. Every minute or so, a car zooms past.

Lion's eyes have flecks of green in them. Her bottom lip has a small tear in the middle. I close my eyes and the small distance between our faces.

One Brief Eruption of Madness

Éric Essono Tsimi

My dear friends,
Ahead of my encounter with a 'confessor' and a lawyer, I can tell you that I no more belong in an asylum than Passi belongs in his prison cell. He belongs here, and I belong there. I want to be heard in a courtroom, not from a couch.

Back when all this began, I was living in a hamlet – the rather pompously named Yaoundé 7. My stay there was only ever meant to be temporary. I was taking a short training course at the Catholic University of Central Africa in Nkolbisson. An introvert by nature, I am unfortunately often perceived as arrogant. Politeness is an overcrowded, frivolous minefield of overblown expectations. In the morning, on my way to class, it would often happen that I didn't feel like wasting time on social niceties, forgetting to return greetings that, in any case, I might well not even have heard. And if, in the evening, I felt like smiling at passers-by, then on my way back to my studio, I'd notice people waiting for an explanation I had no intention of providing. So to avoid disappointment in others, I decided to forgo offering any greetings. It was radical but effective; now nobody spoke to me at all.

No one but Passi. Passi must have been twenty-three or twenty-four years old. He knew my name – I can't remember how he learned it – and always accorded me a 'monsieur'. Monsieur Eric!

You're looking very smart this morning! Good evening, Monsieur Eric! Ah Monsieur Eric, you were with a very beautiful lady yesterday. Ah, Monsieur Eric, all of your lady friends are beautiful, I wish I looked like you, don't you think I look good? I'm more handsome than you are, so the ladies I get should be more beautiful, right? Monsieur Eric, can I help you carry your bag? Monsieur Eric, I have decided to be President of the Republic, and you'll be – I'll appoint you Director General of the National Oil Company. Monsieur Eric, I want to be a singer – and so on.

In reality, Passi was sporadically afflicted with mental disorders. This disability condemned him to hanging around the neighbourhood, never having been able to get to the end of an academic year without a psychotic crisis kicking in. And yet, it was clear that he was exceptionally intelligent. And as he said, he was indeed a handsome man. What with his persistence in talking to me even though almost nobody else greeted me, even though I sometimes ignored him, and his childlike admiration for the simplest of things, I ended up being moved in spite of myself. So Passi became my friend, in a way. He offered me small acts of service, such as replenishing my buckets of water when the supply was cut off, or chasing to find me a bike-taxi when I was running late, picking up my clothes from the cleaner or... but don't get the wrong idea, I didn't take advantage of him. He was a good guy, Passi. He taught me that you can only like people by accepting their weaknesses and faults; not despite their weaknesses, but with their weaknesses. I didn't doubt the sincerity of his admiration or his friendship. He was more than a little nuts, but I liked and admired him in return.

That day, I was in black. A religious service was being held on campus in memory of a student recently struck down by meningitis. Passi saw me walking by slowly and offered to accompany me. He had always wanted to turn up at 'the hill' and show me how talented he was with the ladies. I allowed him to follow me – after all, I was intending to walk all the way to my destination. The steady stream of his babble was just enough to distract me from thoughts of my landlord, who was getting stroppy about my overdue rent. Every student in the world has money problems at some point during their studies, and I was no exception.

The Mass had begun. I was at once both there and elsewhere. As for Passi – a calm seemed to have descended upon him. I tore myself away from my thoughts to note that he was clearly transfixed, the prick of Cupid's arrow having kick-started his emotional-cardiac apparatus with a jolt. His eyes shining with desire, he looked lovingly, indecently, and with comical insistence, at the lovely Laura.

I smiled, reflecting that he was perhaps setting his sights a little high. This madman would never manage to pull a 'go' of her calibre. My condescending amusement soon turned to metaphysical anguish as I spotted the lovely Laura answering his gaze in a way that was explicit, to say the least. Passi didn't actually have the word 'crazy' stamped on his forehead. During the "Brothers and sisters, offer one another the sign of peace" ritual, he managed to travel to the far side of the nave, where he tightly squeezed the hand of the lovely Laura, and she seemed to offer no objection.

Laura! I would have been madly in love with her myself, had I believed for a single second that any approach I made would not have led swiftly to a dead end. In the eponymous play, Molière's Scapin says that he hated "those fearful hearts which, by dint of thinking of what may happen, never undertake anything". I should have acted crazy, and loved her without pausing to measure my chances of success. She was the kind of girl everyone loves, yet whom everyone gives up on in a sort of mass resignation; there is a casual disinterest to the way she walks, an absence of obvious flaws – and men need to know a woman is vulnerable before they attempt to woo her. If she is strong, sovereign, then as a rule, they simply go to pieces. I am but a man! She was constantly surrounded by an aura of simultaneous attraction and repulsion that would inspire doubt in even the most conceited suitor.

Passi's lips were dry. There is no denying it: the poor boy was madly in love. After the "Ite, missa est," he swore blind that his life now made complete sense. And on the square in front of the church, his progress was slowed by Bella, the girlfriend of the deceased, who was accepting words of condolence from all comers. He recognised her – she was from Nkolbisson, his neighbourhood – and could hardly avoid taking his place in line. In so doing, he lost sight of Laura. Literally stunned by the violent, electric shock of this vision, Passi didn't look at me as I walked homewards.

Trying to find Laura, he was panting, becoming frantic as his search became more desperate, refusing point-blank to acknowledge his own level of distress. He went on seeking her until nightfall, his madness allowing him to hope that the sublime Laura might want him or even seek him out, throwing herself into his arms, declaring: "I love you too, let's take off for Limbé, take me to see the Rhumsiki..."

Sunday. There was no water in my shower. I didn't know whether it was a normal cut-off – that reminded me, I hadn't paid my water bill yet – or if the landlord had carried out the first of his threats. I didn't even have any contingency reserves. I got out my containers and hauled them outside – and that's when I saw Passi.

"What's this?" I asked. "I hope you haven't been there all night?"

The day had dawned bleaker still for Passi, as was clear from his red eyes and dulled expression. His quest to find the divine Laura had been fruitless.

"I'm not up for this," I told him, exasperated.

"No water, Monsieur Eric?"

"I have neither water nor money nor peace, so..."

Passi took my containers and pulled a wad of high-denomination banknotes from his pocket.

"Here," he said, offering five ten-thousand franc notes, "just pay me back when you can."

I was flabbergasted and barely had time to utter my thanks before he added, "I'll make sure the janitor leaves you alone until you get back on your feet."

In one fell swoop, Passi had provided everything I craved: peace, water, and money. What else could I contrive to offer him? I was losing my shine!

"So will you put me in touch with this mixed-race beauty – La Métisse?"

"I'll introduce you to another girl, Passi, one who's even hotter."

"As hot as the beauty of yesterday?"

"Even hotter!"

"As hot as your girlfriend the other night?"

"More beautiful than any of them."

"No, Monsieur Eric, you can keep them all. Just tell me how to find La Métisse."

"Listen, I'll be straight with you. That girl is no small fry. Her father is a Minister of the Republic."

"So? I'll be President."

He was raving again. I could not inflict this man on the beautiful Laura, at least not until I had had a chance with her.

"Passi, I can't help you, and that's my last word on the matter."

It was as if something snapped inside him. He said: "This girl was attending the Mass for the funeral of my friend's friend. Had it been my friend that had died, she would surely have attended that funeral too. I'm going to kill my friend, and that way, I'll get to see her again."

Worse was to come. He went on, "Monsieur Eric, I'm going to have to kill you too. I'm going home to think about how best to do it."

I was jolted, but strove not to show it. "Good luck, Passi! You know, the odds really are against you. One minute you want the moon for yourself, the next you think the spirit of Jack the Ripper is within you. Look at yourself: you're big, but you're a lightweight. You're a madman, not a killer."

"That's true, Monsieur Eric, you are stronger than me. But a killer – if he's clever and cowardly – he kills!"

With this, Passi went home, visibly disturbed. His mood had knocked me off balance. My response had of course been arrogant, but there had been determination in his voice as he had promised to kill me. I hadn't believed him, of course – but I almost had, and it was chilling.

Monday. I had spent the previous evening with friends at the Kristel Café, at Titi Garage. I was hungover. It was ten o'clock, and I was late for class once again. I saw that the street was crowded. I had neither the time nor the inclination to hang around, but then I heard the voice of Passi, who was surrounded by police officers armed to the teeth. He was being led towards a police van. "Monsieur Eric," he shouted, all excited, "I killed Bella. Come to the prison and tell me when the funeral is, I must see La Métisse again."

He wasn't much bothered by the loss of a liberty that was of no practical use. It was common knowledge that Passi was mad. Perhaps he would be released. His father, who was never around when he was needed, would nevertheless do all he could to get him out. Incidentally, I had heard that this avaricious father had traded his son's mental health for prosperity. But these stories people tell – you never know how true they are. Passi had once told me that he was an heir, that he'd lost his mother.

After the murder, I realised, retrospectively, that Passi was incapable of lying. I didn't know whether to fear him – or pity him. And that poor Bella! First bereaved and now deceased. Before the police van started up, Passi had time to call out: "Monsieur Eric, Bella lived only for him, she'll be really happy to know that she died for him. Tell La Métisse we'll go to Limbé. She said she wanted to visit the Rhumsiki – I'll take her."

*I*t was break time on campus. The creative writing class had started more than two hours ago. The lovely Laura was there. I approached her, although I didn't at first succeed in catching her eye. I asked her to allow me five minutes, promising that I was unlikely to reach the five-minute mark.

"There's no rush!" she replied, haughty and radiant. The heat that invaded my body was so intense that I was trembling. I told her a true story, the very real tragedy of Passi. She smiled and said I had a vivid imagination, that there was no need to kill to get her phone number, and that she would like to visit Mount Rhumsiki: she deigned to grab my phone from my hand and enter a number into it. Incredulous, I took back my phone (the value of which had just multiplied tenfold) and saw her take flight like a butterfly. "See you soon, Monsieur Eric," she sang – light-hearted, fascinating and colourful. I wasn't sure why, but I found her a little vacuous – though she had never struck me that way before.

*M*y dear friends,
I don't know whether you've seen, or only heard about, my flattering post on Facebook about my oh-so-sweetheart Laura, so recently admitted to full membership of the club of my ex-girlfriends. A girl with such a glowing complexion that I had been fooled into thinking I was somebody – that I could aspire to a destiny as ordinary, and yet as glorious, as the classic fairy-tale ending: marrying and having many children.

However, those of you who have worked alongside me (if only virtually) are familiar with my loathing for public spaces, clichés, ignorance, mediocrity, and ambition. My distaste for such things clearly imposed excessive restrictions on Laura's freedom to come and go, getting in the way of her unexpectedly stupid and pig-headed attempts to consolidate her position.

For many months, I had endured the martyrdom of her plodding views and slapdash use of vocabulary. This worthy child of the neighbourhood of Mvog-Ada would sincerely have had us build a hydroelectric dam at Lom Pangar in a single night – no obstacle was insurmountable to us, just as long as we became husband and wife as soon as possible. Whenever my luck was in, she would put it down to her own extreme devoutness, whereas any adverse circumstance originated (according to her) in my own squalid incredulity. Because I didn't pray, Laura thought me a mystic, and since I described myself as agnostic, she deduced that I had joined who knows what esoteric circle. To her, everything was black or white. In her eyes, for example, my ungodliness was the result of having spent far too much time in the company of 'whites', and when I asked her if Christ was black, if Pope Francis was mixed-race, she simply shrugged her shoulders, gave a wry smile, looked at me with sincere pity, and went off to wash my clothes – as though this was her duty, however far I had strayed, or however mad I might be.

What exasperated me most of all was her critical attitude to my relative eloquence, and her denigration of my work as an author, albeit one poorly paid and of little renown. When I argued that I was working for posterity, she asked me whether she should, in the meantime, satisfy her hunger with the newspaper articles and editors' letters of regret that were piling up in the drawers in my room, like the scars a Sao warrior might have jealously clung to as evidence of his courage and experience.

Oh, you folks and myself: we can all agree that printers' ink and cellulose do not constitute a balanced diet. However, the tone of her criticism was singularly hurtful, and resonated all the more, knowing that she considered writing to be snobbery. That said, Laura was not entirely devoid of intelligence; she very easily guessed when her words had hit their mark, and if I raised my voice even a little, she would counter, mockingly: "Stick it up your arse!" Which, as you will agree, is an outrageously vulgar thing to say in the home of a writer.

Some time ago, to prove once and for all that it is 'by writing that one becomes a writer', the moment I received a cheque from my publishers (for back payment of royalties on a booklet published five years ago), I took Laura out to eat at a chic Cameroonian restaurant in Tsinga. And since eating builds the appetite, the next day, she demanded a meal at the Chinese restaurant in Bastos! On top form, she added (quoting the cabaret singer Chantal Ayissi as though she were an essayist published by Harvard University Press): "A woman is like a car, she needs to be maintained."

Platitudes like this make me literally beside myself with rage, but I managed to contain myself, remarking only that it was precisely because of a letter from a publisher that I had been able to take her out to 'stuff her face' the previous evening.

Your honour, Monsieur le Procureur, ladies, and gentlemen, Laura was so completely devoted to her basest gastric concerns that she failed to understand that I was teasing her. And since she insisted on ignoring a brilliant article I had exposed to her admiration, I became so enraged that I could feel myself weakening, my reason wavering, as she calmly answered me, as though in a monologue, saying that she would not be stuffing her face with my published paper. That article had earned me a more-than-glowing letter from a senior civil servant at the Presidency of the Republic. Laura was hopelessly, appallingly philistine. I looked at her again, asking myself by what historical chance, by which astrological accident, our paths could have crossed. Ultimately – and perhaps this was the crux of the problem – they had crossed without our ever really meeting one another.

The connection was of course Passi. Let me remind the assembly of that misunderstood oddball. He who was writing and singing love pieces inspired by Laura: "Love, bittersweet fruit, which Heaven allows the earth to produce for life's happiness, why is it necessary that you cause madness and death? And why are we Africans abusing everything?"

Before knowing Laura as intimately as I do now, I was convinced that she was a goddess. And so was Passi. Thus, uttering her name, he would shudder involuntarily... Then, resuming his thoughts about love, he would babble: "All these are ways of speaking, Monsieur Eric. One does not die for that thing except in cinematographic turnips. But there are indeed women who stir the souls of men! Laura intoxicates me. My mind is heated by this sole thought, and it's never calm except with the relief of a heady and full-bodied wine. Did you hear anything from her? Did she speak of me? Did you breathe the air she had just exhaled, I'm begging you to tell me! Don't you see that my head is turning on me? She must be mine, or I must leave this life forever. I know people say I'm crazy. What does it matter if love proves it? This love will cure me. Laura is not the girl for you: a temperament like yours does not like to languish. Difficulties irritate you. And obstacles you can't quickly defeat extinguish your soul's passions, rather than inflaming them. People like you must have a perpetual nourishment. If you were in love with Laura today, you would forget her tomorrow, erase her, kill her, if she prevented you from being the centre of the world. The raging madman is not who you think. Look at me! I would kill to win her affection, but beautiful Laura would never suffer for my sake. Monsieur Eric, I look for the 'F' link. Laura and I were destined to be together. I am Passi, she is Laura… we are PassiFlora, the flower my father bought to treat my insanity."

*B*ack to that fateful day when Laura mocked my article. Stretched out on my bed, we were separated by several copies of the daily paper (bringing to mind the old French adage about the wastefulness of giving jam to pigs), and I resolved to actually stuff her face, once and for all, with my paper. She who was capable of admiring nothing could at least be filled to satiety. She acquiesced as I rammed those very pages she so disdained down her throat, undoubtedly believing it to be some sexual game, some kind of artistic quest. My friends, you know that I would never describe this beautiful believer as a pig. But as a result of my serving up this 'paper jam' to her, she suffocated, her eyes on me, her protest scant, and still deaf to my art.

Gentlemen and ladies of the court, allow me then to invoke this particular extenuating circumstance of the case, concerning the weapon used to commit this crime: your humble servant killed his victim using paper and ink. With words, then, ladies and gentlemen! In terms of motive, there was no premeditation: yet this was a crime of passion that should be condemned the more harshly for being, so to speak, a crime of exasperation. If exasperation is a state of ordinary madness, as the well-known Latin maxim would have it (*ira furor brevis est*), then you will concur, my friends, that at the end of the day, I belong not in the Hôpital Jamot asylum as my lawyer has pleaded (and where my poor friend Passi should reside), but on conditional release in search of my lost half – the one who might now be willing to consider something other than doing my washing and stuffing her face!

Per Annum

Mpho Phalwane

$\mathcal{M}$y name is Eko. I'm twenty-three years old, but my memory is not. I have only the last ten years. I dread each new day, because with its arrival, I lose a day of my past. I keep a diary. It's almost full. I carry it with me everywhere. In two weeks' time, it will be the only place that has a record of the man responsible for the deaths of everyone I ever knew. Well, everyone before Luka.

How did I get here? To help you understand, I'll tell you *when* I am; it is more important than *where* I am. It is the year 2119, and memory is big business. People like me don't have the luxury of buying additional memory space annually. So they live one year at a time. I'm lucky I have ten.

$\mathcal{B}$ang! Bang! Bang!
Bang! Bang! Bang!

"OK, I'm coming, I'm coming."

It's Luka. The only person I speak to in this condemned house of eight bedrooms shared with ten to twenty people, depending on relationship statuses and friends in need of couches.

"One, two, three, wait for it, and… four." Luka counts as I

undo each lock. One at the top, one at calf level, one at eye level, and the fourth is the main one built into my ten-centimetre-thick steel door.

"Finally! There's my favourite pair of beautiful brown eyes."

"Ha, ha. And there's my favourite head of blond dreadlocks."

"Hey, they're not blond, more like caramel."

"Well your caramel head will be looking for a place in my little bunk when The Dean unleashes his evil on us rodents occupying the outskirts."

"My door can definitely hold, but I'm not sure about the cupboards up against the windows. Not sure if that's going to stop a rodent annihilation."

This time I laugh for real. The furniture pushed against the windows, the mesh outside – they can't stop it. Not even a concrete slab would be enough. That is why I have to go tonight. But why can't I tell Luka? He's my only friend. The only person left to love.

"Are you ready? You said it starts at eight-thirty. It takes over an hour to get there."

"Grab your bike. I'll lock up."

I follow him out, slam the steel door shut, and push the lock in. It clicks as it latches.

$\mathcal{W}$e emerge from the darkness of the outskirts and into the brilliance of the city. The city is sprawled like a giant eight. It has two hearts. One heart is in the north, the side we are entering from. The difference is clear as soon as we emerge from the two-kilometre tunnel, which is filled with lights and cameras. People who look like me and Luka are subject to random searches while the cleaner-looking folks move about unmolested.

But today the boom light is green and it opens before we reach it.

"It's your lucky day, sunshine," Luka shouts.

There's no traffic so we whisk through with no fuss. The stores with their dazzling displays are still open. Northerners with their ponytails and long silk coats gesture at this and that, and behind the counter the assistants are beaming smiles that look too painful to maintain. Above us the tram whizzes past. They run in loops of eight across the city.

Luka once teased me about how I could get a job in the Northern Eight if I smiled more.

"Like this." He'd grinned and twirled.

"Then a rich Northerner would take me in as her mistress; and what would you do without me?"

That hurt and scared him. I didn't mean to. I never mean to hurt him. Not today, either. I hope he will forgive me. Even if he doesn't, I'll give him a year.

The high-pitched buzz of the bike continues unabated. I relax my arms around Luka, and lean my head on his back. Just as I'm getting comfortable, we pass the heart of the Northern Eight, marked by a golden pyramid. It houses the most exclusive convenience and residential centre in the city, and the most evil man alive, The Dean. The pyramid is said to have one hundred levels, with a penthouse at the top, where he lives. Across from the pyramid, multiple screens play various advertisements, and he is in many of them, including on the largest screen. I force myself to keep looking at it. I picture the day history is re-written, and he is the one in a green labour camp uniform, or strapped on a chair for "medical examination".

"Are you OK?" Luka calls.

"One day." I loosen my grip on him.

The bike whizzes past the circle around the golden pyramid and heads east. I am glad we won't have to go past the Towers at the heart of the old city. The Towers were designed as low-cost accommodation a hundred years ago to cater for urban migration. The original one has seventy-five floors and sides the length of ten soccer fields. In the beginning, people were encouraged to move, with convenience and better lifestyles used as a lure. Before long, electricity and fuel outside the city bounds became so expensive that businesses could not survive on the outskirts. People were forced to move into the Tower or twelve similar but smaller buildings. Today, about a hundred thousand people live there.

I open my eyes as Luka swerves violently to the left, then corrects course. Startled, I lift my face from his back.

"Sorry. Plastic bag."

The lights are dimmer in this side of town, and the buildings are greyer and smaller. We're close.

"You'll guide me from here?"

"Slow down a bit."

I pull out the leaflet I packed with my diary, which I have safe between myself and Luka. I look out for the massage parlour called "The East", two streets before the eastern border marked by the river.

I spot it.

"There. Go left. Stop here."

"Why? You said 'The East' massage parlour."

"We didn't come all this way for a massage."

Luka slows down and we find a fence pole between the massage parlour and the adjacent building. We get off, and Luka chains his bike. There is a window on the second floor of the building adjacent to the parlour.

I go ahead of Luka and knock once when we reach the door. A large man opens it immediately. He also has dreadlocks, although his are black and much shorter than Luka's. He has numerous tattoos, the most prominent being a tiger on this forearm.

He introduces himself as Kali and indicates that we should follow him. I'm feeling nervous and Luka looks worried. There are about a dozen other people in the house. It is illuminated by soft dim lights, which makes it hard to see faces. They are talking in low voices. There are sounds of running water and chiming coming from the speakers. I have not heard this kind of music before.

"Drink?" Kali offers us cups.

I grab one without a word and lift it to my mouth, sniffing first.

It is water. Delicious water.

It is not long before Kali gets a signal, acknowledges it with a head bob, and locks the door.

A woman emerges from the back of the house. Her skin looks smooth, but has folds from loss of elasticity. I try to guess her age. Her eyes lock with mine, and her mouth turns into a soft smile as she moves her eyes to other people.

The encounter leaves my heart pounding. Luka puts his arm around me without a word. I'm not sure whether it's to comfort me or himself.

The woman moves to the front of the room. She sits, legs folded on the wooden floor.

"Sit, please." She gestures to the floor in front of her. Kali is already handing out blankets. We are soon quiet.

"You are all seekers. That is why you are here." She speaks softly but firmly, her head-wrap crowning her head like a queen.

"If you're afraid, you're right to be. What we are doing here is dangerous, and illegal. If we're caught, some of you will be test subjects for science, or sentenced to the mines. If you're old like me, you're lucky, because they'll just kill you."

She breaks into a smile. She must be Rosa: the leader of the underground movement I found, or that found me.

"The quest is not easy," she continues. "However, it is possible to remember. Then you and I will no longer be slaves to memory masters such as The Dean. We will be able to remember long enough to teach our children who we are, rather than the stories the memory masters tell about us."

"This is the beginning of re-capturing our identity, from saved contraband books we still have from past centuries, and our written experiences compiled for posterity."

She looks in my direction. "So I was excited to find Eko, one of our newcomers. She has been doing this for herself for over a decade."

Luka turns to me, with a crease in his forehead.

"Of course they were expecting us," I intercept his question.

"And me?"

I look at him and stand as Rosa introduces me, and tells the seated people that I will be reading from my diary.

I sit next to her, open my bag, and take out my diary. I see everyone's eyes on it, like dogs following a bone. I clear my mind and open to the pages I've already decided to read.

"3 May, 2108. Luka found me two years ago wandering and almost starving. I was ten years old and had been living alone for four years. I didn't know how hard the outside world was. I lived with my mother and aunt in a self-sustaining community over a hundred kilometres north of the city. I think. I don't know exactly how far it is. When I left, I walked for two weeks before I saw any signs of human activity. There were days I thought that I was the only person left in the world, but I kept remembering the soldiers. They came and killed everyone in the village. Everyone I had ever known. My mother and aunt, my two best friends, Lola and Diane. They all died the day the soldiers came.

My mother took me to the bunker when it started. She instructed me to stay there and not to come out until she came to get me. She never came back. On the second day, hunger forced me out. I found everyone dead, their bodies sprawled around like my dolls before my mother made me pick them up. I cried over my mother's body for three days, until the smell became unbearable. Then I remembered that when Lola's mother had died, they dug a hole and put her in it. I was six, and there were thirty dead bodies around me. I dug a shallow hole. It took me three days. In it, I buried my mother. The rest of the people I covered with sheets and blankets so I wouldn't have to see their dead faces.

The food lasted me four years. On my tenth birthday, I decided it was time to find other people if I were to survive. I walked until I ran out of water and food. When Luka found me, I was crouching over a stream, trying to fill my bottle with water. 'You'll die a slow and horrible death if you drink that,' he said.

A few years later, I reminded Luka about that day. He told me he didn't remember.

I laughed. 'Don't be silly. How can you forget how you saved a stupid thirsty girl from killing herself with red acidic mine water?'

He looked at me, his hazel eyes filled with confusion. Then he took me to his friend's friend, Byte. Byte scanned my head and found that I had memory for ten years. I was twelve then, and my new memories were starting to overwrite the old ones.

'And Luka? How can he not remember meeting me two years ago?' I felt dizzy.

'Because he's what we call PA – per annum; his memory only lasts a year, and every year is written over.'

I cried for the rest of the day. That evening, I hugged Luka and told him I'd write down the important memories we had, my past included. I'd write about my mother and my life in the village I grew up in, and everything of importance in our life."

I stop reading to find eyes fixed on me. Luka's face has a softness about it. I go back to sit next to him, feeling self-conscious. No one besides him has ever heard that story. I read to him most nights, to remind him of everything we'd been through. He draws. People's faces, so that we never forget them.

The people around me are reaching out to congratulate me. It's a sad memory, though. I want them to pretend they haven't heard it.

It is Rosa's voice that finally breaks the spell. "Thank you, Eko, for sharing such treasures with us." She pauses, then says, "It is that time of the evening. Let us begin with the remembering practice."

"Your teas are ready, friends." Kali speaks from the back, and we stand and fetch cups of hot liquid. We sit back down and Rosa takes us through the sitting and breathing technique. "It's called meditation. With this you can re-establish a connection to your natural memory path to your brain."

I remember that day eleven years ago, kneeling by the river, trying to fill my bottle. I'm not sure if it's the tea or the meditation or my mind creating it from the story I just read. I come out of my daze to find Rosa gone and the room in a state of quiet excitement. Everyone is sharing their experiences, except for Luka, who is standing apart.

"I need some air," he says.

"I'll get you some water."

A tray with a jug of water and plastic cups stacked next to it stands by the window. The events of the evening are still swirling in my head as I pour water into two cups. A soft thud outside makes me poke my finger through the blinds and press down to peer through. To my horror, a soldier in tactical gear worn by raid squads is leaning on the edge of the window, and the stock of an assault rifle protrudes. And across the road, two men run and lodge themselves against a wall. One of them kneels and props his gun; he's not entirely in the shadows, and I see his eyes fall on the window where I'm standing. Before I pull back, I see him signalling that they've been spotted.

The cup falls from my hand and I turn to run. "Raid squad!" I shout-whisper.

Everyone scrambles to their feet, looking for cover or exits. The first bang! sounds, and I see Luka running towards me.

"No! Back! Back!" I'm screaming now.

When I reach Luka, he grabs my arm and heads for the stairs. I see Kali throwing guns to some of the men in the room. A second bang! sounds and the doors come flying into the room. Then a boom! of a gas grenade fills the room. We see Rosa peering down from the stairs.

"Hurry! Up here!" she calls and turns to run up.

Behind us, the sound of shots and screams fill the room. Gunshot flashes and similar screams sound in my head. The voice of my mother in a hysterical whisper: "Stay here, Eko, and don't come out until Mama comes and gets you."

I stumble and fall. "Get up!" Luka pulls harder at my arm, and drags me until we reach the second floor with three other people. The window. It stands before us; big enough for us to fit through.

Luka smashes it with his helmet. He looks back at me, then jumps. I follow suit. So do the two men and a woman who made it up with us. We land as well as one can from five metres up. No broken bones.

Rosa is the last person remaining at the window. "Jump!" Luka hisses.

"I can't." The others bolt as Rosa stands frozen by the window.

"Jump, Rosa, or we're going to die here!" That jolts her. Luka stands under the window and stretches his arms, showing Rosa he will catch her.

"Sit on the ledge and jump from there. I will catch you, I promise."

She puts her legs over the ledge. Meanwhile I unlock the bike, get it started. Only then does Rosa jump.

Luka catches her like she is a doll. His one-point-nine frame easily handles her one-point-five frame. He slings her across the bike. Above, Kali peers through the window.

"Jump, Kali!" Rosa yells.

"I'll catch up. You go on ahead."

"Nooo! Ka-li!" Rosa screams. Luka revs the bike.

We hear few more shots behind us before we turn the corner and are out of range. A minute later, we spot sky rovers; there's no doubt in our minds where they are headed.

*A*fter half an hour of driving along quieter streets, Luka stops the bike, gets off and furiously kicks the ground.

"What the hell was that, Eko? What have you gotten us into?"

"I'm tired of writing and drawing our days away. It's time we joined the fight."

"And I didn't get a say in that?"

"You knew. You just hoped it would all turn out like a fairy-tale. Life is far uglier than this diary suggests." I lift my diary in the air and my exasperation evaporates when I see the look in his eyes. He's wounded.

"I don't lie to you. I just save you from some of it. Sometimes you're so good and hopeful that I selfishly want to keep you like that. Like I'm your memory keeper, you're my hope keeper. So

KANDIE

that if we win one day, then I'd have a piece of unscathed heaven in you."

He moves towards me with his arms open, and I collapse into them.

"OK. What do we do now? We can't go home."

"We'll go to your secret village," Rosa speaks up. I'd forgotten about her.

"What?" Luka and I say together.

"I don't know where it is. I was a child when I left."

"And how will we get there? This bike certainly won't do the job," Luka adds, gesturing at the bike.

"You might not remember it, Eko, but I do."

"How?" I felt like I could hear my mother's voice again. The tea is not completely out of my system yet.

"I've been practicing remembrance, since long before you were born. Like your parents." Rosa says softly, like her mind is transported to a faraway place.

"Who are you?"

"I'm your aunt. You father's older sister. I met you before. Only once. Just before your home was attacked."

She looks down, her face twisted by pain.

"Your father had sent me to go check on the progress of the new plant species your mother and her colleagues were working on. It was a better strain of the anti-neuro-inhibitors that I gave you as a tea back there. The new strain was supposed to last longer, and have fewer side-effects.

"But once I got there, they needed more time because a storm had damaged the generator and fixing it had created delays. They needed a week or two more. That's where I saw you. I left, intending to return. But a week later they were attacked, and we heard that everyone in the village had been killed."

She pauses to cry, then composes herself.

"So when I heard you read that passage tonight..." She sighs and laughs with tears still rolling down her cheeks. "I got fresh hope. For the resistance, and for myself."

The implications of Rosa's words are slowly making their way into my head. Her arms are around me before I can ask any questions. I hug her back, and think about what she said – my father. Could he be alive?

"But someone else must have realised who you could be. I think there are spies in our movement," Rosa says, breaking from the hug. "The raid was unco-ordinated and small. Only one unit, I think. Otherwise we wouldn't have been so lucky."

"So? What is your plan, Rosa?"

"Go to your village. Find the strain of anti-neuro-inhibitors your mother was working on. A lot more people would join us then, and we could have a real shot at ending the era of The Dean."

"Luka? What do you want to do?" I ask.

"I'm in." He smiles.

"Let's get going, then." I smile back.

Sew My Mouth

Cherrie Kandie

$\mathcal{M}$y lover can only love me behind drawn curtains. The bed must not creak or the neighbours will hear us. On Friday evening, when her parents come to visit, my lover cannot love me because they want her to marry a man. We all sit at the small brown rectangular dining table beneath the high serving-hatch that opens to the kitchen. My lover and I sit on one side, her parents on the other. She sits facing her father, who is tall and meaty. He laughs like a big drum. He eats like a big drum too; his inside is large, empty and hollow. He is shoving big ugali mounds into his mouth.

I think that her mother must know, because mothers see the air that mixes between lovers. Her mother must know because she is studying me like a specimen. She narrows her eyes, tightening her brow at the same time. Crow's feet choke the mole next to her left eye. Her face is lined around the eyes, but is otherwise as smooth and deep brown as a loquat seed. Small greyish bushes peep from beneath her blue headscarf; hers is a good strong hairline, just like her daughter's, one that extends far down into her forehead. I turn to my left, and my lover is making concerted conversation with her father, nodding, smiling, matching his raucous laughter, pouring extra words into the natural silences that occur in conversation, pouring her father wine and more wine until his speech slurs and his light brown cheeks turn pink and shiny with sweat, until his big-drum laughter grows and grows and threatens to swallow our little matchbox flat.

We are eating ugali and creamed sukuma, with kuku kienyeji that I bought at the butcher's for one thousand shillings. I know that my lover's mother likes avocado, so I bought ten of them, each for forty bob. But my lover's mother does not touch them, and neither does she touch the plate of food that I served her.

When I first met her she was pleasant, jubilant even, because I had found her daughter a place to stay near the university. Over and over again, she had said, "God bless you." After seven years, however, her genuine and earnest god-bless-yous had disintegrated into a liquid and guarded hostility, which now seeped through her narrowed eyes as she studied me. Three hours ago she had bustled in, just before my lover's father, a dark blue mermaid kitenge hugging her hips and flaring at her calves, her hair hidden in a matching scarf, her arms laden with baskets of produce from the farm, hugging and kissing us on the cheeks and saying, "How are you, my daughters?" "My daughters, I have brought you cabbage and potatoes and peas..." "You look well, my daughters..."

My daughters, my daughters, another person would have thought that she loved me like a daughter, but I had known otherwise. I had known because I had learned to unearth true intentions, gleaning them like long translucent bones buried deep within tilapia fish. My lover's mother had not been speaking with her mouth, from which her many *my daughters* had fluttered out. She had been speaking with her eyes, which had refused to surrender to the smile on her mouth.

She is still staring at me, eyes equal parts curious and hostile. I think that perhaps she thinks that dreadlocks are unbecoming, even if I have pulled them up into a ladylike bun that make my eyebrows feel unusually high; even if I have clipped Magda's dangling earrings onto my un-pierced earlobes. Perhaps she can tell that the black dress with a pink flower print that I bought for today was bought for today, and that I am not in the habit of wearing dresses. I wonder if she can see, with those narrowed eyes, that the dress is too small, that the fabric is cutting into my armpits, that I am sweating under my arms. The food is growing cold, and white Kimbo droplets begin to float on the soup. My mind is running here and running there, out of breath, offering me one reason or another for this woman not liking me. It is trying to convince me that I do not know what she is thinking, it is running careful circles around the truth, it is telling me that she hates me for reasons I can fix.

But I know. I know what she is thinking even before the curiosity in her eyes evaporates, leaving hard hostility behind; before she flings heavy black tar into the air mixing between my lover and I, before she flattens that tar with a roaring steamroller, when she turns to my lover, smiling, full lips flattened against gleaming teeth, asking, "Mami, when you will get a husband? And a nice house?"

The skins of the unwanted avocados shine like my lover's father's light brown cheeks. He is drunk.

*O*n Friday night, after her parents leave, we hold hands and pretend that we are outside. We walk in Nairobi. Our matchbox flat becomes the large sprawling city. The two bedrooms are the suburbs. We live in the bigger of the suburbs, the one with generous pavements and many trees. We leave home and walk along the corridor, which is the highway to town. The kitchen, found just before we get to town, is Fagi's wooden Coca-Cola box-shaped shop. We lean through the serving hatch and ask for a one-litre Fanta Orange that we put in a paper bag. We hold hands again. We imagine that Fagi says, "What a lovely couple!"

Then we get to the Central Business District. The sitting room, which is also the dining room, is the CBD. The wall unit that almost touches the ceiling is the Times Tower. We look up and say, "How tall! How long did they take to build that?"

At last we go back to our house in the suburbs after spending the whole day bumping into rough fabric sofas and smooth aluminium matatu chests, into polished wooden stools and grey concrete buildings, into sweaty people and dining chairs with proud long backs, all of these fitting, as if by magic, in the small CBD of our flat. When we get to our bigger room, we lie on the same bed. If our lover's mother were to come in and find us, she would exclaim, "My daughters!" This time, her mouth would slacken, unable to smile. Her eyes would become round, un-narrowed, because whose arm was whose? Whose skin was whose? Whose leg was whose? Our body parts would be mixed up together like pieces of meat in a stew, in a sufuria without a lid, exposed because the lazy blanket had fallen off in the middle of the night.

❧

*T*he next day, Saturday, Magda is gathering water in her palms and lifting it onto her body. The wide blue plastic basin is perched on a stool, the whole arrangement a castle chess piece. First she is gathering up only as much as a dog's tongue because the water is cold, then she is gathering up more, then I hear no more water because she is scrubbing, and then I begin to hear larger and louder water as it pours over her body, and the thirsty drain, as it drinks it up. She comes out wrapped in a white towel and asks me if I have seen the nail-cutter, and I want to tell her that it is in the second bedroom, on the desk by the window. Keep your nails short: school rule or *lesbianology*? But this is when Magda's vibrating phone stirs us. It is a text from Thomas, our neighbour, to say that he is at the door. As Magda rushes to dress, I rush to mix the blankets on the bed in the smaller second bedroom, trying to make it look slept in, tossing some of the red towels that clutter the bed into the cupboard, throwing a pair of jeans onto the floor, opening the curtains. Magda and I scamper around our matchbox flat like rats; I think of green rat-poison pellets floating in a glass of Fanta Orange. I want to lie down for a bit, and cry for a bit, but I hear the sound of the door opening and I hear Magda saying loudly: "Thomas! Mambo!"

And thus, Thomas has fractured our gentle reverie. Magda is

louder now, fussing over him, very much like her mother, "Sasa wewe, what will we cook for you? Do you want tea? How is job?" Her crotchet-braid weave bobs as she rushes from the kitchen to the sofa to the dining table, reheating food and setting a stool before him. "Tom, dear, how much chilli do you like in your food?" – "Maji ama Coke?" – "I'm sorry that this is taking so long!"

Thomas glows under Magda's uxorial light; he is smiling as he watches her shuffle about. Madga smells like Nivea body lotion, good food and three fat future children, two boys and one girl. Thomas, twenty-nine, wants to be with her, would marry her, on his thirty-second birthday, at the Holy Family Minor Basilica in town, him dapper in a black suit, her veiled in all-white, his family on the pews on the right and hers on those on the left. I know all this because I trawled through the WhatsApp messages he sent Magda, all of them unanswered, arranged one after the other like rectangular stones on a stepping-stone pathway. He would marry her, but here I am. I sit quietly on the adjacent sofa. I know how to shrink myself to live. My father taught me how to make myself smaller. First, he taught my mother, then me, then my three little bald sisters, one after the other, each of us with big-big eyes yearning to be enough for a man who wanted a son but got four daughters, each next one with rounder eyes and a bigger forehead, foreheads made to look even bigger because any trace of hair was promptly shaved off. To look neat for school, my father had said, to keep boys away, my father had also said. My mother promised me hair as soon I finished high school. I and my egg head had made ourselves so small that our father could not see us. I know now that if I make myself small enough to almost disappear, I will be left alone to live.

But Magda swells up, she is swelling up now, big like her big drum father, big like her afro weaves, hiding herself under loud layers, showy like her fabulous mother. When her parents are far away in Eldoret, when Thomas leaves, when I have fallen asleep, and when all the lights are off, my lover goes into the smaller bedroom. There, with the steady, solitary and painful focus of a chicken trying to lay an egg, she peels off all those layers. Perched on her red towels and locked away from me, she prays, shakes, and rakes razors across the skin of her inner thighs.

There is nothing like Magda's hair. It is the darkest of clays, which she moulds into many shapes. Buns, braids, cornrows, weaves, mixtures of two or three or all of these, shrunken tiny afros or picked spherical ones, wigs, hats, sometimes with her front hair showing, and finally, cloth hair – scarves twisted and bunned at the back. My hair is weak and fine, and can only grow long in dreadlocks, and even then, it is never voluminous. So Magda's hair is even more beautiful to me, the good strong hairline, the many shapes, the balls of shed hair like cotton strewn all over the dresser. The only thing that I like more than her hair is her skin. It is darkest between her thighs, and there, on each side, I find short, black and precise scars, arranged like gills.

On TV, a politician says that there is no space for gays in Kenya. Thomas says, "I support him. Can you even imagine a *dick* in your *ass*?" He takes a slow sip from the glass of Coke that Magda has set out for him, and licks his lips. With a prodding half-smile, he adds in a lower voice, staring straight at Magda, "But I *support* the L. That one I most definitely *support*." He is the kind of man from whose mouth sentences slide easily, ropes curling into nooses encircling women's waists. My jaws grow hot as I imagine him masturbating to *lesbian porn*. He adds, "But how many letters are there in that thing again?"

There is a stilted pause in the conversation. There is too much to ignore, even for Magda. Perhaps she is thinking that he knows. What would follow then would be to wonder what the implications of his knowing would be. In the end, Magda recovers from the brazenness of it all, strangling the too-long pause with a big laugh, flinging it under her loud layers, almost screaming-laughing, and saying, not even sarcastically, "Thomas you are so funny! Oh my gosh! *How many letters are there in that thing!*"

Marionettes are sinister because they are controlled by strings that lead up to the devil. If I were to pinch a normal person, they would frown or slap my hand away, or cry out or pinch me back. But if I were to pinch a marionette, its empty eyes would just stare back at me, wooden and smiling, dancing and clapping.

Magda turns to me laughing, repeating, "*How many letters are there in that thing!* Don't you think that's so funny?" Her eyes are clear and round, her mouth stiff and stretched into a smile, straight teeth arranged dutifully, kernels of white maize on a cob. Her voice is thick brown, millet porridge, rich and homely; sugary and buttery, but tinged with something bitter – very likely lemon juice, straight from the lemon.

Underneath puppets' veneers are knives that will slice your throat in your sleep. White wriggly maggots under a lush and pretty log.

Thomas interjects, "Magda, you look so pretty when you laugh like that. Let me take a picture of you. Where is your phone? Mine's just gone off."

I am shrinking, crawling, deeper under the bed, Thomas's words trailing after me. I am thinking of the night months ago when Thomas had banged on the door, speech slurred, *I want to see Magda, I want to see Magda*, how we had put off the lights and tiptoed to the smaller bedroom, waiting under the bed for the banging to stop and for him to leave, how the thick puddle of low thrum anxiety nestled at the base of my throat had exploded into hiccupping panic as I had heard the door burst open, as I had clung to precious Magda, under the weight of her red towels, the dusty underside of the bed choking the both of us. How my mouth had remained sewn.

The next morning Madga had mopped up the muddy footprints that tracked from the door through the sitting room all the way to the corridor. He had not got to the bedrooms. I had gone out and found a serious fundi with a pencil behind his ear. He had fixed the broken door and added a new grill, with fat metal bars, standing tall and straight like askaris.

*O*n Sunday morning I wake up, and Magda is not next to me. I try to open the door to the second bedroom but it is locked. I feel faint, so I go to the balcony for some fresh air. On the street below, at the bus stop just outside our building, matatus snarl in the dust like wild cats. It is hot. There are hardly any trees or pavements. Then I notice that all the red towels are gone from the hanging line. I rush back to the second bedroom, and through the door I say, "Magda, are you OK? Open the door, please."

"Give me some time alone, please."

Her voice is weak and watery, like strungi, poor people's milk-less tea. Worry makes it difficult for me to reply calmly, "OK How much time?"

No response. I coax some more, but not even the watery weakness reappears. I want to bang on the door. I want to scream MagdaMagdaMagda, but the neighbours will hear me. So I sew my mouth. But the trapped Magdas remain at the base of my throat, popping like fried oil. Then they are flowing downwards, still popping, burning the inner walls of my body, shaking me. I think that I should cook some tea that I will not drink, because perhaps the smell will calm me down. I am shaking as I cut open the plastic milk packet with a knife, and halfway through this, the packet slips and bursts on the floor. I drop the knife, I forget the tea, I am sobbing, sinking to the tiled floor, the hems of my heavy cotton sweatpants wetting with milk, like wicks.

*W*hen Magda and I had talked about God, she had said, "You don't understand. It is God who keeps me alive." I had wondered where I could get some of this God of Magda's. He had sounded like the beef cubes I add to potato stew when it gets too bland.

Still I had not understood. This God business had outgrown me. It was like an old sweater I wore as a child, now too small and scratchy. My God was not gentle like Magda's; my God was like my father, whose house breathed only after he had left. But now staring at the diamond patterns on the ceiling, crying-convulsing, with milk soaking my scalp, my back, my panties, my legs, I begin to mutter, God please, God please. It is now only me, and Magda, and Magda's good God.

*M*y heavy cotton sweatpants are stubbornly wet, but the milk on my cotton T-shirt is drying and sticky on my back. I am no longer convulsing but I am still sobbing softly, kneeling at the door of the smaller bedroom and trying out each of the keys in the pile I found in a basket on top of the fridge. The sixth turns the lock. The door flings open. The room is dark, the curtains are drawn. There is a smell of zinc. I switch on the light. Magda lies naked on her red towels, her dark thighs a mess of red. I kneel beside her. She is breathing.

But my lover's mother will love her and will crush her. She will take her daughter's heart and crush it between her narrowed eyes, between eyelids heavy and strong with love that cuts with the strength of diamonds. Magda, twenty-seven and weary of this crushing love, will grow louder and bigger to hide her crushed heart. Like an agitated turkey, her feathers will fan out, her face will fill with blood. Later she will think it unfair that a heart should bear this crushing alone. She will make her thighs bleed again. At least this is what I tell myself because even though she is lying there bleeding and barely breathing, I do not want to call her parents without her consent. But mostly, I am afraid that if they take her away, I may never see her again.

*I*t is like she has given birth to the devil.

I mend her thighs. She leaves after two weeks. In the end, her mother is the person that she goes back to, tail between legs, heart in hands, wanting it soothed. After she cut herself, a quiet voice told me that it was my fault. That it was the thing that mixed up in the air in between us that was cutting her. That it had grown too big for the only place in which I could love her. It had become too much, too raucous. It had swallowed us. It had shrunk me. And it had cut her thighs, every year for three years, always a few days after her parents' visit. I stopped meeting her eyes when I changed her bandages twice a day. I stopped talking to her, responding wordlessly to her needs for drinking water, the toilet, bananas, the bhajias fried in a shack directly opposite our building.

I expected her to leave. When the rain went and the sun came, my father did not fret that the rain had gone. It was time for the maize in the fields to ripen. And so after the scars had healed, like the rain, like a patient discharged, Magda put on her red maxi skirt and left with a small bag.

But the house is heavy with my beloved. I cannot sleep in the bigger bedroom because her hair is on the dresser, not to mention in the smaller bedroom, where she had given birth to the devil. I sleep on the rough fabric sofa, maroon with gold-thread flowers. I refuse to touch the mixture of towels, blood and red dye in the basin on the balcony. One day I feel that I do not want to see anyone, not a soul, not even a cockroach, ever again. So I call my boss to quit my PR job where I am obligated to wear short grey skirts. He tells me he has already given away my job because I did not show up for three weeks and didn't respond to his calls. I cook and cry. From the sofa, I begin to design websites for a living. When money gets tight, I take up Magda's old job at a DVD shop a few minutes' walk from the flat.

*O*ne evening, two months later, I come back home from the DVD shop and know that Magda is back because the towels hang stiff and foul on the balcony, now a dull orange after bleeding out all their dye. I expected that she would leave, and now I accept that she has come back. She comes out of the kitchen. Her hair is gone, cropped close to her scalp. I am not sure whether her cheekbones had always been so high, her eyes so big, her irises so large, floating like cocoa beans in milk. It had been seven years of seeing only her hair.

That night we sleep heads touching, breathing each other, arms around each other. I roll over to face the other side and Magda moves with me, her nose at my nape, her arm still wrapped around me. Even though neither of us had contacted the other, I had spent all this time expecting that she would come back. So I am glad that I no longer have to expect. But I am also stifled by the suddenness of her return. I know that it is the rain's place to come unannounced. But I also know that Nairobi November skies tend to be heavy and cloudy like grey wet blankets, ones that mother spirits wring to drench the city. The question is: is the coming of rain in Nairobi in November expected or unexpected?

It is perhaps a matter of weather in relation to climate. The weather is mercurial: in the morning it wants pink lipstick, and by noon it has decided that today is a red-lipstick day. Some days it ties its arms around me, and other days it cannot meet my eyes. If the weather is a yellow banana peel racked with black scars, then the climate is what is inside. It is the way Magda squeezes my hand under tables when I have sewn my mouth so tightly that I can hardly breathe. It is the certainty that is the great big engine that is her heart: how it runs on butter and Baringo honey, and how it warms me, melting open my stitches.

Therefore, if a particular Nairobi November day appears sunny from inside the house, then what do we say to someone who goes out to the salon to flat-iron their hair, expecting that the straightness will last for at least a week and a half, and then does not have an umbrella in their bag on the very day that the rain decides to come the way that Jesus said that he would, kinking their expensive straightness? Is the coming of rain in Nairobi in November expected or unexpected? We can say, yes, it is your fault, the rain was expected, this is November, why didn't you have an umbrella, you just go home and style your afro. We can also collect in a corner and decide that no, it is not your fault, the rain was unexpected, it has been sunny for the whole day, imagine, it only decided to rain once you stepped out of the salon, pole sana, let us curse heaven together. There are things that are both expected and unexpected, and the rain is one of these things.

Waiting

Harriet Anena

*M*aa told me to keep my legs together until I got married. I had turned fourteen the last Saturday of June 1990, and sex education was my birthday present.

"Men are like termites," she said, handing me a jerrycan.

"Yiyi Maa, do men live in anthills?"

"Silly girl! I meant there are so many men out there. No need to rush."

Two years earlier, Maa had stuffed her obegu with my clothes and hers, held my hand and led me out of Paa's house. She was tired of a jelly-kneed husband who couldn't defend her against a mother-in-law who dictated how much salt and water to put in her son's food, how and when to have sex with him, and who to befriend or begrudge.

For eight years, Maa had been putting away forty thousand shillings every season she sold maize and millet, and now she had bought a half-acre piece of land in Laliya.

"Enjoy wifeying your son, old woman," Maa spat.

Grandma slumped on the verandah; you'd think her knees had taken a disabling hit. Even after seventeen years as daughter-in-law, Maa's words always hit Grandma like a bullet.

I cried all the way to the taxi park in Gulu town. On any other day, Maa would've pulled my ears or spanked me. But there I was, a kid used to my Grandma's smooches and Paa's coddling, being hit by the rain, on the way to an unknown place. She must have felt sorry for me.

I cried even harder when I arrived in Laliya, 4.2 kilometres from Gulu Town, and realised that our new home was a dry grassland. Maa watched me from the corner of her eye as she cleared the grass with a panga she'd carried along. After an hour of sulking, I helped Maa build a temporary shelter; then she walked up the hill to borrow fire from the only house in sight.

She returned, carrying hot coals on a metallic ladle. A girl my age walked closely behind her, two ten-litre jerrycans in hand. The girl, Acen, would become my best friend.

Acen handed me one jerrycan and with a smile invited me to follow her. The first part of our journey to the well was dotted with questions from Acen: Which class was I in? What was my other name? Would I be studying at Laliya Secondary?

As I walked, I heard loud chattering from the crown of a large mango tree. I could make out four boys seated on the branches. They appeared older than me and Acen by maybe three years. Their chatter subsided to whispers when we approached.

"Acen, what is your friend's name?" one of the boys asked.

"What do you want to do with her name?"

"Anyaka, what is your name?" another asked.

I quickened the pace, but Acen told me not to mind them.

At the well, we filled our jerrycans in silence. I was about to start the journey home when Acen motioned me towards a nearby palm tree, our gossip haven, as she would later christen it. She told me how the mango-tree boys always threw stones at passersby, touched young girls, and insulted old women while hiding in the bushes or on a tree. The villagers, Acen said, believed the boys would be more disciplined if their fathers spent more time teaching them manners instead of drinking arege.

Sensing my discomfort, Acen told me never to allow the mango-tree boys to sense that I was afraid of them, otherwise "they will pee on your head." We burst out in laughter.

As we started the journey home, I hoped they would be gone. They weren't. They hopped down and demanded that I tell them my name. When I didn't, they started chanting:

"Anyaka cak kori opong
Anyaka cak kori neka woko!"

They followed us, singing about how my full, beautiful breasts were killing them.

This happened every time we went to the well. Acen told me to abuse them. I did. They didn't stop. Acen joined me in pelting them with stones. They didn't relent.

"One day, I'm going to do something terrible to those boys."

"Is it the monkeys Acen told me about?" Maa asked. "What did they do this time?"

"What they always do. They sing about my—"

"Your what?"

"My breasts."

"What about them?"

"How my breasts are killing them."

Maa laughed. "Is that why your lips are as long as a train?"

"But they disturb me."

"And you allow them to disturb you?"

"Even when I abuse them, they don't stop."

"Then abuse their mothers."

"Maaaa!"

The next time the boys started to chant, I stood for a moment, stared at them and blurted, "Ngwiny cet pa megiwu."

They stopped chanting, unable to believe that I had just insulted their mothers' asses. They seemed to recover, though, because they resumed their chanting, louder this time. I turned and ran back home.

"Where is the water? And why are you wailing as if you have lost a child?"

"They are still singing about my breasts."

"Did you abuse their mothers?"

"Yes."

"Come."

"Maa, I don't want to go back there."

"Come. We're going back."

I followed meekly. Once the boys saw me approaching with Maa, they jumped down and attempted to flee.

"Stop right there. Why have you been disturbing my daughter?"

"..."

"Am I speaking to stones?"

"No..."

"If you don't stop disturbing Aleng, I will cut off your tiny penises one by one. Do you hear me?"

"Yes..."

"Twaca!"

They turned and sprinted like relay runners, their heels tapping their bums.

*M*aa walked into my room just as I was tying a latambara around my chest. I turned away from her and bent to retrieve my school shirt from the floor.

"Maa, you should have knocked!"

"This is my house, young woman."

"But this is my room, Maa!"

"What are you hiding? You think those are breasts? Ask me who has breastfed three children." Every time Maa mentioned the siblings I never met, her face fell. I didn't know how to ask her about it.

"So, you don't think my breasts are that big?" I asked, changing the subject.

"Those are not breasts," Maa said with a smirk. "These," she said, cupping hers, "are breasts."

But the boys at Laliya Secondary School, on whose account I had started flattening my breasts, were worse than the mango-tree boys. Although they didn't chant, they made suckling noises whenever I passed by. One of them even christened my breasts

"Fresh Dairy".

I couldn't complain much to Acen because she'd have loved my troubles. She longed for the boys to whistle after her and tickle her and rub her bum like they did to other girls. She giggled and wiggled every time we walked past a group of boys. They didn't seem to notice her, though, maybe because her breasts were the size of groundnut pods. Although she faithfully pointed a mingling stick at her breasts every morning because her mother had said that doing so would make them grow faster and bigger, they only showed up four years later, when we were both in Senior Four.

*K*eeping my virginity was not as difficult as I had feared.
I began to believe what Maa always said: "You can't crave what you have not tasted." She'd also said that sex before marriage would make me as worthless as bitter cassava that is only eaten during famine.

"But, Maa, is sex really that bad?"

"Who said it is bad? I remembered the 'talking post' in primary school that advised to 'Say No To Sex.' Better keep those legs together," Maa continued, as if she hadn't already made her point.

"I just wanted to know."

"Wait until you're married. You will be glad you left that garden to fallow."

"Garden?"

"Aleng, why do you even go to school if you can't understand simple things?"

"I have understood."

"Men are born with extra appetites. Your garden is better off fallowing for now."

"I have heard you, Maa."

"Who knows whether what you heard through the left ear hasn't passed out from the right one?"

I knew the conversation would never end if I kept talking and challenging Maa. So I said nothing.

*I*met D at the Makerere University inter-halls cultural gala. Our eyes met as we both stood in the University Hall compound, waiting for the next group from Africa Hall to perform. I looked away, but still felt his eyes on me.

I remembered I had seen him at Laliya Secondary School Old Girls and Boys Association meeting. I remembered how most of the girls kept hugging him. As a fresher, I was still too self-conscious to offer unsolicited hugs to men. In fact, I hadn't hugged a guy that entire semester.

I also remembered that during subsequent association meetings, D sat opposite me and stared at me. Although his eyes were big, they did not bulge. Although he had fleshy lips, they were not repulsively thick. I thought his face was attractive, but I suspected it was his height and toned body that made the girls so eager to hug him.

He wasn't standing that far from where Acen and I stood. He could easily have walked over to where we were if he had wanted, but I suspected he was too proud.

"Let's go stand on the other side," I told Acen. Acen had a round face, a dark complexion, big eyes and thin lips like mine.

I was studying literature and she was pursuing a Bachelor of Arts in Education. We stayed at Herbatin Hostel, shopped from Kikumi-Kikumi, prayed at St Francis, and ate government-sponsored lunches in CCE Hall.

"But this place has a good view."

"Let's leave, OK?"

"Why?"

I hesitated. "Some guy is staring at me."

"So?"

"So he's making me uncomfortable."

Acen asked if the guy in question was handsome and, if he was, where he was. I motioned, as subtly as I could, towards D.

"Haaah!" Acen exclaimed as soon as she'd seen D. She poked my ribs. "So you wanted to run away from Mr Handsome's eyes, uh?"

I rolled my eyes. "He's not even that handsome."

"The guy is easy on the eye, ba."

"To you, every guy is easy on the eye."

"Are you saying I have poor taste in men?"

"Those are not my words."

"See how he is looking at you, his eyes glittering with love-love."

"Shut up."

"If only he could look at me like that!"

"Go away!"

Acen giggled.

Much later that day, after Livingstone and Africa Halls had emerged winners of the inter-cultural gala, I let Acen drag me to Ground Zero. I had never been to a nightclub before, I hated crowds, and I didn't drink alcohol.

"I should be in bed, enjoying sleep," I complained, shortly after I had been waved in by the bouncers.

Acen wouldn't let go of my hand. "If you don't live this life on campus, when will you?"

"Not everyone who goes through campus has to go to a club."

"Anyway, you're here now. Don't embarrass me."

"Embarrass you how?"

"By looking miserable. People will think you're here against your will."

"But I am here against my will."

Acen rolled her eyes and told me to get myself something to drink.

"What about you?" I asked.

She said she'd spotted someone she wanted to say hello to, and would join me at the bar. I walked to the bar, sat on one of the high stools, and ordered apple-flavoured Novida. I scanned the shelf behind the barman, and then started to mouth the names of familiar liquor brands: Jameson, Jack Daniels, Jonnie Walker, Uganda Waragi, Four Cousins. The rest I had never heard of.

At the top right corner of the shelf was a cocktail menu with big lettering: Painkiller, Bloody Mary, Dripping Queen, 4-Some, Big Cock, Between the Sheets, G-Spot, Rough Rider, Sex on the Beach…

Sex on the beach? How does one even do that? When everyone else is gone? What happens when sand gets in the way? That would be one bloody … Mary! Hmmm! shouldn't the name Mary come after pious ones like rose, hail and holy? Of course naming a cocktail Holy Mary would be more scandalous…

Somewhere in the corner, Acen was dancing with a guy I didn't know.

How do you meet a stranger and paap! – a few minutes later, you're already squeezing each other like that?

I sat for what seemed like an hour before Acen walked over to ask if I was OK. She smelled of liquor. "Blue Ice," she called it.

"Blue Ice? Sounds like the name of an aftershave," I said.

"You look pathetic sitting here alone. Come, let's dance."

"I'm OK here. You dance. I'll watch."

"Are you sure you're OK?"

"I'm fine. Go back to your love-love."

She stuck her tongue out at me and then crossed over to the other side. Her dance partner stretched his arms out when he saw her approach.

I had just turned to the barman to order another Novida when someone stood behind me. I felt hot breath on my neck. I turned to find D smiling at me.

"I want to string the cords of your heart like the adungu."

"How long have you been rehearsing that line?" I asked.

"Long enough."

"Next."

"I want to drink you like a well-brewed kwete."

"Next!"

"Let me be your magician… make you a lily so that… my dew can fall on your petals… let me be your nimbus cloud… so I can rain on your garden…"

"Next."

"Try me in your court… find me guilty… sentence me to life…
in your heart."

"Won't you credit the poet?" I ask.

"I was hoping it could pass off as my—"

"—Thief!"

"Can you at least admit I tried?"

"I can admit that you're a good thief."

"You're as big-headed as people say your mother is."

"What do you know about my mother?" I asked.

D said nothing.

I wondered if he'd heard the rumour that Maa killed her
children, if that story had followed me from Gulu to Makerere.

"What kind of woman kills her own children?" Paa's relatives
had said.

Maa put Okello to bed, but when she woke to breastfeed him,
he was dead. Just like that. In-laws and neighbours offered their
condolences in the morning, but found her guilty when she was
out of earshot. After Okello, Kidega died in a similar manner.
People hadn't even poured soil on Kidega's body before they
started calling Maa lajok. Even children called her a witch.

When I was born two years after Kidega died, everyone counted
the days. Everyone asked Maa when she planned to kill me too,
so that they could prepare for my funeral. When, eight years later,
there was still no funeral, they said Maa had changed her mind
about killing me. They said she could stay in Palenga after all. But
they said she had better not kill Paa once I was older, and eat my
dowry alone.

In the last month, I had googled infant deaths every Friday I
had lectures in the computer lab. *What kills children in their sleep?*
Mysterious death in infants. What drives a mother to kill her children?
The only article that seemed to explain my siblings' death was what
Google called cot death. Maa was loudmouthed and headstrong,
but not a killer, I told myself.

I shook myself to reality as D turned his back to me and began
speaking animatedly to a chick in a short red lace dress. Their

laughter and the scanning of each other's frames made me think they were having a reunion. She planted a lingering kiss on his cheek when they disengaged from a hug, and she walked towards the side of the room where Acen was still dancing.

"I'll be on the other side," she screamed. D nodded before turning to me.

"Has your mind returned from the forest it had wandered to?"

"Does your mind wander to the evil forest too?"

"So what are you thinking about?"

"None of your business, just like it's none of my business that it took just a minute for you to disappear in the arms of Miss Red Dress."

"Are you jealous?"

"Oh D! Don't give yourself too much credit."

"Hmmm, if you are not careful…"

"What will happen?"

"You'll end up alone and bitter."

I slapped him hard. Then I jumped off the stool and disappeared into the crowd, looking for Acen. When she saw the look on my face, she followed me to the exit without asking questions.

*T*wo years after I had slapped D, he was kissing my cheeks as we sat at BBQ Bar and reminded each other of that day. Even the music blaring from the speakers couldn't dull the sound of our laughter.

"Whack! Whack!"

"Hahaha. But I slapped you only once."

"Of course! Then you fled like a chick that had seen an eagle."

"If I'd stayed near you for another minute, I would've knocked your head off."

"Lol. This head is too big for you to just knock off."

"Just thank me for sparing you."

I nudged him in the ribs as he rose, pulling me off my seat. I joined the throng of sweaty bodies gyrating on the dance floor. At 4am, we took a boda boda to D's place.

Three months after graduating, D had rented a two-roomed apartment in Buziga. He'd got a job with Standard Bank and he needed his privacy.

The next day, D took me shopping at Oasis Mall before driving me back to Herbatin.

The moment I entered the room, Acen jumped up, grabbed the shopping bags in my hands, and emptied their contents on the carpet.

"Jal, this one fell straight from heaven!" Acen said.

I laughed. "Which heaven?"

"How many do you know?"

I chuckled.

"Some of us are yet to get PK chewing gum from our boyfriends. You are here with a week's worth of shopping!"

"This is normal stuff, Acen!"

"If you let your stubbornness get in the way—" Acen continued.

"Don't start!"

"Make sure no one snatches him!"

"He's a grown man. How can he be snatched?"

"See!"

"Whatever!"

D picked me up from Herbatin Hostel, as he always did every fortnight.

I watched him dodge boda bodas and taxis with a calmness I doubted I would have if I ever learnt how to drive. The madness on Kampala streets was the reason I had consistently, in the year since he'd bought the blue Rav4, declined his every offer to teach me how to drive.

The heavy traffic made the eleven-kilometre journey from Makerere a nightmare. D held my hand most part of the journey, kissed it occasionally, and steered the car with his right hand.

When we arrived in Buziga two hours later, the air smelt of night rose – the kind Maa planted at the back of the main house. D walked into the dining room and lit candles.

"What's the occasion?" I asked.

"Can't a man spoil his woman?"

I smiled, and took his hand as he led me to a seat.

"When did you prepare all this?"

"I took the afternoon off."

"Wow!"

"Anything for you."

We ate mostly in silence, my chest tightening with unease, D looking at me like I was lapena – his favourite dish – and he couldn't wait to eat me. I smiled every time our eyes met, but the unease never left, not when he kept pressing my hand and thigh under the table.

I didn't realise how scared I was until my hands started shaking as I changed into a nightie. He must have noticed that something about me was off, because he kept asking if I was OK.

"I'm just tired," I lied.

I declined his offer of a massage, saying I didn't wish to bother him. He said it was no trouble at all, but I closed my eyes and willed my heart to beat slower once I was in bed.

He wrapped an arm around my waist and leaned in. His breath, warm against my cheek, smelt of wine. I tasted it when he kissed me. I wanted to tell him his beard was tickling me, but he started to fondle my breasts and the words retreated back to where they'd come from. He lifted my nightie and caressed my thighs.

I had no idea I had made a sound until he whispered, "Do you like that?"

I was too worried about where else his hand might wander to say, "Yes."

His fingers slipped into my underwear. If he was disappointed by how dry I was, he did not show it. I could feel my body stiffen at every touch. I took deep, slow breaths to calm my nerves.

"You like that?" he asked again.

I nodded, knowing that if I spoke, he would sense the lie or the hesitation.

"I want you." His voice was a deep-throated rasp. His tongue probed my ear.

"Hmmm."

When I felt my underwear slide down my thighs, my eyes flew open and my hand found his wrist. "Wait."

"What is it, babe?"

I tightened a grip around his wrist. "Can we wait? Just a bit."

"Wait? For how long? A week? A month? Six months? A year?"

"I don't know."

"What do you mean, you don't know?"

"I can't think properly right now."

"Do you want me to stop?"

I tried to steady my breath. "For a while."

D withdrew his hand. "OK," he said in a high-pitched nasal voice.

"I'm sorry if my pace is too slow for you."

He was silent for a while. Then he said, "Don't worry."

*F*rom then on, whenever D asked me to sleep over, I offered one excuse after another. When I couldn't come up with a good excuse, I timed my visits to his house to coincide with my periods.

Acen worried more about the state of things than I did. "Is everything between you and D fine?"

"Everything's great," I said.

"You don't talk about him that much any more."

"Everything's fine. I was at his house just three weeks ago."

She gave me a curious look. "And?"

"He wants chao."

"I sense a 'but' coming."

"There's no but. I just asked if we could wait a bit."

Acen laughed so hard that she slumped onto the floor. "Oh, Aleng! I had no idea your mother's warnings had damaged you this much!"

"Leave Maa out of this."

"Eh! Why are you starving the guy? What hasn't he done for you?"

"I'm not starving him: I'm giving him something to look forward to."

"Aleng, be serious. Good men are hard to find, ba."

"I know that."

"Stop playing childish games."

"It's my body, OK?"

"You're twenty-one, for heaven's sake!"

"Besides, D has no problem with it. He said we'll wait."

"That's what he says. But how sure are you that he's not running around with some chick as we speak?"

"Well, if the plan is to run around with some chick as we speak, nothing I do will stop him. He's a grown man."

"Hmn! At this rate, your thing will grow cobwebs nga no one has entered it yet."

"You're disgusting."

Acen laughed. "But, seriously, for who are you keeping it?"

Two weeks later, when Dr Mukasa said he couldn't deliver the lecture on Literary Criticism that Friday afternoon, I took the opportunity to go to D's house. Even though he'd given me a spare key, I'd never been to his house without him.

I let myself in. I cleaned, cooked, lit perfumed candles, sprinkled red and white roses in the corridor, and showered. Then I lay on the sofa, with my eyes closed, wondering what sex would feel like. Maa had said once you tasted it, there was no turning back.

Acen had said the pleasure would knock me down like a hurricane. I knew that Maa and Acen often exaggerated, so I kept my expectations low, just in case.

D arrived at 6:30pm, half an hour later than I had expected him. The door was open, as I had said it'd be. I was still lying on the sofa when he walked into the living room.

"How are you so beautiful?"

I suppressed a smile.

He proceeded to the bedroom to undress and shower.

Ten minutes later, he was carrying me to the bedroom. He kissed me. Then he lay next to me. He caressed my face and removed my bra. Then he trailed my skin with his tongue from my nipples to the navel. He was quiet, gentle, unhurried, not nearly as excited as he'd been the last time. Either he didn't want to raise his hopes in case I chickened out again, or he wanted the moment to be as memorable for me as it would be for him.

By the time he slipped off my underwear, he was shaking uncontrollably.

"Are you OK?"

He knelt between my legs. "Yeah. You make me OK."

He lay on top of me, his boxers and vest still on, held me tight, his body wracked with stronger tremors. I knew he had climaxed when I felt a dampness on my thigh.

*M*aa had noted with curiosity the frequency and length of my phone calls since my return from campus. She teased me whenever I excused myself to answer a call outside.

"There's network here, you know," she would say, chuckling.

I smiled, deciding to joke about it. Whenever D called, I would look at Maa, smile or laugh, and say, "I'm going to look for network."

"Good luck finding it," she'd say. Sometimes she suggested that I stand on an anthill or climb a tree.

When she realised that I was never going to voluntarily offer details about D, she asked, "So, who is that person who makes you look for network every evening?"

"Just a friend."

"Just a friend? Aleng, you now think I am too old for your Makerere self?"

"Old? Maa, you just like being old."

"So, who is he?"

"How do you know it's a he?"

"Only a man would make a woman hide behind her mother's house whenever she answers his call."

"He's called Dean. Dean P'Oloya."

"Oloya, the head teacher of Laliya College?"

"Yes."

"Well, at least you're not dating a relative."

"Maaa!"

There was an uncomfortable silence. Then Maa asked me what kind of job he had, whether he had introduced me to his mother, if he planned to marry me soon – after all, my graduation was just two weeks away.

"We are taking it slow, Maa."

"Good. You need to be careful, Aleng."

"Dean is a nice guy."

"Even nice guys can make you pregnant. Even nice guys can abandon you for some young city girl."

"Maa, he's not like that."

"How do you know? Do you know what he is doing in Kampala behind your back?"

"Maa!"

"Ahaa! I'm just lightning. I won't rain here."

"What does that proverb mean?"

"It's not up to me to decide."

The next day, Acen called asking why I had left my man to Kampala's temptations. "You should come back and mark your territory," Acen had said.

"How is your own territorial marking with the new guy going?"

She chuckled. "He is still behaving. You know how they are."

D was waiting for me at Kisenyi Bus Park two days later. He was leaning against his car when the Homeland bus I had travelled in turned into the terminal. I waved at him through the window, but he didn't see me. He only saw me as I was carrying my suitcase out of the bus minutes later. He moved towards me and stopped momentarily, a smile on his lips. Then he scooped me up in a hug that lasted longer than was comfortable for me in public, and I feared taxi louts would make snide comments about us.

I pulled away.

Once in the car, he hugged me again and tried to kiss me. I pulled away, saying I was tired from the long trip. "But I missed you," I said, drawing a smile on his face.

D was on annual leave. We spent the few days to my graduation together, re-watching *Scandal*, kissing, going out to eat or just lounging on the sofa.

The day ended with D either attempting to have sex with me, begging me to rub him, just a bit, or pressing me under his weight in an attempt at arousing me.

He apologised every time it happened, saying he would keep his promise to "wait".

"It's me," I would say and tell him not to apologise.

"What do you mean, it's you? You say that all the time."

And I would smile or caress his cheek or change the subject.

And when D knelt, the day after my graduation, a ring in his hand, waiters and waitresses oohing and aww-ing and begging me to say yes, I also knelt, hugged him, and whispered, "Let's get out of here".

We ran towards the parking lot, arms around each other, excited voices rising afresh behind us.

"She said yeees," a woman's voice screamed.

"She's going to give him chao," a male one added, drawing laughter.

D's steps were light with excitement, mine were unsteady with nervousness. My hands were quickly getting sweaty around the ring I'd received and clasped.

Limbo

Innocent Chizaram Ilo

Life begins when everything starts to fall apart.

I

*I*feoma's life begins on a Monday morning when a mauve-feathered raven tucks an envelope containing her monthly bill into her mailbox. The bird lingers on the porch, pacing around, waiting for a tip. A sly gurgle escapes Ifeoma's throat. It is plain silly – not her gurgle, but the sight of the raven waiting for a tip. Ifeoma has never understood this whole business of ravens sticking around after delivering bills until the house owner stuffs a wheat cracker or two under their right wing.

"Get going!" Ifeoma shrieks from the kitchen where she is bent over a smoky charcoal stove, warming leftover beans porridge for breakfast.

"That's why nobody likes delivering your bills," the bird gibes before flying off. It drops a medium-sized mound of ordure on Ifeoma's roof to vent its frustration.

The fire hisses as water and oil from the pot's chipped bottom leaks into the stove. Ifeoma digs a spoon into the pot before setting it on the floor with a heat pad. She goes straight to the mailbox and snatches up the envelope. This month's bill came in a rose print envelope. Last month, it was sunflower. The month before that was lilac. Mr Osondu, from Town Council, has a knack for packaging messages of doom in flowery envelopes. Ifeoma calculates how many times she left the shower running for too long or forgot to turn off the lights and the heat when leaving for work, as she opens the envelope.

The crinkling paper on the table, with figures printed in bold font, glares at her:

SELEMKU TOWN COUNCIL

JANUARY BILL

ADDRESSED TO MS IFEOMA AMA

NO. 24 BLUE CRESCENT

WATER: 50 Buzas

LIGHT: 100 Buzas

AIR CLEAN-UP: 70 Buzas

TRASH DISPOSAL: 15 Buzas

HEAT: 45 Buzas

RENT ARREARS: 500 Buzas

PLEASE PAY UP ON OR WITHIN A WEEK OF RECEIVING THIS.

There is no way Ifeoma is going to cough out 780 Buzas in the nearest future, at least not with her measly job as a scarecrow. She has managed to pull through these past months with her mother's help. At twenty-five, Ifeoma is sick of mopping her mother's kitchen with her tears. The dirty white tiles in her mother's kitchen exhaust and darken her knees. Last month, Ifeoma's mother had chortled as her daughter mopped until the tiles assumed the shimmer of salt crystals.

"Trash disposal didn't come last month. Why are they billing me for it?" Ifeoma grumbles over the rumble in her stomach.

This is not the first time Town Council has billed Ifeoma wrongly, and no matter how much she raves at the Local Complaint Booth, it reoccurs each month. It used to be much easier when Kelechi was still living with her. Kelechi had exceptional tact when handling the eye-rolling secretary at the Local Complaint Booth. With her feathery voice, she always sweet-talked the secretary into correcting the bills.

Stony rage trickles down Ifeoma's throat at the thought of Kelechi and how things would magically fall into place if she was around. Ifeoma crashes her balled fist on the table to calm the tornado brewing inside her head. The rotting mahogany rips, sending the haphazardly stacked china bowls crashing on the floor.

She knew this mess would happen. Mama Ojay's ouija board said so.

✄

II

*O*uija boards are not really Ifeoma's thing. She prefers pendulums and crystal balls, things that submerge the truth in saccharine. But since Kelechi left, Ifeoma has had a hard time figuring out whether she likes something because she likes it, or because Kelechi liked it. Kelechi is exotic. She knows which Okirika boutique sells the smoothest rolls of silk, which bottle of wine is vintage enough, and identifies colours like marine-gold, maroon-red and oyster-silver. Ifeoma is plain. Red is red to her, and not wine-red, ox-blood or fuschia-pink, the rolls of silk at the Okirika boutiques all have the same texture against her skin, and wine is wine as long as it can knock one over.

So, in the spirit of trying new things, Ifeoma had shambled into Mama Ojay's shop last night, after having a drop too many at Tombo Bar, and joined the long queue of people who wanted the spirits lurking inside Mama Ojay's ouija board to reveal their fate. Mama Ojay was sitting surrounded by a ring of aromatic candles, stroking the fine edges of a black ouija board.

"Your spirit is too feeble for the storms of life," Mama Ojay barked at the girl in front of Ifeoma.

Ifeoma stepped back and allowed the man behind her to take her turn. Mama Ojay gave the man a sultry wink, and told him that fortune would smile on him. Ifeoma stepped back again, and allowed a freckled woman, whose hair had a pepper-fruit stench, to take her place. Mama Ojay shook her head and asked the woman if she knew how it felt to bury one's children at an old age. This is how it works, Ifeoma said to herself: Mama Ojay alternated good news with bad news. So she stepped forward and chanted the inane incantation Mama Ojay compelled everyone to sing.

Your mother's left lap is stuck in an onion ball.

Mama Dura is frying oranges for dinner.

Spirit children cook their mother's womb at Bambi Lake.

"Your spirit is brittle. It looks tough, but is easy to crack. Your days will be rough."

Mama Ojay's unflinching voice had made Ifeoma wonder how long the woman practiced those words just to say them to her. Ifeoma stood up, gathered the pieces of her pummelled self and nearly knocked the freckled woman over on her way out. When she got home, she fed the cats on her rooftop with worms. Maybe you also deserve rough days, Ifeoma whispered to the furry ferals as they nibbled at the worms in the shallow cup of her palms. The cats meowed until yellow streaks of sunlight came knocking on the jalousies.

III

*A*ll night, Mama Ojay's voice replays at the back of Ifeoma's mind. Ifeoma refuses to give it much thought; after all, her world roughened the day Kelechi slung two duffel bags across her shoulder and walked out of her life.

Their breakup was mechanistic. One night they were puffing plastic darts into cumulonimbus, and the next morning Kelechi left. Puff. Just like that. She said Ifeoma was not *deep enough*. A week later, it spread all over Selemku that Kelechi was getting married to Afam. Rheum-clogged-nostrils Afam. Inky-splotches-on-white-jogging-shorts Afam. Spindly-legs-that-look-like-they-will-snap Afam. Maybe Kelechi saw Deep Street from another end, Ifeoma had scoffed when she heard the rumours.

The alarm clock goes off, jolting Ifeoma back to the present. It is 7.30am and she has barely half an hour to get to work if she does not want Miss Ude, her boss, to have her head for lunch.

She grabs a towel and tries to get rid of the sawdust on her dress, but succeeds only in smearing it all over the fabric. She browses through a pile of clothes at the bottom of the bedroom closet before settling for the only clean dress in the heap – a woolly gown with puffy sleeves and washed-out neckline. Throughout this process, she wills herself not to think of how Kelechi made sure they did their laundry every Friday evening.

The alarm clock blares again. It is 8.00am. Miss Ude will definitely have her head for lunch. To sprinkle vodka on Ifeoma's wounds, the pair of gossamer wings she hung on the hibiscus hedge are still wet. Although getting to Miss Ude's farm on foot will cost Ifeoma another hour, she still takes the route through Cold Tunnel that is longer, lonelier, and stinks of sun-dried mercury. Cold Tunnel means she does not have to face the townspeople's *I-knew-it-wouldn't-last* smirks. The last time she took the main road to work, a tiny man had walked up to her and asked if she was going to get a new girlfriend or start *swinging like normal people* now Kelechi has left her.

Kelechi is gone, and Ifeoma does not need the whole town to rub it into her face.

IV

Selemku Town has long shaken off the bugs on its sleeping-blanket, rubbed the reddish soreness off its eyes, and slid into a new day by the time Ifeoma hits the road for work. The tawny owls perched on the Iroko have woken up and are bragging about how many children they scared last night. Nro, the woman who sells dream potions, is scraping up dewdrops stuck to ferns in front of her house. She uses the liquid for her sweet-dreams potions. Kelechi and Ifeoma used to buy Nro's potions. They would mix the sickly yellow liquid into their dinner, usually mango rice, cuddle on the sofa, and dream about getting married and having children.

As Ifeoma walks past the heap of rotting prawns near Bambi Lake, she draws up mental algorithms to find alternative ways of paying her bills. Maybe I should ask Miss Ude for a raise, Ifeoma hums to herself; it has been three years since I got a raise. However, this plan does not sit well because she knows she is neither the ideal employee, nor Miss Ude the benevolent employer. She considers selling her eyebrows to the voodoo women at Bini Market. Eyebrows stave off nightmares, but Ifeoma can live without them, especially now her life shares a lot of semblance with nightmares. Worst-case scenario, she'll use her childhood memories as surety for a loan from the moneylenders near Ruboji. The moneylenders are going to ask for her delightful memories: when her father taught her primary colours in the garden, her first fishing trip with him, or the time she bruised her knee in the backyard and he kissed the sore spot. But no matter how valuable they are, she will never use her memories of her time with Kelechi for fear that some moneylender might ogle the holograms of their kisses, fondling, and caresses stashed in his file cabinet.

"Look who finally showed up," Miss Ude announces as Ifeoma trudges through the gate. The older woman is milking her favourite cow, Efi, a rotund mass of flesh with thin legs and black-spotted skin, in the shed. Mud and milk are splattered on her once-white apron.

"I had to walk all the way here because..." Ifeoma's voice trails away.

"Your cat died?" Miss Ude throws Ifeoma a quizzical glance. She holds the pail close to the cow's udder to prevent the milk from spilling.

"No."

"You had to change your cheekbones?"

"My wings were wet this morning so I had to walk all the way here."

"Go get started." Miss Ude says after a long, condescending pause. She looks Ifeoma over as if she wants to sniff something else, apart from the truth, out of her.

Ifeoma changes into her work-cloth, a sack-gown frayed at the hem, before heading to the rice farm. She assumes her regular position, near the bamboo cluster, and yells at the pigeons pecking the rice stalks. The baulky ones not cowed by her screams catch the fury of her stick. The rice stalks are ripening fast, Ifeoma observes. They tower above her, almost reaching for the clouds. If she can stomach the right amount of pride and ask, Miss Ude will save some bushels for her when she harvests the rice next week.

Being a human scarecrow is probably the worst job in Selemku. It is not even a real job. Miss Ude gave her the job because of the friendship she shared with Ifeoma's mother. People do not employ human scarecrows when they can buy the ones Aliyuh makes with wooden poles and raffia. Truth be told, Aliyuh's scarecrows are more effective than Ifeoma's pretty face, and as a bonus, they never come late for work.

V

*W*ork finishes at 8pm when the pigeons retreat to their nests. Ifeoma goes straight to shower in the bathroom behind the granary. The lead-scented water soaks into her pores, and she scrubs her skin until it bleeds. *But there are things we cannot scrub off our bodies; like the grime of a job we don't like, or the memories of a lover we will never forget.*

"I have something to tell you," Ifeoma says to Miss Ude later that evening. The two women are seated under the avocado tree. Ifeoma is eating the bits of cold sardine Miss Ude served for dinner.

"I also have something to tell you," Miss Ude says.

"OK, tell me yours first."

"Ifeoma," Miss Ude begins. "I bought a scarecrow from Aliyuh this morning."

"Yippee! So I'm finally getting an assistant?"

"No, I'm letting you go."

"On a vacation?" Ifeoma swallows the spittle clinging inside her throat.

"You are fired. Paying you is like giving to charity, and I don't like charity."

A lumpy air blanket sucks up the space between the two

women.

"What if the pigeons notice that the scarecrow is fake?" Ifeoma is not sure whether her voice conveys a threat or a plea.

"Don't be silly. Pigeons have enough of nuts and earthworms to worry about. After all, scarecrows are meant to be fake."

For two nights in a row, Ifeoma sulks off to her house. The men sipping akpeteshie at Tombo bar whistle at her and threaten to slap her backside as she crosses Bolingo Junction. She remembers last night and how her drunk self had let those men fondle her breasts. Thinking of it now leaves her dirty.

"You may want to try the board again. Fortunes can reverse," Mama Ojay calls out as Ifeoma passes her shop. There are no customers today, so Mama Ojay is sitting outside trying to coax passers-by in.

Slimy, green puke from the cats she keeps feeding worms drips from the roof when Ifeoma reaches her front door. She gasps as the door swings open when she turns the knob. Someone is in her house. If it is a burglar, she says to herself, she will light a lamp and show him her unpaid bills. Who knows, the burglar might be magnanimous enough to share his bounty with her. In exchange, she will tell him which houses in the neighbourhood have the shiniest gems.

But the lock is not broken. The person inside the house must be either an expert lock-picker or someone who has a spare key. Ifeoma steadies her pulse and pushes the door further open.

"Good evening. You're back."

Flakes of imaginary ice prickle Ifeoma's skin as she recognises the voice. "What are you doing here?"

The room is pitch-dark but she can see Kelechi's shadowy outline standing beside the tapestry because the fire in her eyes is still undead.

"I tried putting on the lights, but they wouldn't come on. Are you short on your bills again?"

"How is Afam?" Ifeoma asks, ignoring Kelechi's question.

A choking calmness.

"I came to drop my spare key and formally invite you to the wedding. It's this Saturday." Kelechi breaks the ice.

"Pfft! I can't come. Girl has to work overtime to pay the bills."

"Good night, Ifeoma," Kelechi says and makes for the door.

"Does he love you more than I do?" Ifeoma grabs Kelechi's arm and pulls her to her chest.

"Does it matter?"

Kelechi's lanky frame throbs in Ifeoma's arms, like a leaf desperately holding fast to a branch on a blustery night. When their lips meet, it unravels memories buried under cobwebs. Their tongues tingle as they recognise the distinct flavours of their lipsticks: Kelechi's wild cherry, and Ifeoma's tomato.

"I should be going. This never happened." Kelechi tries to pull away.

"Do you enjoy hurting people? You still love me, don't you?" Ifeoma says, breathing hoarsely into Kelechi's ear.

"Love is very complex."

"And to think that you left me for a man."

"Would it have made any difference if I left you for a woman?" Kelechi shoves Ifeoma aside and slams the door behind her.

Ifeoma had promised herself she would not cry when Kelechi called it quits with her two months ago. She understood that some people grew out of *this kind of love* quickly. But now, as she stands in the emptiness of her house, crumpled sheets of grief dance around her eyes, and large beads of tears flow undisturbed. She collects the tears in an old nail-polish bottle. One day, when she finally finds bliss, the tears will remind her of love's bitter sweetness. She gropes her way through the darkness until she reaches the sofa. There, she falls into a troubled slumber.

VI

*G*rey is the colour of waning love.

Roughly stitched, grey clouds splay across the skyline. Two women are walking, hands locked into one another. The slender heels of their stilettos go knock-knock on the tarred street surface. They stop at the train station and buy a ticket to the next town. When they get to the next town, one of the women leaves the train with a strange man. The other stays in the train.

Light fades.

Ↄ

VII

"Not again!" Ifeoma untangles her body from the blanket and scrambles off the sofa. Her spine is sore from all the twisting and squeezing she did while sleeping. Something saps air out of her windpipe. She pulls the window open and sticks her nose outside for fresh air. The dream always comes back, each time vaguer. It started the night Kelechi left.

Scattered beams of dawn, filtering into the parlour through the open window, light up the room and show Ifeoma how dishevelled her house has become. The cockroaches have fattened from licking the piles of unwashed dishes. Layers of mould flourish along the ceiling boards and the floor has acquired an extra coating of dust.

"No one saves you, Ifeoma Ama. You are going to glue the battered bits of your life back together."

The rest of Tuesday washes the air with the drabness of a gravedigger's funeral. Ifeoma removes the thick mesh of cobwebs strung along the wall and ceiling, dusts the photographs in the spiral-bound album, and burns all the photographs in the house that have Kelechi in them. She struggles not to stand close to the fire, afraid that the burning memories will possess her.

Wednesday almost slips away as if it never came. Ifeoma arranges the books in the shelf, moves out the broken table, and mends the torn tablecloths. In the evening, she goes to her L Support Group meeting. She has missed two consecutive meetings and doesn't want other members to see her as weak; someone crushed by a break-up.

Throughout the meeting, Ifeoma wishes someone would lower

her down a spike. Soliat, the woman sitting beside her, jabbers about her *wonderful relationship*, how her life has transformed since she met a woman called Ndiwe. Soliat's black braids slap against Ifeoma's face as she turns.

"How long is the relationship?" Ifeoma asks Soliat.

"Two weeks."

"And it's already wonderful?"

"Yes!"

Ifeoma smiles, almost grateful that Soliat did not get the sarcasm.

During AOB, two women ask those present for suggestions on spicing up their sex life.

"What does a woman walking around with a depressed vagina for months know about spicing up someone's sex life?" Nonye, the woman Ifeoma dated before Kelechi, mumbles as Ifeoma stands to speak.

Everybody laughs.

"Maybe because my vagina is talking from experience," Ifeoma says when the laughter dies down.

"Ifeoma, you know you are not allowed to use the v-word during meetings," Oby, who is also called Madam President, cautions.

"You didn't hear Nonye use it first?"

"No."

Of course Oby did not hear Nonye use the v-word because she started dating Nonye several weeks ago. Ifeoma grabs her purse and storms out of the meeting.

Thursday tinges the air with an unfamiliar staleness. Ifeoma washes the plates, does the laundry, and mops the floors with water she borrowed from Mrs Ginika, her neighbour. She sits on the porch and waits for the clothes to dry because the neighbours' children have a longstanding reputation of soiling people's laundry during their evening football game.

Friday is reluctant to come. When it does arrive, Ifeoma sings 'Valerie' until evening: "...and I miss that ginger hair and the way you like to dress."

VIII

*K*elechi does not have ginger hair; hers is dark–dark like the bottom of a porridge pot. The two had met two years ago at Ogbete Market. It was April. The dusty raindrops had already filled the cracks on the ground, and an eye-stinging petrichor was spreading itself like nectar over people's noses. Kelechi was standing beside the butcher's, waiting for the rain to stop, while Ifeoma was buying okra in the next shop.

"Do you have a spare umbrella?" Kelechi asked her. "My hair stinks when it gets wet."

"We can share," Ifeoma had offered, baffled by the possibility of someone actually carrying a spare umbrella. "Where do you live?"

"Nwampa Street, near the bakery."

"I live at Blue Crescent. It's a few blocks away from your street."

They tiptoed around the huge muddy puddles, squeezed through the tightly packed crowd, and still managed to hold on to the umbrella. The umbrella, with a pattern of red parrots and yellow ducks, had a weak frame and let in raindrops through tiny holes.

"I've never heard of a human scarecrow," Kelechi said when Ifeoma told her where she worked.

"Trust me, it's not as fascinating as it sounds. What about you?" Ifeoma asked.

"I'm a struggling painter. I moved to Selemku a month ago." It was then that Ifeoma noticed Kelechi's feathery voice.

At Soles Alley, Kelechi slipped on a banana peel and fell. Ifeoma would forever remember the sight of Kelechi's hair soaked in water. Weeks later, when their love blossomed, Ifeoma had described it as *love in a time of wet hair*. Their love had the newness of spring onions and scent leaf. Kelechi moved in with Ifeoma the next week. They were moving too fast. They liked it that way.

Kelechi painted all day: pictures of girls cuddling, nude women wrapped in rainbows, girls bathing in the rain, men in floral gowns, and women wearing trousers. She sent her paintings to the Art Council and waited for their response. The Art Council rejected most of them with comments like *it lacks form, the propaganda comes before the art, it's too chic, why are you emasculating men.* The sparing few accepted did not have royalties or payments attached. The Art Council felt they were doing Kelechi a huge favour; giving her a dose of exposure that would help her paintings find the right market.

Afam changed everything.

Kelechi met Afam at an art exhibition six months ago. They had babbled the whole evening about art revolutions, movements and expressions. They compared Leonardo Da Vinci and Michelangelo, which Afam said was an insult to Leonardo's impeccable reputation. Ifeoma gaped at them, praying the evening would end.

She thought it would be the last they'd see of Afam, only to come back from work one evening to find Afam and Kelechi chattering like old friends. Ifeoma waved this off, thinking it was a one-time thing. It was not. The more Afam visited, the more Kelechi became a stranger to Ifeoma. A stranger who painted rocky landscapes, wildlife and potbellied politicians. The Art Council started to accept and pay for her paintings. She began to foot all the monthly bills. When Ifeoma complained, she told her to stop being such a child.

It was this same stranger that woke up one morning and left Ifeoma.

IX

*M*ama Ife calls the ritual dinner she has with her daughter every Friday evening *bonding*. Ifeoma flies all the way from Blue Crescent to her mother's house in Maitaima for this. People in Maitaima live longer than the folks in other parts of Selemku because the glowing streetlights do not allow bats with crumbly grains of death under their wings to fly over their houses. Ifeoma grew up here, in one of the fancy stone mansions with glossy lawns. She still remembered those weekends when her mother would force her to sit in the garden and watch her smoke electric-cigars with her friends from the Tinted Madams Club.

Mama Ife is already at the table when Ifeoma arrives. Ifeoma murmurs her greeting and sits six chairs away from her mother. The clanging of the stainless-steel spoons on the ceramic plates and the occasional entrance of a servant drown the silence in the room.

"Anything new in your life, apart from Kelechi leaving you?"

"I lost my job." The words escape Ifeoma's mouth. "Miss Ude must have told you."

The older woman wipes her mouth with a napkin and says, "Coincidentally, my kitchen floor needs to be mopped. You know a thousand Buzas can always put you through until next month."

Ifeoma pushes her plate away, says her thanks, and stands up to leave.

"I told Miss Ude to fire you."

Ifeoma stops in her tracks. "You think that will make you own me?"

"Pfft!" Mama wrinkles her nose. "Aren't daughters meant to hold fast to the ends of their mothers' lappahs?"

"Little wonder Papa chose death over staying with you. You will grow old in this big house. Alone and unloved."

"At least I kept your father for fifteen years. You couldn't even sustain a woman's love for two years."

Ifeoma's fist tightens around a breadknife lying on the table. "You don't know anything about Kelechi and me."

"While I couldn't care less about your silly relationship, I knew you were no match for Afam. He is an Art Professor. All Kelechi needed was a lecture on Expressionism and Cubism, and she was his. I'm telling you from experience, no woman wants a human scarecrow who earns 300 Buzas every month."

"What do you know about women wanting their fellow women?"

Ifeoma's mother darts her face away from her daughter's gaze.

"You think you're the first woman to love another woman? Miss Ude is my lover. She has always been. Even since before I married your father."

"Your what?!"

"Do you now see why I couldn't bring myself to love your father? He always reminded me of the life I left behind."

"Why did you marry Papa if you didn't love him?"

"Who says you need love in marriage? A little dab of compromise here and there, and I let the man slip the ring on my finger. I deserve more in life than to end up as a farmer's wife. A woman farmer at that."

"You are cold."

"Cold? I just didn't want to lose everything – my father's bequest, my—"

"It's always been about the money for you?"

"You think it's just about the money? How about walking on the street and seeing the people you are better than call you *femmo*? Looking at you in the most condescending way because you crave a fellow woman's breasts and toto; things you have yourself."

"Kelechi and I are different."

"You and Kelechi are not different. There is nothing like you and Kelechi. It's over. Once I thought you guys would marry and be together. I imagined how your victory will smear shit on my face. But here we are. Goodnight Ifeoma, catch some rest. Your arms and ankles will need all the rest they can get to mop my kitchen floor tomorrow."

Ifeoma's head is too clouded with thoughts for her to fly, so she decides to trek home. She bumps into Miss Ude at the gate. The two women stare into each other's eyes. Miss Ude breaks the stare and begins to walk into the house.

"Why do you still come to her?" Ifeoma's question stabs at Miss Ude.

"You're young. You won't understand."

X

*W*hen Ifeoma gets home, she kicks off her shoes and slumps on the sofa.

"I am not going to be like my mother. One day, I'll find someone and things will work out with her. I'll be happy. I'll find love. But first, I need to pay my bills."

The words lure her to sleep.

XI

*O*n Saturday morning, while the wedding bells are ringing at St Lucy's Chapel, Ifeoma goes to her mother's house to mop the kitchen floor. Her mother chatters about how her friends prod her to tell them what detergent she uses for her kitchen floor. "I told them *my daughter's tears*. Foolish women! They went scouring every mall in Selemku for a detergent with that name."

Ifeoma taps into her memories at intervals – the sepia images of the love she shared with Kelechi, and a few from times shared with her father – to produce more tears.

"She'll give you 1000 Buzas. You'll pay your bills. You'll come back next month because you are good at mopping floors with your tears!" Ifeoma chides herself as her mother's throaty cackle hangs around her like fog.

Unblooming

Alexis Teyie

*A*nnette was the sort of girl who did not deserve a nickname. There was no universe in which you might look up at her midway through early morning prep, and think to yourself, that Annie, what a girl! Only a strange and broken person would call out across the field during lunch, Anne, nikuletee chips kutoka tuck shop? This was clear to me from the first day we met outside the head teacher's office when we both transferred into Fuzu Primary School. I looked into her eyes (nicely brown, with long lashes – wasted, I tell you!), and I knew Annette would remain Annette to me, even if I were to cut the umbilical cord of her first-born son and watch her shit during childbirth.

Now, look, I'm not saying a person couldn't love Annette. My cousin Jojo says everyone is lovable, unless you're a witch, or Lucifer, or that shopkeeper who says to come back for your balance, but when you return, turns up the volume on his radio, insisting he knows nothing of your so-called change.

So, yes, Annette was probably lovable. She was even funny sometimes, without trying. The thing with Annette is that she just did not know how to sit in her body. She was always jumping up and into your business, stung by chilli that had not even touched her own tongue. And maybe it's because we were always having to remind her to stay calm inside her skin that it was difficult to shorten or change in any way that name 'Annette'. Saying 'Annette' was not just a way to ask for Annette's attention, it was a reminder of how not to be. When Teacher Lucy said it, you understood she meant, Annette, you there, stop fidgeting at once, and everyone else better swallow your inner Annettes and repeat after me, "Sir Evelyn Baring declared a state of emergency on October 20, 1952." And so we would swallow all the Annettes itching in us, wanting to ask, isn't Evelyn a girl's name, and we would recite: "Sir Evelyn Baring declared a state of emergency on October 20, 1952." All this could be true. Maybe not. But I held to my commitment to never call Annette 'Annie' or 'Anne' or 'Anna' or 'A' or 'Netty' or 'Nessa' or 'Netnet', or even 'Sweetie', like Jojo called everyone she met. I held firm to this commitment because Annette, this Annette, single-handedly destroyed my world in Standard 6. Bloody Annette.

In the middle of second term, right after mid-term exams, Annette wrote up a list. I can't begin to imagine what drove Annette to create that list. It's too easy to say, well, that's just Annette pulling an Annette. If you had asked me the week she started talking about the list, I would have said, I think she's a little lonely, a little bored, and immediately I said this out loud, I would have known, deep inside, that this was exactly something Jojo might say. Now if you had asked me the same question three months later, I would have looked you in the eye, which I rarely did, and said: this Annette of yours is possessed by a water demon, and there would be no telling me otherwise. I cannot believe I didn't see from the very beginning how mad it was, this list, and its devout priestess, Annette.

*O*K, so Annette walks into class at break time. Her tie is knotted so tightly around her neck that her collar looks like the wings of a cock on heat, but in she strolls, cool as you please. The rows on her hair look fresher than all the other girls, even Zawadi, whose mother is a hairdresser. We only have twenty minutes, so no one bothers to look away from their bhajia, their assignments, or the latest gossip from Khadija, who knows everything, like when the PE teacher picks his nose during the national anthem at the very back of parade. Annette walks right up to the teacher's table, digs into her tunic pocket, and pulls out this large paper, like from an artist's sketchpad. She says, "Ehe, pay attention. Noisemakers, mkome. I have something to say—"

"Ala! Ukistaajabu ya Musa... Madame Annette can speak Kiswahili? Since when!"

"Khadija, why are you always interrupting? Just keep quiet there in the back."

"So, say what you are saying and leave us alone then."

"Mark, aki you are so rude. Can you not be a gentleman? Anyway, as I was saying, I have made a list so we know who are the girls and who are the women. You boys better pay attention."

No one says anything, and this is clearly not the reaction Annette was hoping for.

"Did you hear?"

Again, the only sound is Goody-Goody Jimmy scribbling Agric notes at his desk near the door.

Khadija starts laughing before anyone else, and now Mark is laughing, and Auma, and Zawadi, and I'm laughing too, a little too eagerly maybe, a little too keen to steady my precarious position on the inside of this joke. But Annette, true to form, knows just who to poke, and the precise pressure to apply.

"Ehe, OK, just laugh, but it is interesting that the first girls to laugh are the ones whose names are nowhere on the list. Kwanza you, Peninah Juma, always acting as if you are better than everyone, bouncing for us here like some rapper. So you continue like that, just continue and see where your husband will come from if you can't even—"

"Eish, there's no need for that jameni! And can you not call her Nina? How many times must you be told?" Solo intervenes, and slides me one of his quiet looks, as if to say, hey, I see you. In that moment, warm under Solo's gaze, I honestly believe that this is going to be just another silly thing Annette got into her mind, an interlude before CATs that no one would remember – except me, of course, because I have a talent for hoarding grudges.

That evening, I go down the road to kina Jojo's house. Aunty Lizzy puts me straight to work washing the dishes, but I don't mind; I like their new house, with the wide verandah and the soft blue kitchen tiles. Anyhow, I have a good washing up strategy: I start with the cups, because they're easy. Jojo is kneading dough for mandazi, and she can tell I have something to say. When I get hot water for all the greasy stuff, and feel about for the Scotchbrite in the sink, she turns up the volume on the radio. The Fugees come on. We both like Lauryn. She seems like the sort of woman who smokes Marlboros on Sundays. I start to say what I have been trying to say since I walked through the door and Aunty Lizzy pointed me towards the kitchen: "Jojo, you know—"

"Uantenimiraa! Waria uantenimiraa!"

"Acha ujinga, that's not what they are singing. It's Juan tanamera. It's about a boy called Juan. Watu waSpanish husema 'ha' instead of 'j'. Why would they be singing about Waria? There are no Somalis in Europe!"

"Kwenda. As if you know. Let me tell you something," she says, pinching off rolls of dough, "wazungu sing all kinds of nonsense."

"Wyclef and Lauryn are not white. They are black!"

"They are American. If you are American, you're a mzungu hata kama you are the colour of charcoal."

"Ah, I guess. Anyway, what's it like?"

"What? I'm not a mzungu."

"No, not that. The period." I pull out steel wool from the cabinet and start to work on the sufurias and pans. Usually the steel wool has caught the rust, and Jojo says, "Tetanus, sure thing." I don't mind, really. I like the smell of the wool coated in all that orangey-reddy-brown, like fermenting beer. "Does it feel like you're peeing?"

"Why are you asking?"

"Annette—"

"The one and only?"

"The same one, yes. So she said this stupid thing today. She is keeping a list of all the girls who started."

"You're just a late bloomer, Nina."

"No, it's not that. It's just, I guess I didn't really think that... but anyway so there are those girls who only get it a few times, and then it dries up, ama?"

"Kwani, it's a borehole? How can it dry up?"

"You know…"

"But then you won't have children."

"So?"

"I mean, OK, I guess then you could be one of those mamas driving around in a red Starlet and sleeping with the boss."

"Yeah, maybe," I say as I place the plates on the drying rack.

"Nina? You won't even notice it. Really, I promise. And your chest will catch up and all that."

"Sure, yeah." I find it a little hard to breathe, but I raise my eyes to look at her. I inhale carefully, somehow certain I would need to remember this exact moment: Jojo perched on a stool, elbow-deep in dough, neck moist, and eyelashes weighed down by flour; Awilo Longomba's "Coupe Bibamba" slithering into the kitchen, wrapping itself round the rich scent of burning sugar. Beneath this all, the sound of cooking oil – jittery, uncomfortable in its own body.

*O*f course, I was wrong about Annette's idea. Our little universe in Standard 6 Blue got knocked out of orbit when Khadija learned, before anyone else, that Zawadi's mother had given her tampons. Now, the CRE teacher had mentioned to some of us how those things could break the hymen, and anyway, why would good girls stick things in there that God had not created? The speculations about Zawadi's virginity exploded into a full-out inquisition, with detailed research, character witnesses, and somehow Annette emerged as the Inspector General. The list ceased to be just a silly diversion. Who had started 'raining' and when, shaped everyone's conversations over lunch, when the Music instructor's back was turned, during warm-ups for sports. The more people talked about the list, the more zealous Annette became. There she was, lingering outside the girls' toilets, and there again, hawk-eyed during PE, and again, looking up during drama rehearsals, vigilant. And then, one girl's name after another followed, with Annette meticulously documenting the exact dates. And me? Zuzu wa Fuzu Primary, that's who I was. When Clare, tiny Clare who always got mistaken for a lower primary pupil joined the list, Annette became unbearable, unfolding her paper dramatically, underlining the dates with a flourish.

Four months in, I felt certain I would never get on that list. I thought I was safe. I figured the red lorry might have passed me over, that my novenas had reached someone wherever prayers go. And then I felt it. It was a Tuesday, during History, the last class before lunch. Teacher Lucy was going on about the Kapenguria Six, and this warmish moisture started to spread out underneath me. I did not know how to get myself to the toilets, or if I even wanted to leave, because then I would have to tell someone, be something, something different. So I sat.

I sat as Teacher Lucy made us repeat: Achieng' Oneko, Bildad Kaggia, Kung'u Karumba, Jomo Kenyatta, Fred Kubai, Paul Ngei. Tepid, that's it. Like too-sugary tea poured from a thermos for a guest that never came. Again! Achieng' Oneko, Bildad Kaggia, Kung'u Karumba, Jomo Kenyatta, Fred Kubai, Paul Ngei. That feeling, like someone was walking over my grave. A fat person stomping all over my grave. I couldn't breathe. I felt like I was inside a hollow tree, a big one like the old trees on the main avenue. I looked up, and there were these branches, my branches, rich and heavy with fruit, flowers. Me, there, inside the foot of this tree, and then, a branch withering, and another falling off, and another while I sat there, cross-legged, wondering why this tree was running away from me, and if it had to collapse, why didn't it take me with it? Again! Achieng' Oneko, Bildad Kaggia, Kung'u Karumba, Jomo Kenyatta, Fred Kubai, Paul Ngei.

The bell for lunch eventually rang, and everyone rushed out. Solo paused by my desk, waiting for me to shout which team I'd be on for football. I couldn't move. I shook my head and hoped he wouldn't ask me anything. I must have managed to stand. I must have somehow found a pack of Always. I must have gone to the toilet. I must have somehow made it through the afternoon, packed my bag, walked out into the 5pm sun, out all the way to the stage, got into the right matatu. I must have remembered to get off at the right stop, walked past Jojo's house and reached home.

The next thing I remember for sure is deciding that I wouldn't let anyone know, not even Jojo. I would unwrap the pads very carefully so no one would hear in the stall next to me. At home, I would wait until everyone was watching *Esmeralda* on TV to slip away to the bathroom. I would remember to spray myself with the eau de toilette I stole from Jojo to mask the vigorously dainty smell of Always. I would do all this for two days.

*A*nd then Jojo found out. She must have told my mother because I walked in from school that Friday evening, and Mum called me into the kitchen. Her wrapper was sliding down her hips, and she didn't look up from plucking feathers from the chicken when I entered.

"How was school, basi?"

"Kawaida tu, nothing new."

"All right. Can you help me chop those tomatoes? And don't do big pieces, you know Dad doesn't like that."

"Sawa."

I knew something was wrong from the way she kept sniffing, like she always did when she was nervous.

"I heard that something happened this week."

I kept chopping, and wouldn't look up.

"Peninah, you are now a woman. You can give birth, eh? You have to watch yourself now, around those boys, OK? You can't be running around with them like you have been doing. This tomboy business has to stop."

TEYIE

The proper response, I suppose, is all right, yes, sure, but after few tomatoes, I had fallen into a gentle rhythm: the slicing of the air, the whoosh down, the first digging into the tomato's skin, the slide through, the final thummm on the wooden board – like an old lullaby. My eyes focused on the chopping, the up and down, the throbbing on the board. I started to feel as I did looking down from the top of our flat.

"You can't trust these boys, Peninah. You hear?"

The roof was its own universe – a Lego house with Lego people and their nice colours and their hands like blunt pincers. What I liked was the hard concrete pushing up at me, the delicious threat of air just over the edge. All around, bright uniforms hung to dry flapping in the wind, arms and legs hollow, now inhaling, now deflating like interconnected mouths of tilapia, screaming silently. The smell of wet shirt in my nose, crisp with OMO detergent and clean, clean sunshine. The antennas of TV sets on our entire block twitching above – dark straws sucking in air, or siphoning out something else, I don't know. Faraway, sounds of children laughing, coming and going. I would stand at the very edge, barefoot, and curl my toes over the rough stone, the edge biting into my skin. Somewhere inside, a cricket jumping up, tickling my throat. If I swam forward, right over the edge, would I maybe float a little?

"Peninah, you know we care about you, Dad and me. So you have to listen to me when I say you can't trust these boys at all, at all!"

You know, once in Music class, I thought, when people die, we should attach their hearts to a huge bouquet of colourful balloons, and let them loose.

"You have to watch yourself around them. If they think you're easy, they won't be able to control themselves. I mean, even with your father, you know he chased me for two years? Two years! That's how they know you mean business. Only the serious ones will remain, you understand?"

Imagine that: you'd be in the kitchen, doing the dishes maybe, shoulder-deep in foam and left-over githeri. Pausing from scrubbing a particularly grimy pot, you might look up and out the window. Right there, urged upwards by the clouds, a flamboyance of balloons. Like rainbows about to hatch. You might even cry a little.

I wanted someone to see a flock of rogue balloons, and to feel something for me, even if they didn't know me. The knife I was holding dove into my palm, over and over and over, leaving deep skid marks. I looked at the knife, and saw it plunge in, and for a second, I could swear I felt I could give it the whole hand, if it wanted it.

"Nina! Aki bring your hand to the sink! Kwani, you weren't seeing?"

Sluggishly, as if I was waking from one of those malaria dreams, the kitchen came back into focus. Blood shot out of the puckered skin in my hand, like a teasing tongue: nyenyenyenye, the last one there is a cockroach.

"Ei surely, it's really deep. And it's not just one. What was going through your head, Peninah?"

Time stretched taut like a bladder, shuddering lightly. It all suddenly seemed ridiculous to me: Kienyeji chicken boiling on the gas cooker, and right next to that pilau and beef stew chortling in the pots, and the mandazi for evening tea still browning in the pan. I didn't know what to say, where to look. I stared instead at the tomato that had fallen out of my hand, and onto the white tile – a crimson smile splattered on the floor.

Mum thrust my hand underneath the stream of water, and held it there while the blood circled the drain.

The Things They Said

Susan Newham-Blake

*I*t was a long time since you'd done anything gay. And to be honest, you weren't really in the mood to go to the lesbian book reading and hear coming-out stories, or first-love stories, or stories about hearts bruised by disappointment.

When you'd come out, they'd said you were brave. That you were a warrior. Not everyone follows their hearts. But your mother had sat with her face in her hands. Your father, his face ashen, had shaken his head, then announced it was just a phase. Neither of them had had any idea. It made you wonder whether you'd always been this invisible.

When you moved to a bachelor flat and fell in love with the girl who worked at the corner coffee shop with her witty turn of phrase, her eyes that shone with curiosity, the small gap between her front teeth, people said how happy they were for you. How you deserved to find love, to be happy like everyone else. And for a while you were. In love. Happy.

You painted your bodies with peonies and butterfly wings, scribbled large letters on cardboard placards, joined the rowdy crowd at Gay Pride. You hung out at the new lesbian bar in town, where you were safe from raised eyebrows. Sometimes you'd go nowhere at all, just stay entwined beneath crumpled sheets for an entire weekend. Even when she went back home to her family without you because she wasn't ready to tell them yet, you stayed home alone uncomplaining because she was worth the wait. And it was only a matter of time.

You were patient for weeks, then months. And then you weren't so patient any more.

You grew sullen at having to sit alone, the empty chair next to you, knowing she wouldn't arrive. It was hard not to take it personally even though she said it would break her mother's heart, that her baby brother would hate her.

You fought. Why couldn't she just do it? It hadn't been easy for you, either. Why couldn't she? For you? So many arguments, hours of exhausting debates into the early hours of the morning, spiralling in circles trying to understand, to make things better. Until it was all over. She wouldn't, couldn't, and then she was gone.

Nobody said much then. You could touch the silence. Some said it was a pity. That maybe she'd come round. But you knew better.

You went to therapy. Dealt with your abandonment issues. Came to realise many folk feel like they don't fit in. You got a new job, something you enjoyed, took out a lease on a ground-floor flat, brought home two puppies nobody had told you would keep you awake at night with their whining.

Then you met someone new through a friend of a friend. The best way, they said. She was different. Unapologetic about who she was. She'd hold your hand as you walked through bustling shopping malls and sometimes she'd stop and kiss you full on the mouth. She didn't care that people stared, so why should you? Just what you needed, they said. Things all happen for a reason. This was someone you could really settle down with.

And you did.

You found a bigger place. You moved in together, you with your dogs, she with her Persian cat. It didn't matter that you were allergic to the white hair strewn all over the new sofa.

She introduced you to her parents. They were liberals, open-minded. Her mother hugged you and asked if you were a vegetarian. You weren't. Her father handed you champagne, the glass so thin you held it like you might cradle a bird's egg.

You went away for weekends, just the two of you. You'd lie in the king-sized bed with expensive sheets and stare into each other's eyes, amazed you could be so happy. You had so much in common. Books. Politics. Eating out. Walking. Watching back-to-back series on a Sunday afternoon. There was talk of marriage. A civil union. Allowed now, one of the few places in the world. You weren't so sure at first. You'd never thought of it as an option. Your mother was Catholic. God, what would your grandmother say? This wasn't about them, she said. Any of them. This was about you, the two of you.

So, you drew up a guest list, Googled wedding venues, thought about dresses. The date was set. The wedding invitations sent. How wonderful, they said, how exciting. They'd all be there. Your colleague said she'd never been to a gay wedding before. You wondered about that. What *was* a gay wedding? The only thing that made it gay was the two of you. Don't bother about her, your fiancée said.

Your mother didn't reply. Not at first. You took her out for coffee in exchange for an answer. She and your father had discussed it. There was something about the sanctity of marriage that complicated their decision to attend. It wasn't what they believed in. They would get back to you.

Later that night you threw a glass against the back of the closed bathroom door so hard that the splinters appeared on the floor for weeks afterwards. Your fiancée tried to comfort you, but it didn't help. You didn't want the freak show wedding any more. It had been a stupid decision.

But your parents came round. Of course they did. They loved you, though please could your father not walk you down the aisle. I'm sure you understand.

They wanted to know where you'd find a priest to bless such a thing. You told them it was not a religious wedding; there would be no priest. They nodded at that, satisfied, like it wasn't a real wedding after all.

On the big day, you both wore white dresses. You'd chosen them together. Everyone said how lovely you both looked, but you were self-conscious. You wondered if what you really looked was comical. Two women in matching billowy dresses walking down the aisle, fatherless.

Your parents arrived late, hung back from the crowd. They did not bring your grandmother. After enough wine, you no longer cared, you danced outside on the verandah, your dress hitched into your underwear so it wouldn't get torn. In the morning, it was a relief to have it all over.

You got a promotion at work. You bought a house. Put it in both your names. A small Victorian, with black-and-white tiles and a ball-and-claw bathtub. The cat died. You argued about whether to get a new one. What about having a baby instead, you suggested. There were ways to have your own. Sperm donors, inseminations, fertility clinics. It was you who drove these discussions. It was you who wanted to be pregnant, and she was relieved. She'd never had the desire to carry.

There was a mutual friend who might be keen to donate his sperm. A data analyst. Never married. You took him out for lunch to ask. He said yes easily. Too easily. You wondered how it would all work, what effect your cosy triad would have on the child, on your relationship. You wondered if he'd keep up his end of the bargain of not being too involved, of not caring too much. You argued that evening, and the next, and then agreed to go another route. You visited a fertility clinic. Decided on an anonymous donor. Made an appointment. The procedure was not too uncomfortable. Just like a pap smear. Quick, painless. Afterwards you lay with your legs in the air hoping it would work. And it did. Two blue lines on the disposable pregnancy test.

Congratulations, they said. What pioneers! You're an inspiration, proof that if you put your mind to it, you can get what you want. And you were proud. Excited about becoming a mother. You felt lucky, too. In the old days you wouldn't have been able to have your own baby. What a wonderful thing, modern technology.

But as you lay awake in bed at night, looking into the darkness, your mind raced. Was this the right thing to do? Would your child be all right without a father? Would your wife love a child that wasn't biologically hers? Would you feel like a real family?

You went for the foetal assessment, holding your breath. The baby was healthy. A healthy boy. Your wife seemed pleased about that. Boys were easier, she said, and you nodded.

Your parents accepted the news quietly. An anonymous donor. Your dad repeated the words slowly. It's not really what we believe in, your mother said, in case God was listening. But of course we love you, of course we're happy to be having a grandchild.

A colleague at work said she thought it was cruel to bring a child into a gay family. Again, you wondered what a gay family was. Afterwards you kicked yourself for not defending your decision; for not having stood up for yourself and your unborn child.

You carried to full term. You gave birth naturally, your wife, standing on your right side, the nurse on your left, the gynae poised ready to receive your newborn child. He was a healthy weight, received full marks on his Apgar test. You touched his tiny fingernails, his soft ears covered in fuzz. You held your mouth and nose against the top of his head, breathing him in, unable to get enough of him.

He took to your breast easily, though at nights he was colicky. He could scream for an hour, unable to accept comfort. There were long nights without sleep. You noticed she was busier than usual at work. Coming home later. You fought. He was her baby, too. But it's you he wants, she said.

He grew bigger, stopped crying so much. One day she picked him up and nestled him against her neck. You smiled. Mommy's here, she said. You were taken by surprise at the unexpected urge to grab him out of her arms and shout: I'm the mommy!

It was hard going back to work and leaving him with the nanny.

It was tough juggling the responsibility of work and baby, coming home tired, then having to change nappies, push spoonfuls of mush into his defiant mouth, cope with nights of interrupted sleep. You argued. It felt like you were doing more than your fair share. Completely normal, they said. Normal for the birth mom to feel like that.

Over a bottle of wine one night, she admitted she sometimes felt invisible. You are so clearly his mother, she said. People never address me when they speak about him. No one ever refers to me as his mom. Do you know that at the baby shower hardly anyone congratulated me on my coming child? You reassured her. He *is* yours. It doesn't matter what anyone says. According to him, you're his other parent. She replied: I feel like the fucking au pair.

He grew into a toddler. You both laughed at his quirks, the way he liked to hang upside down from your lap. How he tried talking in sentences before he could say words. How he ran instead of walking. How he tried to pick up the dogs, who were twice his size.

And then he was ready for nursery school. You wondered whether you should tell the teacher he had two moms. Whether it would make any difference. The teacher was unfazed. I've had all sorts in my class, she said. I once had a little girl with two dads. She was a very well-rounded kid. You wondered if that had surprised her.

He got invited to his first birthday party. You bought a present. Wrote in a card. Arrived on time, but when you stood at the table helping yourself to a pink cupcake covered in hundreds and thousands, the hostess said: How long have you and your husband been living here? You froze, unsure of how to answer. You stammered, went red in the face. You knew you should say: I don't have a husband, I have a wife. But you didn't want to embarrass her. I'm married to a woman, you said apologetically. She blushed. Sorry, she said. Then she looked at your son. Is he adopted? No, I carried him. You felt proud when you said it, like somehow it made you more legitimate.

You had that conversation many times after that, so many times it felt like you were discussing the weather. You no longer felt embarrassed, you no longer apologised. You often corrected with the words: wife, not husband. Sometimes you even spoke about the sperm bank, the anonymous donor. Wow, they said. What an interesting family. Your son's best friend said he was so lucky to have two moms, that he couldn't think of anything nicer.

Now that your son was older, you left him with the babysitter, went on date nights. Romantic movies or ones that made you laugh, sushi at your favourite seafood restaurant. A bottle of wine. On one of these evenings, you raised the idea of having another baby. You wanted your son to have a sibling. Maybe you'd have a girl this time. She wasn't sure. Things are easier now, she said. Why rock the boat? Being a parent was harder than she'd imagined. Let's wait, she said, there's no rush. You lay awake at night thinking about the other moms at your son's school, how most of them had two kids, some even three. You wondered if having another child might complete your family. Make you feel more normal. Just like everyone else.

You were included on a WhatsApp group of moms from your son's class. Friday night, pizza night at mine, one of them texted. It became a ritual, going to each other's houses for an early dinner, the kids running around the garden or hiding in tree houses, you and the other moms talking about your struggles to get them to eat, to get them out of your bed, to get them to wear their shoes.

Why don't you come along? you asked her. But she was too busy at work, needed time alone in front of the TV to unwind without the nee-nawing of your son's fire engine, his crying from being overtired. But sometimes you would come home, and she wouldn't be back yet. It seemed like she was never around any more.

At times, you were lonely. There were more and more arguments. I don't want another child, she said. I'm happy with what I have. You didn't believe her. She seemed so distant these days. Was she having an affair?

She laughed at the suggestion. Of course not, she said, then suggested you take a break from your boy. Go away for a long weekend, just the two of you.

When you checked in, the receptionist looked worried. Oh dear, this cottage only has a double bed, she said. Your wife spoke: That's exactly what I asked for. She'd nodded, her face reddening as she'd comprehended.

The cottage was in a valley engulfed by steep mountains on either side. In the late afternoon, they turned pink from the setting sun. After dark, it grew cold and you made a fire outside, sitting next to the hot flames, beneath the sky sprayed with stars. A bat flew above, giving you both a fright. You laughed after that, and then grew quiet listening to the soothing hum of crickets chirping.

She put her arm around your shoulder then, pulling you closer, and something about the way she held you made the tears come. What is it, she wanted to know, why are you so sad? I just want to be normal, you said. I just want to be like everyone else. She didn't understand. You want to be straight? she asked. No, I just don't want to be different. Sorry to disappoint you, she said, but you're a suburban married mom. What could be more normal than that?

You sat unable to stop the tears because you realised that after all these years, you still longed to know how it felt to move through the world like everyone else. What it must feel like to be in a marriage where you were both biologically related to your child, where you were the mom and he was the dad, where no one ever stared or commented. Where you were not a pioneer. Not interesting. Not inspirational. Not different. Just like everyone else.

If it's that important to you, she said, I'm happy to try for another kid.

Back home weeks later, your best friend was insistent. Come to the lesbian book reading. Go, said your wife, I'll look after him.

And so you put on mascara, caught an Uber and met your old friend at the door. The bookshop was bustling when you arrived. People milling around with glasses of wine, chatting. Others moving slowly, heads bent, poring over the shelves of books.

You grabbed a glass of wine, found a seat and waited. There were four women reading, published authors, all lesbian.

The first had warm skin, big gravity-defying hair. Her voice smooth, unwavering, as she read. The voice of the second was softer, but clear. Her blonde bob fell into her face as she recited the words from the book she'd written. The third was voluptuous, with frizzy black hair to her shoulders. The last wore a trouser suit, and had cropped hair framing a striking face. Her voice was deeper than the others. She had a tattoo on her hand, a line of words you couldn't read from where you sat.

One by one they read tales about love and loss, about friendship, about childhood, about their dreams. They shared their innermost thoughts, expressing their fears, their longings, unfettered. They spoke without fear of reproach. As they read you felt something quieten inside you, something settle. You smiled at your friend.

After the readings, the applause was deafening. As the audience dispersed in no great hurry, you sat watching the women around you, young and old, different shades and shapes. Some married, others single, some with kids, others newly in love. You imagined them leaving the bookshop, going back out into the world. You sat until it was just you and your friend left in the emptied bookshop. Your breathing had quieted, your body relaxed. And you thought: the things people say, whether out of kindness or a need to control, are simply words that could float unattached. They had nothing to do with you.

South of Samora

Farai Mudzingwa

The only thing worth writing about is the human heart
in conflict with itself.
— William Faulkner

I wake up in Budiriro. Winter morning. The sun is an orange
glow at 6.23am. It doesn't bother me that I am in a township.
In the chilly stillness, I can hear a low rumbling. The railway line
is less than a mile to the north. A low drawn-out blast from the
locomotive horn disperses the last remnants of sleep. I step outside.
A second one sounds louder, nearer; a long, lazy bellow from an
iron bull. The blast rides over the crumpled sheet of houses rolling
out in the distance. The orange ball is rising behind me, and the
weak light reveals the unmade bed of asbestos linen, roughly slept
in. Untidy dreams embedded in the creases. Roofs jut up on sharp
angles and threads of power lines streak across and between folds.
A haze nestles between the peaks, and in the distance, blends into
the grey sky, still dark, and blurring the edge of the bed. It is a
dusty, smoky fog. Cold and pressing.

I stand outside, exposed on the bare concrete slab of this partially
built house. The air is cold and still. A light dust hangs in the air. I
part my lips and breathe out. A puff of steam emerges and quickly
dissipates. The orange is thinning into a cleaner light, and a ray of
sun bounces off a solar panel on an angled roof in front of me. The

crumpled linen now stands in sharp focus, and the electrical cables become shiny strings racing in fours, between bare, grey plastered walls, piles of bricks, and sharp asbestos roofs. A third blast sounds from the train as it rumbles past. The tremors I feel are not from its passage. They are within me.

Last night was my first night here. I had the uneasy sleep of new surroundings, a narrower bed. First, I woke up in a sweat. Too many layers, and I had steamed up the windows in the tiny bedroom. It was dark outside. And the solitary light from the house across the road added to the eeriness. The darkness painted a boundless canvas with a lonely amber glow illuminating a door from across the street. Leaning back on my elbows, I searched for my bearings. The darkness was inside my room. My eyes would not adjust, and it persisted. I peeled off a blanket and pushed it to the foot of the bed. It slid onto the floor. I reached towards the curtain-less window, opened it a crack, and lay back, feeling the chill crawling over my damp skin. After a while, I was dry. I pulled the second cover back up to my ears and drifted off.

I couldn't tell how long I slept, but the second time I woke up shivering. A presence was passing through the room. The cold it had brought in was transient, rousing me just enough to feel the trails slipping out. Next, the shrieks came in short bursts. My bedroom door faces my neighbours' bedroom window. Their little boy Shalom's voice came at irregular intervals, sliding in under my door. In the darkness, I could hear slippered feet scraping on the floor and the sound of doors shutting and opening.

And then came the prayers. I was now fully awake, but still in bed with the covers up to my ears. I was breathing lightly and slowly, pausing at the top, and again at the bottom, of each breath. I wanted to catch every sound coming from the house next door. The steady fast-paced rhythm of the prayers filtered in. A woman's voice in Shona, Shalom's shrieks accenting the prayer every few seconds. Two more voices joined the ensemble. One deeper, male, and the other higher-pitched, female. They kept up the tempo, and in the darkness the shrieks came at longer intervals until they gradually reduced to whimpers, and then it was just the murmur of muffled prayer. At some point, I drifted off again. A long drawn-out moan from a distant train lifts my eyelids, and when I see the orange tint filtering through the bare glass, I slip on my morning shoes and step onto the concrete slab outside my door.

$\mathcal{T}$his is temporary. I'm here for a short while, and then I'm going back to Greystone Park. But I don't mind it here. And it's not like I'm a snob or anything. People live here too. Real people. I've never taken part in the WhatsApp group banter about "people from the other side of the tracks" or whatever. I mean, I may laugh here and there, if the joke is really funny, but for the most part, I'm not like that. And for some reason, the guys like using Budiriro as the setting for their condescending quips. Privileged boys from the suburbs. Budiriro is an abstract concept to them. Some generic location that represents everything inferior and less affluent.

For them, 'other' people live here. The people riding to work in the stuffy and packed commuter minibuses; the people peering into TV cameras behind reporters on the evening news; the people affected by typhoid and cholera outbreaks; the faces at political rallies; the bodies running away from teargas and riot police; the people who speak English with the bad accent; the people who stand too close behind you in supermarket queues; the people queuing for hours outside banks; the people bending over to buy second-hand clothes from imported bales; the bodies crowded on sidewalks downtown; the eager pavement barbers imploring "Togera here?"; the fruit and vegetable vendors taking over the pavements in the centre of town; the youths making a career out of installing WhatsApp on phones; those brash people driving cheap Toyota Altezzas; the people who somehow slipped into private schools when the economy lost shape; the people who landed in 'new money' and almost became our neighbours; the people lacking that intangible 'something' – which may be found next to whiteness; the people with body odour.

The statements, the assumptions, are casual, and Budiriro is cast well. It is a long name with enough harsh native syllables to invoke the image of township undesirability. The only place with the same billing is Mabvuku, and for the same reason. The residents of a new housing development refused to have a Shona name for their neighbourhood. When the city council jokingly advised that their utilities rates would be higher if they had an English name, the residents earnestly agreed to be renamed Westlea. The Westlea story might be embellished, but the facts do not change the truth.

Highfields and Mbare, two of the oldest native townships in Harare, have escaped ridicule. Enough politicians, business people, and popular musicians have come out of these two, and speak so delightfully about them, that they are almost mythologised. There is a Mbare Club of successful people who were born or raised there. Forged in that crucible. Are your parents really achievers if they did not grow up in the dusty streets of Mbare, and then through sheer hard work and determination, made it out to the suburbs? Each generation keeps moving forward, across the railway tracks, and then further north. You had to start off in Mbare, you see, and then your success is measured by how far north of it you settled. There is a popular song whose lyrics are a long list of all the successful people to have emerged from Mbare. There are no songs about Budiriro.

*I*have now been here for three months, four days, and a little over seven hours. This is longer than I planned, but it's still temporary. I'll go back soon, things are just taking a while. I haven't changed my Twitter location and I don't post much on Instagram now. I'm not embarrassed or anything. It's just that I don't want to cause any confusion, or have to explain all the time. So for now my online location still says Greystone Park. I'm really still there, in spirit, so it all makes sense. It takes me forty-five minutes to drive to Budiriro from town. I am living right on the edge of the city. My testicles and pride are dangling over the line that runs between Harare Province and Mashonaland West

Province. When I walk down the road to buy cigarettes from the kiosk I am making a border run. Or maybe I just feel like an alien. Or look like one. I don't have airs or anything, but the man in the kiosk greets me in English. He greets everyone else in Shona. I respond in Shona, but he persists.

I live exactly 38.4 kilometres south of the city centre, and if I slip past the traffic police 'spot checks' at Kambuzuma Road, Gleneagles Road, the Stadium, the Showgrounds and Herbert Chitepo Street, I can make the trip in under an hour.

I get home in the afternoon, and Shalom and a kid he plays with (whose name I don't know) are kicking a ball around in the dirt that is their front yard. I made the ball for Shalom a couple of weeks ago. I made it out of dry grass, an empty five-kilo plastic mealie-meal bag, and discarded shoe laces. In truth, he started making the ball, got stuck, and then asked me to finish it. I've never had to make a ball before, but I did a decent job. I'm good with my hands. Shalom sat quietly, watching my fingers working, and then only spoke again once I was done.

"You should give me that cereal box when it is empty," he declared.

"What cereal box?" I asked.

"That one." And he pointed through my open kitchen door, at the Cerevita box on the counter.

"OK," I responded, "but why do you want it?"

"I want to make a car," he said.

They are kicking the ball around, and every couple of minutes Shalom grabs the ball and changes the rules of their game a bit to make sure he keeps winning. The ball is the shape of the ringworm fungus spread over his scalp. You can't really see them until he comes within a few metres, and then the rings, little embossed circles, stick out in relief on his sharp little bald head. The rings came on as a parting gift when the zvishiri stopped tormenting him. The night I lay in bed listening to the attack, my first night here, was one of the last attacks he had. After pulling him out of school for a couple of weeks, his mom finally found a prophet who could shield him from the night visitors.

That first night, when the presence had floated through my room, had left me more curious than scared. I spent much of that morning lingering outside, hoping to catch a glimpse of the boy I had heard, and to put faces to the praying voices. The boy came out first. Flannel pyjamas, fleece sweater, fleece hat, and a bowl of cereal in his hands. He walked round to catch the sun and came to an abrupt halt when he saw me. His eyes were large and clear, and he had striking long lashes. Dark rings framed the large eyes. We stood there, him sizing me up, and me taking him in.

"Hesishaa," I quipped at last.

He just looked at his porridge.

"Unonziani?" I persevered.

"Shalom," he finally spat out.

His voice came out stronger than I had imagined after the whimpers I had heard the night before. I think he saw the relief in my face, because he dropped one shoulder and shifted his weight.

"Imotayako here iyi?" he asked, turning his attention to the car which stood between us to the left.

"Yes, it's mine. Do you want to drive it?" That seemed to do it.

He grinned and squealed, "I can drive my car, not that one!"

"Where is your car parked?" I asked with all the sincerity in my skinny frame.

"I can't find it ... but I'll make another one." His eyes dropped.

"Your porridge is getting cold." I decided to change the subject. I was still curious about last night, but not sure how to bring it up.

"I don't like porridge," he muttered while kicking a stone.

I stretched my neck to look around, and then did the same, looking into their kitchen window. He looked at me amused and a bit confused, then I gestured to the pile of garden refuse in my yard. He looked up at me, shocked, and then a grin came over him. He didn't need a second prompt. In movements that took a bit too long and threatened to jeopardise the whole operation, he spooned out the entire bowl onto the pile and then placed a handful of raked grass over it. When he was done, he looked up at me and I gave him the nod. He returned it, and then I went my way and he went his.

In the late afternoon, Shalom's mother often sits on the raised manhole cover of the main sewage line that runs between our houses. We don't really talk. Just the polite greetings in the mornings, afternoons, and if we both happen to step outside after dark. She catches the fading rays of the dipping sun and watches her boy running around in the sandy grey dust. Every few minutes she warns him not to get himself dirty, and threatens to beat him and bathe him in cold water. The sewage line she sits on runs further down between the rows of houses and under the main road. There are similar lines running at intervals from the different sections of Budiriro, all headed across the main road, across the railway line and to the sewage plant on the slopes a short distance from the tracks. Not all the sewage lines make the journey across. A few disintegrate in the corridor between the road and the railway tracks. The grey water collects in stagnant pools with a sickening stench of human shit and laundry soap. In one of the drier openings between the main road and railway tracks, and well embraced by the sewage smell, Shalom's mother found the Apostolic Second Rising Deliverance Church of Prophet Madzibaba Emmanuel.

I told only two close friends, Rodney and Ishe, that I had moved from the suburbs to the unclipped toenails of the southern townships. They have not kept my confession to themselves. I can feel the looks of pity or disgust or ridicule when I meet acquaintances I have not told. They skirt the subject, and the awkwardness makes it difficult to breathe with any regularity.

Last Friday we were at a Circuit Party at Jam Tree Restaurant in Mount Pleasant. Rodney insisted. The evening was going quite well until we met some guys I hardly know, but regularly meet in certain bars. I've had many wild nights with these guys, but would be stumped if I had to name any of them. By and by, some girls came over, and I started talking to one of them. She soon asked which high school I went to. I left school ten years ago, but somehow this is pertinent information to strangers in a bar at 11.23pm on a Friday. This was the easy part. I told her I went to Falcon College, which elicited the usual "oohs" and "aahs", and she leaned closer. It was also nearing closing time, and when I remembered my looming 38.4-kilometre drive home and announced my imminent departure, she purred seductively, asking me where I lived.

I couldn't. The words would not come out. I opened my mouth, and the stench of sewage filled my nostrils and the pale dust dried my throat. She tugged playfully at my sleeve, and the rumbling of the train thundered in my ears and drowned out the music. The train runs on that railway line that cuts down the middle of the country, dividing each town it slices through. The suburbs, the shops and the town centre on the left, and the industry and high-density townships on the right, downwind, with the sewage dams and the zvishiri. A running train is a rare sight these days, though, unless you live far south of the city and right by the tracks, like I now do. The human bodies, the dust, the stench of sewage, the loud voices and the lack of respect for personal space have moved further north. The railway tracks no longer separate North and South; they are now firmly in the South. The line that now separates the affluent from those merely surviving is Samora Machel Avenue, a long, broad road running parallel to the railway tracks, but a few miles to the north, cutting across the city centre of Harare. I did not tell her that I live south of Samora. I was not embarrassed or anything. I just didn't want to have to explain. Besides, I'm only here temporarily.

Shalom's mother is not sitting at her usual spot on the raised sewage manhole this evening. The line is clogged somewhere downstream and it is overflowing here. The grey water is seeping out and the pool is spreading into my yard.

The refuse truck comes by on Tuesdays – when it comes – but when it doesn't, she burns her plastic waste in a small pile in her front yard. Earlier I saw her lighting her pile, and the plastic bonfire has brought glee to Shalom. He is poking a stick into the fire and watching the plastic melt and burn on the end of the stick. The dark puffs of smoke find their way into my bedroom, their pungent smell mingling joyfully with the sewage smell.

"Hesi!" The little face pops up at my window, and I know my solitude is over.

"Hesishaa." I save the online application on my laptop and turn to face the welcome intruder. "What is that?"

"Chimutichangu! Huya!" The delight on his face could power my lights for three days. I have no option but to follow him outside. He is waiting at my door as I step out, and then he drags me to the fire.

"Why aren't you in school today?" I ask him while he scans around him with all the seriousness of a crime scene investigator.

"I'm not feeling well," he mutters without halting his search. That explains the sounds I've heard over the last few nights. I have been staying up late applying for internships and bursaries, and then crashing into sleep, only vaguely aware of sounds in the early mornings.

He bends down quickly and picks up a long stick and presents it to me. "This is yours," he says, and proceeds to demonstrate how to poke a stick into molten burning plastic and then brandish the flaming end in circles. I decline politely and think about telling him not to play with burning plastic, but I'm still thinking about the attacks. I notice that he has lost weight, and his skin has lost its brown lustre. It has taken on a tinge of ashy grey. He is still illuminated, but he seems to be running out of breath easily.

"Have you been to the hospital?" I ask him, knowing the answer.

"Uh uh," he shakes his head, "Muporofita ndivo vanouya nemvura." And he points to the bottles of the Prophet's blessed water, which are dotted around their yard to ward off bad spirits.

When I was six, Shalom's age, I had an illness that turned out to be a bad ear infection. I spent a night in the Avenues Clinic, and then a few days at home playing PlayStation games and being a nuisance. I have hated hospitals ever since, but I also have respect for the things that medicine can do. I just don't like how it is administered. Needles.

That was the last time I spoke to Shalom. I was still up later just after 1am, riding out the discomfort, adjusting, but not regretting the move here. I have routines to work around the lack of privacy, and even have a standard address to stop random people proceeding up to my doorstep. I felt the wave of cold air, not as a chill going through my bedroom, but as a mass over the whole yard. I recognised it instantly. They floated over my house and descended over Shalom's house with no regard for the bottles dotted across the yard and around the house. This time they were swift. There were no shrieks, no prayers, and no hurried footsteps. A quick descent and when they took off, they took Shalom's light with them, and left an empty shell of a boy. Mute, motionless, and only able to stare into space.

"Cobra! Cobra! Cobra yema floor!"
My parents were born in Guruve and Nyazura, both rural colonial outposts, moved into Mbare Township in the 1960s, and progressed to Greystone Park in 1985. I was born in Greystone Park in 1991, and in twenty-six short years, I have gone back to the 1960s. My train is moving backwards. I stormed out of my parents' house because I wanted to be my own self-made person, and here I am: 'making it on my own'.

Budiriro means 'progress' or 'development', and yet it is on the fringes of the city – one foot in the open grasslands, the other in the remnants of a defunct township. I stand in it. It is named in jest, optimism or cluelessness. The city moves forward in the north, companies fighting to install fibre internet in homes, while down here on the edges, life floats in a bubble of soapy sewage. The fights here are between vendors and their improvised carts.

"Mbaaaaaaatata! Mbaaaaaaaatata! Fresh mbaaaaaaatata!"
The air is still today. There are no clouds in the sky. Just the bare sun glaring down and the occasional slight gust of wind. But the dust still drifts into my rooms. There is no regular transport this

far out, and so every half hour or so, a mshika-shika speeds past hooting for passengers and sending clouds of dust over the road and the houses.

"Hove! Fresh hove!" An old man rides past, with much labour, on his rickety bicycle with suspicious fish in a front basket.

My neighbour two houses down has a flimsy work bench in his front yard, and he places a speaker outside the door as he grinds, drills and welds door frames, window frames and security screens. He produced my washing line, and after that job I learnt to get someone else. He plays old-school reggae, and he is playing some song by Culture as two guys walk up to my door and peer in, hoping to sell solar power units.

An ice-cream man rides past on his tricycle. He is wearing overalls the blue of the popular Dairibord, but there is no Dairibord inscription on his hat or breast. The cooler box on his tricycle also has the Dairibord blue and white bands, but no words or logo. He doesn't need to shout, his distinctive bell draws kids from their play and sets them tugging at their mothers' skirts.

Two girls shuffle lazily past where the fence would be between my yard and the neighbour to my right. One of them is sucking the last bit of ice from a Freezit. She tosses the empty plastic wrapper on the ground. As they disappear down the street, the packet is nudged into my yard by small gusts of wind until it catches on the grass.

I am not a snob. I really do not have a problem living here, even as the blast of an approaching train sounds in the distance. I still have the determination and youth to prove my parents wrong.

Shalom's mother carries him out and places him on a reed mat in the sun, his back propped up by two pillows and his neck at a crooked angle. His vacant eyes do not blink. I turn and see the Cerevita box standing on my kitchen counter. In that moment, I understand one thing at last. I can no longer be here.

Transubstantiation

Genna Gardini

NOUN.

*the conversion of the substance of the Eucharistic elements into the
body and blood of Christ at consecration, only the appearances of bread
and wine still remaining.*

BAPTISM

*Listen to me now, Diana. It's not a 'christening' in the Catholic
Church, we call it a baptism. What happens is the baby must be
named after a saint or someone who has passed, God bless. Now, you act
like your name is Diana because of that tarty Princess in the blue bikini.
But actually I named you after St Diana because she gave everything
up to be a nun. Then for good measure, I also gave you another name –
that's the one that only you and me and Father Murphy and God know
about. It's not even your second name because why must Home Affairs
now get involved? I called you Ruth. That's your secret name that no
one else knows.*

Diana walked slowly towards the Rhodes Drama Department's
notice board. It was, she could already tell, plastered with
fresh casting sheets. They beckoned to her the way her mother's
hands did: white, stiff and as likely to smack as redirect her.
"Please," Diana implored the higher power her whole parish

suspected she'd forgotten. "Please just let me get into one. Anything, even if it's just chorus, please Lord, let me get into one play." So far, all Diana had gotten into, after deciding to go to Drama School instead of the Mariannhill Monastery, was trouble.

"And in the Eastern Cape, God help us!" Mrs Marrah, an Extraordinary Minister of Holy Communion at Our Lady of Moab, had shuddered when she found the Rhodes application forms folded in her daughter's missal. Later at Mass, she had administered communion to Diana, maintaining full eye-contact while aiming the wafer straight into her mouth. Diana had tried to believe that the thin flake refusing to dissolve in her spit, solid as a stone in piss, was the body of Christ. She'd willed herself to see him baking in the warm oven of her maw, softening to become part of her. Then she choked on the Host and had to be escorted to the bathroom. Her mother had not been impressed – Diana's performance hadn't been convincing. And this was exactly the same feedback she was receiving from the Drama department one year later.

"In the beginning was the Word," Diana continued praying. "And the Word is Diana and the Word will be on a list," Diana neared the board and added, "And, uh, world without end, amen." The papers pinned to the board rose and stayed like a cloth smoothed across an altar, like the fitted sheets she fixed flat on her res bed every morning. "You'll need a… what do they call them now… a mattress protector," her mother had sighed, pressing her finger to the plastic Mr Price Home packaging like she was giving it a benediction. "You can't let anything get past that first layer or you're done for."

A large group of undergrads was clustered in front of Diana, clamouring to check if any Honours or Masters students had noticed them at the last open audition. Diana caught sight of Avani, her former best friend and now reluctant guide through the complicated social structure of the department, and stopped. Avani had been a year ahead of Diana at the convent, back then a pious prefect with braces. Now, some twelve months and two dramatic haircuts later, she was an agnostic second year and too cool for Diana. "You're out of the convent now, Di," Avani would hiss whenever they ran into each other by accident, her eyes skittering around to see if anyone had seen them talking. "Retire the Toughees, make new friends, whatever. This isn't matric any more."

It certainly was not, Diana thought. At school, the two of them had been inseparable, taking turns to star as Gabriel in the nativity show each year. Both of their blazers had been braided in that specific private school code that meant Humanities Honours. "Joseph and his technicolour dream-coat," Mrs Marrah had grumbled, her needle negotiating the latest intricate row. She'd referred to her daughter as a 'culture vulture', reminding her that there was a type of pigeon, a far more obedient bird, called the Nun. But Diana liked the idea of being a vulture. Vultures worked in pairs. She'd always imagined herself and Avani picking and gnawing at the carrion of whatever biblical story their Drama teacher chose for the school play. At varsity, however, Diana was now surrounded by a flock of ambitious scavengers. She had learnt fast that there was no room for coupling within the Drama department. Here, she wasn't a bird of prey. She wasn't even a pigeon. She was the carcass.

Diana did not want to deal with Avani. She'd come back to the board later. She tried to wriggle past the classmates she was too afraid to talk to outside the pracs where they all struggled to locate their diaphragms together. "Breathe out your anus," their Movement tutor would intone before yelling, "If you're tempted to be childish, just expel that impulse on the outbreath! The outbreath!"

A hand grabbed Diana, then, as quickly as it had found her, let go. "Come here, man, don't be arb," snapped Avani, pushing past the huddled first years. At the front, Diana scanned the papers. Avani moved a finger from line to line on the lists. Finding her name on not one but two sheets, she made a shrieking noise, and her clutch on Diana's arm returned. "Did you even see!" she said, and then added, "Oh, look, sorry, Di, but you shouldn't take it personally. They're doing like a full Sarah Kane season this term and you basically have to hand in your virginity with a plagiarism form at the audition to get in." Seeing Diana's expression, Avani paused. "Listen," she whispered, "let's go have tea soon, we can order cheesecake and have a proper DMC like old times, how's that?" Diana nodded, doing one last check just in case her surname had been misspelt somewhere. "It's not there!" Avani snapped. She took a deep breath. "Oh, fuck it. Look, I'm going to be late for Voice, must dash."

CATECHISM

Stop whingeing, Diana. Catechism is special Catholic school, and it's even more important than Sub A. You'll learn all about the bible with Auntie Stephanie and your colouring-in book with all the pictures of Jesus, isn't He so nice and clean in His robe, not like you with half a KitKat melted down your jersey. I don't care if it's boring, God said suffer little children and that means you have to go to catechism.

*I*t was her Wednesday theatre-making prac and Diana was crouching in the wings of the Rhodes Theatre while the rest of the class stretched on the stage. Their usual tutor had been cast in *African Footprint* and had left Grahamstown without a backwards glance. He'd been replaced by Kay, an MA student who inspired both terror and awe in the class. So far, she'd spent each tutorial sitting in the far back of the theatre, giving impossible tasks and watching the first years through dark sunglasses. "I heard her say, 'The threat of this so-called light blinds me', how hectic," one of the students reported back to the others, pointing at the dormant rig above the stage.

On this day, Kay reclined in the cue box, considered the auditorium in front of her and said, "Be anything that is not you."

Almost all of the participants were confused. The prospect of not being themselves was the opposite of what twelve years at various Waldorfs had taught them. Kay sighed. "All right. Don't transform," she said, "*transubstantiate.*" Understanding slapped Diana like the bishop at her confirmation. In her secret squatting spot backstage, she closed her eyes. She saw an image of the Holy Communion, slivered, moving towards her via the missile of her mother's hand. Diana breathed in through her nose and compelled her body to exist within the wafer. She sat with her arms folded underneath her knees to help lose the sensation of having limbs. She rubbed the soft skin of her cheek against the rough floor, scratches delineating parts of her face, making them lined. A pattern pressed into unleavened bread. Pain heated through her like she had touched a stove or, no, like she was being grilled under one. Then someone coughed, and Diana jerked up. Her classmates had made a circle around her, a few struggling with their backpacks to find plasters and lost Panados, but most staring, silent. She knew that silence. They were waiting for the grown-up in the room to tell them if what they'd just seen was good.

"Well, Diana," Kay started, walking down to the stage. The capillaries in Diana's sternum bloomed – the tutor knew her name! "What do you think you did there?"

Everyone was watching Diana now. Then one of the pockets of her cargo pants began to vibrate. She knew the screen of the Nokia would be flaring "MOM". Diana ignored it, shifting her position to try to hit the red button with a buttock.

"I think I… transubstantiated?" she replied.

"You think or you did?" Kay asked.

Were they two different things? Diana felt a surge of certainty. Something real had happened, she'd felt it, sure as the buzzing of the phone against her thigh. "Ja, I did," she answered, louder. "I transubstantiated."

Kay smiled. "Nope," she said. "You didn't."

FIRST HOLY COMMUNION

You stand in line with all the other Standard Ones. I don't care if it's chock-a-block, you have to be patient, you don't hear Jesus telling those two thieves who were crucified with Him to get a move on, not that He was in a hurry. So, when you get to the front, you open your mouth, don't worry about your retainer. When the priest blesses it, the bread turns into His body and the wine turns into His blood. And you eat Jesus so you remember that you killed Him with your sins. Then afterwards, if you're good, we'll go to the Spur and we can have some spare ribs.

"*I* don't know how to explain it, Di. You've got to, like, go on a journey." Avani stared at a point just beyond Diana's head, right at the back of the tiny restaurant. "It's a great place, you'll love it," she had assured her earlier. "Very *Hillcrest*." She'd over-enunciated the words so that Diana could tell that what she meant was *not very Grahamstown*. This, like the places they'd frequented as teenagers, was meant to have good cheesecake and boring customers. A blast from the past, Avani had said. Diana suspected that she'd chosen it because she didn't want to hang out with her at the theatre café, where future Embeth Davidtzs drew painstaking puffs from rollies. Their heady smoke always reminded Diana of Mass, where altar servers had swung incense around in large, dangerous circles.

"Urgh, this incense is killing me," Avani had whispered to Diana as a slightly singed altar girl sought refuge in the same bathroom they were hiding in. "Come to Rhodes, Di," Avani had mouthed quietly so the server wouldn't hear. "It's just a year. Everything will be the same."

But it wasn't. Diana ate her cake, which was nothing like the confectionary they had once smuggled back into the convent. This cheesecake tasted like it was made of maggots crushed on top of old Marie biscuits. "Stop moaning!" she could almost hear her mother shout.

She looked around, trying to find a serviette to discreetly spit her mouthful into, when she noticed Kay sitting alone, her sunglasses still on, writing furiously. The tutor cocked her head up, a sliver of her eyes showing. Diana swallowed and looked down at the rug, stained the way all things in Grahamstown were, accidentally and permanently.

"Di, are you actually even listening to me?" Avani barked over her hot water. "Basically, what I was saying is it's not like school, where we'd get all those Eisteddfod prizes and whatever for just *acting*. You can't just act now."

"Aren't we studying acting?" Diana asked.

"No, I mean, obviously you have to act, but you can't just *pretend*."

Diana moved her fork around the plate, trying to keep an eye on Kay in the corner. "Isn't acting another word for pretending?"

"You just don't get it. No wonder you're not getting cast in anything," Avani snapped. Her mouth dropped in immediate regret. "Fuck, I'm sorry." She leant closer.

The last time she'd been this near Diana was two years ago in the church bathroom. They'd ducked down into their cubicle and Avani's face was suddenly too close to Diana's. Her elaborate headgear had pushed between them like electric fencing and Diana had breathed in the gummy smell of unsuccessful orthodontistry. "Di," Avani had giggled and Diana had shushed her by applying her face to the intricate, metal patchwork threading her mouth. After the altar girl had flushed and left, the two had sat, looking at each other.

Avani didn't move now either. "I know things have been weird, it's just—"

Diana's phone began to hurdle across the table, indignant as a Grade Ten forced to attend athletics day. They both watched it and then Avani bucked back, stuffing her Ché Guevara purse back into her bag. "She phoned me on Saturday, you know, trying to find you. And I was at a *digs party*." She shook her head in disbelief. "I told her signal is shit in Grahamstown, that's probably why you're not answering your phone. Obviously I didn't say it like that, but you know what I mean." Avani stood up, readjusting her hemp headband, angling to see if Kay had spotted them. "I'll see you later."

CONFESSION

This is now the sacrament – Diana! Pay attention, I'm not going to tell you again. This is the sacrament of penance. Here you tell Father all the bad things you did that week, like when you back-chatted me yesterday, and you say your Act of Contrition. Then you go back outside to the pew and you kneel and you do the sign of the cross and you pray and then you do the sign of the cross one more time so He knows you really mean it. And you don't do the sin again. Or Jesus won't forgive you.

"*F*orgive me Father for I have sinned," Diana bleated, the words dinging automatically out her mouth like she was typing a number she forgot she still knew. Father de Silva sat opposite her in the cramped rectory, biblical artworks mosaicing the walls like Nirvana posters in a res room. His face was open and encouraging. But his clerical collar looked a bit dingy, Diana observed. She wondered, not for the first time, how laundry worked in the clergy. Did the vestments have to be dry-cleaned or hand-washed or what? Was there a special liturgical laundromat? And who did the daily load? Probably the nuns. It was always the nuns.

"It has been…" Father de Silva prompted.

"Shit, sorry." Diana reddened – she'd sworn in front of a priest! She could feel the hellfire of her mother's outrage sizzling across provinces. She took a moment to compose herself, then tried to make eye contact with him and failed. The absence of confessional booths always caused Diana severe performance anxiety. Without the scrim of the partition between them, she couldn't get in character, she couldn't transform into the kind of girl who left confession with two Hail Marys and a quick Glory Be. Not that she could transform into anyone, though.

"It's all right," Father de Silva said. "Take your time." This was a tone she was familiar with. It was how high-school drama teachers spoke, their voices warm as a cup of Horlicks next to an IEB mark-sheet filled with As. Her lecturers did not talk to her like that. They did not really talk to her at all.

"Not since I came to Rhodes," Diana said.

The priest nodded. Here it comes, she thought. He'd ask her why, she'd say she wasn't sure, he'd tell her a relationship with God was like any relationship, you had to put in the time, she would mumble an apology and get her rosary ready – and it would be done.

But what he said was: "Do you know this painting behind me?"

On the canvas flanking the priest, two women embraced. One was in a veil, her face marinaded in the middle, pruned by grief. The other woman was younger, wearing the blue Diana thought of as the Virgin Mary's leisure-wear, slightly less susceptible to stains than her ascension white. This woman was clinging to the older, her expression bovine in comparison to the other's anguish. In the back, another figure, dressed in red robes, was hightailing it into town.

"Ja, I know what that is. The Book of Ruth," Diana answered.

The priest nodded. "A devoted daughter follows her mother-in-law after her sister leaves."

And her mother knew best, she thought. And God blessed Ruth because she didn't cause any shit, amen.

"You know, that mother always seemed like a very difficult character to me," Father de Silva continued conspiratorially. "She changed her name to Mara, you know. It means bitter."

"I'm aware of that," Diana replied.

"Back in the seminary, I sometimes wondered about the other sister, the one who didn't go with them. I have a secret theory about her. Maybe she and Ruth are the same person. The same girl, just two different choices. One stays with her mother and follows her to Bethlehem. But the other makes her own way and has a whole other life. I think that they're the same girl, but each decision turns them into someone else."

Diana considered this for a moment.

"You're away from your family for the first time," Father de Silva continued. "In a new place filled with new people. It brings its own challenges. Sometimes it can be difficult for our loved ones to understand that we must make our own way. Does your family support you coming here?"

"My mom didn't want me to come here and study Drama," Diana said. "She said actors are enemies of God."

"Mass is a sort of theatre," Father de Silva announced after a long pause. "The entire congregation sitting there is the audience, and I'm up at the front like an actor. I'm going to tell you a secret." He leaned forward. "Sometimes I get a bit of stage fright and I forget my lines. One Palm Sunday I even made up a Psalm! I don't think God minds, really. In fact, I think God knows all about acting. It takes a bit of acting to always be good and to love your neighbour. But if you keep doing it after a while, you'll find that it doesn't feel like acting any more at all."

He followed this by smiling at Diana. "This is a safe space, my child. You can say anything you want here. Only God can judge."

Diana swallowed. "My friend," she began. "Or she used to be my friend. Or something. I don't know. That's why I came here. She said she wanted me to come with her. But when I got here, everything was different." Diana felt the words build up in her, spilling like a Lent box stuffed full of fifty-cent coins. Fingered cardboard, replete with old hopes, bursting at the edges.

"Now she doesn't want me around, she was just pretending, it didn't mean anything, and I don't know what to do," Diana trailed off, not sure how to finish. The respite of finally having said all of this winded her. It dislodged something that had been stuck in her chest for the last five months, and she felt, for the first time in longer than she could remember, a beaming. Like the bright patina searing off of Jesus in pictures. Diana breathed and looked up. Father de Silva was nodding, supportive.

"You have a demon," he said.

"I beg your pardon?" Diana asked, polite out of habit.

"A demon," he repeated. "There's a demon in you that has made you think about this girl in unnatural ways. It's not your fault. Satan tempts even the strongest among us. The power of prayer and devotion will bring you back to God and to your real self."

Diana stared again at the painting behind the priest's head. In it, she could see now, Ruth was being grabbed at the wrist by Mara, who was ready to haul her to Bethlehem. She wasn't gazing serenely into the distance, she was looking back at her sister-in-law absconding towards freedom. She looked like she was ready to bolt, too.

CONFIRMATION

Catch a wake-up now, Diana! When you're sixteen you stop going to catechism, and now is the time when you confirm your faith. But you can't just snooze through class, it's called a confirmation, not a sit-around-twiddling-your-thumbs. This is when you tell God, in front of everyone, that you commit your life to Him and you know the consequences if you ever change your mind. And nothing good is ever called a consequence, believe you me.

You have a demon. Diana had been echoing this to herself for two weeks. She said it now as she lay sprawled inside the Nun's Chapel, her favourite building at the university. Her dress was hitched around her waist so she could air her chafed thighs after the downhill walk from res. Or maybe she was just blithely exposing herself in a holy house because she had a demon, she thought. Demons probably loved showing a bit of leg.

"You OK?" someone asked.

Diana opened her eyes. Kay was standing over her. Diana scrambled up and smoothed her dress below her knees. "Yes, sorry, hi, sorry." She realised that this was the first time she had ever spoken to the tutor outside of class. Kay's face, circled by a series of braids, was round and pressed, as if she had just woken up. Diana felt the sudden urge to apply her tongue to the crease of her tutor's cheek, like the iron her mother took to her Sunday pantsuit, and felt her own face redden in response.

"Why are you sorry?"

"Um, I don't know. Because I shouldn't be here, I suppose? Sorry."

"Well, neither should I," Kay shrugged. She sat down on the cold ledge next to Diana, her legs bare under the bright swathe of her skirt, and fished a box of Provitas out of her satchel. The top few were broken into small shards. "Want one?" she asked, passing a fragment to Diana, who held it in her fist like a panic button.

"You waiting for someone?" Kay asked. "Your girlfriend, what's-her-face, in second year?"

It was like someone had pressed burning cotton wool into Diana's ears and then shoved her head into cold water. "No, uh, just visiting the building." She shoved the bit of biscuit down her throat like a plug.

There was a pause.

"That's fucking weird," Kay laughed. "But maybe I'm visiting the building, too. Trying to figure out my play, and no one's ever here to bug me. My flatmates are so loud."

"What play are you doing? Is it the Sarah Kane festival?"

"Nah, it's a thing I'm going to workshop with the cast, they'll all play themselves. You know what the postmodernists said: God is dead, kill the playwright, blah blah blah." Kay removed her sunglasses and blinked repeatedly at the stone light of the ceiling. "My ex gave me pink eye," she explained, wiping the lenses, when she caught Diana staring. "Took me forever to get rid of it. And to get rid of her too, but don't quote me."

"How was I meant to transubstantiate?" Diana asked.

"Hey?" Kay said. "What, you mean in class? Fuck man, I came here to think about my show and smoke a joint, not to give you feedback."

"Isn't it your job to give me feedback though?" Diana said in a small voice.

"It's my job to teach you when I get paid to," Kay snapped. "I'm not going to spend my free time explaining how acting works to you. Do I look like Grotowski? I just liked the word, I didn't expect anyone to actually transubstantiate. That was the point. You think Jesus really turns into a cheese roll and crackling every Sunday? Doubt it. Now can I please just work on my play?"

She saw Diana's hurt expression. She rolled her healed eyes, then passed the Provitas, a peace offering. The two sat next to each other, quietly eating biscuit fractions.

"Do you think I have a demon?" Diana blurted.

"Fucking baby gays," Kay muttered under her breath, grabbing the box and stashing it back in her bag. "Knew I should have gone to Bots."

"I don't get into any plays." The words rushed from Diana. "Everyone thinks I'm a bad actor. I can't transform into a protea in the veld in Movement, and Avani is going to digs parties, and my mom hates me. And now I have a demon."

Kay, who was already getting to her feet, stopped and measured Diana up for a moment. Then she sighed.

"OK. I'm going to explain life to you and then I'd like to get on with my own," she said. "It's only going to happen once, so make sure you take it in."

Diana held her breath, ready. This was it. Sure as the pause before the sign of the cross, sure as the inhalation of the audience before you stepped onto the stage.

Kay squinted at her. "Grow up." Then she fixed her sunglasses, used the pulpit to straighten herself, and left.

RECONCILIATION

*W*ell, *have you ever. The prodigal daughter finally bothers to phone back. It took you long enough. You know, it was the St Thomas procession on Friday, and Auntie Stephanie always fasts so I thought I'd show her this year. I didn't eat for three and a half days and when I saw your miscall on WhatsApp I thought I was having the devil's visions, like Jesus in the desert. But it was just you—*

What?

I know you don't have a demon, Diana. I had you soaked in holy water within an inch of your life at your baptism. Any demon that wanted to possess you would have to be a scuba diver. Honestly, I don't know how you come up with this nonsense—

Calm down. Diana, take a deep breath. Listen, I know you've been struggling. It's a struggle for me, too, I won't hesitate to tell you. But you can't just pretend I don't exist. I'm your mother. Firstly, I pay your MIP, don't forget that. But also I made you, I know who you are. And the Pope says it's fine now, what was happening with Mrs Chetty's daughter, so there you go—

Sherbet, my girl! Don't call the Holy Father problematic when I'm trying to help you, that's blasphemous. The bloody nerve—

What do you mean?

Of course not. It's just a wafer, Diana, don't be ridiculous. If it was dripping pus and what have you, do you think I'd be wearing my slacks and serving it? You can think again—

Your whole life hasn't been a lie. Why must you always make such a palaver out of everything? Listen, koeks. Who knows what happens? I was told that it turns into His flesh and I'm certainly not going to call the CSI to get it investigated. I choose to believe it. Maybe it's all fun and games, who can say. The point isn't that you go to church so you can eat our Saviour tartar. The point is you go there and you remember who you are. And you keep doing it so you don't forget. Like answering your mother's phone calls.

HOLY ORDERS

*D*iana had to walk past the notice board on her way to the Movement room, hidden in the bowels of the Drama department. She was headed towards the usual humiliation of her Physical Theatre tut, where she was still forced to hunch and bend in an approximation of various plants every week, but before she got there, she thought she'd just have another quick look. She lifted up the pinned foolscap pages reverently, as if they were a veil.

"Diana!" Avani, who, it turned out, had actually failed this module last year even though she'd said she got a first, bellowed. "Come now or you'll get DPR! Everyone's already being fynbos on the mountain!"

"Shit," Diana mumbled, but before she crashed down the steps, she allowed herself one more look at the cast list for Kay's show. Her name was there, buried deep, deep in the chorus section. But, still. There it was.

"Diana!"

She let the flurry of papers fall back down on the board, final as a stage curtain. "Here, here, I'm here!" she yelled, charging towards Movement.

What We Could Have Been

Heran T. Abate

"What do you want to be when you grow up, Ami?" He watches as his big sister picks the white fibres off of the mandarine, just the way he likes it.

Almy smiles at how he still mispronounces her name. They are sitting off the side of the verandah at home in Dire Dawa, the orange glow of late afternoon sun warming their bare feet. Dani wriggles his toes, trying to get them to touch the ground the way Almy's do.

"You see those leaves over there?" She points to the branches of the mandarine tree draping the fence. "How they shimmy and whistle when the wind passes through them?"

The ten-year-old nods.

"I want to be that."

Dani breaks into laughter, his small voice galloping in a fit of giggles. She splits the fruit and hands him the bigger half, which he separates in three pieces.

"You're a human, silly. You can't be a plant." Almy may be eight years older than him, but he thinks she's his equal.

Before she can respond, he jumps off the verandah and runs to where Muna is bent over a washbasin doing the laundry. Muna smiles at him before washing the suds off her hands to receive his gift.

Almy rolls a mandarine slice on her tongue. She hasn't told Dani that she'll be moving to Addis in September; he only knows about the short trip this weekend. But she can't play music if she stays here, not the way she wishes to, anyway. In Addis, she can get a Biology degree just like Ema and Abba want, and get proper music instruction just like she wants. She would rather not go to university at all, but it's a compromise she's willing to live with.

Dani skips back and plops down next to her. He swallows the rest of the fruit and beams at Almy.

"Fine, I want to be music," she says, looking at him, eyes wide and earnest.

"Like a singer?"

"No, like music."

Dani makes a face at her.

"Forget it." She rolls her eyes at him playfully.

A few days later, Almy arrives at her aunt's place in Addis. Auntie Bizu, in her excitement to launch Almy's music career, announces that they'll be meeting her theatre friends that very evening.

Almy spends the rest of the day fretting about what she'll wear, how she'll act. If Auntie's friends are anything like her, they will be sophisticated, otherworldly. Almy wants to play the part. She decides she'll make her hair up all fancy like she has seen Auntie sometimes do.

She walks into the bathroom and stands in front of the mirror, staring herself calm. She places a pile of hairpins on the sink below the mirror. Once her fidgety hands have quieted, she picks up a hairpin and parts it between her teeth. She takes a breath. With her other hand, she takes a strand and holds it to the back of her head, her right hand following with the pin. One strand at a time, she fixes her hair into a crown of curls, spiralling and unfurling like waves dipping in and out of each other. One faint ripple around her forehead frames her face, smoothing out the sharp angles of her jaws.

Her arms collapse at her sides. Outside the frosted glass windows, she can tell it has become dark. She panics, thinking that Bizu might have left without her. She rushes to throw on her clothes, and darts to the door leading to the salon.

Bizu is apparently in no rush. She is reclining on the couch; her slight frame making not so much as a dent on the plush surface, as if she's hovering just above it. Her eyes are closed, a sly smile dancing across her face as she sings along to the hit on the radio.

Almy sighs in relief. She pads ahead on light feet towards the kitchen, careful not to disturb Auntie.

"Who are you hiding from, child?" Bizu's eyes shimmer open. "Turn around and let me look at you."

Almy is nervous, twirling before her aunt in the outfit she has chosen with painstaking care, the loose material of her trousers swaying about her. Beneath her silk blouse, her chest caves.

Bizu springs to her feet and inspects her niece. Her one hand cups her chin in thought; the other holds her waist, where a brooch cinches her dress. "Ah," she exclaims, clapping her hands.

Almy giggles, her eyes darting around for something to look at. On the walls are framed pictures of Bizu in one elaborate costume after another, in the different roles she played at the theatre.

"How modern of you," Bizu says, pleased with Almy's choice of trousers.

"Thank you, Auntie." If Bizu approves, then her friends might not be such a hard crowd.

Bizu continues to hum along to the radio. The song ends abruptly for a news intermission.

"The date is August 11, 1969, folks, and I am Shimelis Retta bringing you breaking news. Seven university students have hijacked a plane and forced the pilot to land in the Sudan. The Emperor has condemned their acts as…"

"*These* are the people Ema and Abba want me going to school with?" Almy blurts out.

"Ah, fools," Bizu waves her hand. "Ruining all the fun." She walks around the coffee table to pick a cigarillo out of its box. She plays with it as she walks into her room. As soon as Bizu closes the door behind her, Almy dashes to the phone. She calls home and hopes that Dani will be the one to pick up. It rings a few times and Almy is about to give up when—

"Hello?" Dani's small voice chimes.

"Dani!"

"Hi Ami!"

"What are you doing?" Almy only called for reassurance, but even so she plays big sister with him.

"I got us a new cat."

"Dani, what, from where?"

"Outside our house. She looked hungry."

It's Sunday. Ema will be at the railway hospital, doing an afternoon shift. Almy imagines how Dani would have carefully watched Ema's movements, waiting for her departure before ushering his new pet into the house.

"So you're feeding her?"

"No. Washing her."

"Dani, where?"

"In our tub."

She can already hear Ema's voice, complaining that this child is turning their home into an animal sanctuary. And it will be up to Almy to discipline her little brother.

She sighs. "Dani, cats don't like water. Please take her out."

"Wuro does. And she must be cold now. I gotta go."

Almy hastens to tell him to be careful, but there's already a dial tone on the other end.

"Ready, darling?" Bizu says, posing in the doorframe.

*I*n the Fiat seicento on the ride over, Almy struggles to train her thoughts on Auntie Bizu's advice. "So the person you'll want to talk to," Bizu says, "his name is Haik. A giant of a man, looks like a school-boy these days with his curly hair grown out."

Almy's heartbeat pulses in her ears as she follows the flourishes of Auntie's manicured hand in the air as she speaks. How regal

Auntie looks, tucked into the end of the seat as if it were a throne, her legs wound like elegant origami.

"He's trained everybody who's anybody in music."

"Will you introduce me?" Almy is already in awe. She tries to sit up straight, emulating Bizu's grace.

Bizu nods, amused by Almy's nerves.

Almy reminds herself to breathe and turns her head to the window, to the fog obscuring Chercher Godana's sweeping avenue, casting a halo around the streetlights.

"How long did you say you've been playing the piano?" Bizu asks.

"Six years."

"Good, tell him you're looking to play with the national orchestra, eventually."

Almy has no idea where she wants to play. What she knows is that she's done playing variations of 'Für Elise' with her music teacher in Dire.

Approaching the Haile Selassie Theatre, Bizu directs the driver left towards Arat Kilo. Once at the back gate of the old palace, they turn into a residential neighbourhood with gangly eucalyptus trees swaying on either side of the street.

"With anything else music-related, you can ask Tegest." Bizu winks. "That girl owes me more than the holy water she sprinkles on her porch."

Almy continues to watch the changing landscape. A slapdash of houses stand next to each other. A cozy villa behind high concrete walls, the next a mud house with a fence drooping from the weight of weeds growing into it. One tukul in particular makes Almy shudder. One side of its whitewashed walls is coming off like a scab picked too soon, exposing earthen flesh and a skeleton of wooden rods beneath.

The house strikes her as something Dani would comment on. "Who lives here? Why? Can we go inside? Can we take them home?" Almy wishes he were here.

The seicento slows to a stop in front of a black gate. Bizu speaks to the driver in that voice, plush as the cashmere coat on her back. Had Almy been listening, she would have heard him lower the fare – his own voice cooing under her aunt's spell. But Almy has already stepped outside. She is soaking in the neighbourhood, trying to brace herself for who knows what.

She hears the muffled clatter of wind instruments being tuned at a distance, banter and giggling closer by. She draws in her breath, and with it a waft of warm air and the sound of crackling firewood. Bizu emerges from the cab, smoothing the hood of her coat over her head before taking Almy's arm under hers.

Almy tries to keep her hands from shaking as she pushes the gate open. It gives onto a trail carved out of enormous polished stones, trees on either side of the path. Every few metres, a solitary flame dances in a kerosene lamp lighting their way forward. They walk towards the chime of voices. In a clearing, Almy sees a crowd gathered around a voluptuous fire, its glow bathing them in a warm light.

All eyes are on Auntie Bizu as they get closer. The circle opens up to take aunt and niece into its fold.

"Always playing the part of the queen." A man with sculpted features gives Bizu a kiss on the cheek.

"If only to honour His Imperial Majesty," Bizu flirts back, curtsying ever so slightly. "This is my niece Almy." She keeps Almy tucked under her elbow like a clutch.

Almy recognises only Tegest. She worked with Auntie at the Haile Selassie Theatre. Almy knows this from the framed picture in Bizu's apartment; Auntie as Cleopatra, Tegest as her chambermaid. A sonorous voice catches Almy's attention. A tall man is lecturing to a stalky fellow about the music coming from indoors. He looks Armenian, like a fellow pilot Abba once brought home for dinner. From his height and curly hair, Almy knows this is the Haik Auntie spoke about.

"Do you hear that riff?" His index finger pointing towards the house.

"Yes, yes, a racket more like." The other man's tone is jocular.

"Just listen," Haik signals, then pauses. "The piano montuno backs the five-tone scale. The five, that's what gives it its Ethiopian sound. It floats on top, just over the montuno." With one of his slender hands, he makes a wave-like motion while with the other he snaps his fingers at intervals.

Almy is careful not to betray her interest in their conversation. She hasn't the slightest idea what these fancy terms mean. Nor does she know how she'll approach Haik, much less what she'll say to him.

"If you ask me," the man says, "they should either stick to our traditional music or play their jazz elsewhere. Mixing the two is absurd."

Haik is hardly listening, fixated as he is on the music wafting from the open windows, his head bent towards the house. Almy imagines he is holding his breath, waiting until the song ends to exhale. She strains to hear the music above the chatter.

Haik begins to walk away and Almy's heart bounces into her ears, thinking this may be the only chance she has. But by the time she has unglued her feet from the ground, he has disappeared into the crowd. She'll find him again, she reassures herself. She pauses for a moment, then extricates her arm from Bizu's and walks towards the house.

The living room is a vast expanse of wooden floorboards with the furniture pushed against the wall. Three men have improvised a stage out of a corner. One man has his back to the rest of the living room, bent over a piano. Another is lightly tapping on a vibraphone with what look like fur-balled microphones. The most lively of them is tap-tapping on what she will later learn is a conga drum.

Almy stands at the far end of the room, her hands tucked behind her back, palms plastered to the wall. The lightness of the vibraphone flitters through her ears. The tum-tum of the drum eclipses the quiet thump of her heart. The keys of the piano swing the distance from the makeshift stage to the wall behind her and tether back. Together they make a concert of sound like nothing

Almy has ever heard before.

For a second, she forgets her nerves.

There are three women watching from the sidelines. Though their features differ, their shared corpulence gives Almy the impression that they are triplets. The musicians with their instruments, the ladies with their bodies. They are testing the sound to see how well their instincts respond to the beat. They clap to harmonise, their shoulders and necks snapping in time.

They wave Almy over to join them. She shakes her head shyly. She is relieved when they turn back to themselves, shimmying and gliding into a seamless circle. The music picks up speed and carries their joy with it. Almy can no longer hear herself think. She glides into step with them, and once she does, it is as if she had been there all along. Carried on a wave of the sound, she feels weightless.

The song ends, and a loud laugh calls Almy back to her senses. It's Haik standing in the doorway facing the makeshift dance floor. His face is bright with unconcealed mirth. Almy hadn't imagined him to be a laughing man. The three ladies greet him. Almy doesn't know whether to return to her place against the wall or walk over and introduce herself. She's sweating, unpresentable.

Now he raises his hand, beckoning her. Almy wipes her forehead with the back of her left hand and walks over cautiously.

"Bizu's niece, no?"

"Yes, my name is Almy." She wipes her right hand and extends it to shake his.

"I take it you enjoy this music?"

"Yes. I've never heard anything like it," Almy begins. Their conversation carries on with an ease Almy hadn't anticipated.

The next weekend, Almy is so keen to return home to Dire Dawa that she almost dashes onto the train without the sheet music Haik gave Auntie Bizu for her. He has agreed to instruct her in music theory and piano practice once she starts university.

Abba picks her up at the train station in Dire. In the car, she tells him about her week; how Bizu helped her find an instructor, and that she'll *gladly* do university as long as he and Ema pay for her piano lessons. Abba assures her that they will. He is happy that she's happy. Almy is ecstatic. She cannot wait to get home to tell Dani all of this. Abba drops her at the gate before driving off. She dumps her stuff on the verandah, kisses her mother, and runs from room to room in search of Dani.

She finds him in the salon, belly on the ground, legs in the air, his fingers clamped over a crayon. He is singing, drawing in his colouring book. His kitten leaps behind his legs as she stampedes into the room.

"Hi, Ami." He smiles with his gangly teeth, eyes lighting up at the sight of his sister.

"I was music!" She hugs and shakes him.

He crinkles his nose at her.

"You asked me what I wanted to be when I grow up, remember?"

"Oh, that." He sits up to face her, crossing his legs to get comfortable. The kitten, a calico ball of fur with patches of grey and orange, settles in his lap. "Go on."

She tells him how glamorous Auntie is, that her friends are more handsome than Roger Moore or Shashi Kapoor, whose movies she and Dani have watched together at Haji Mohammed Bomba Cinema. That she heard a new kind of music that isn't even on the radio yet. That when she danced, she felt like music.

He watches her without blinking, the kitten purring in his arms.

"Do you believe me now?"

There is a twinkle in his eyes. He says nothing. He gently puts the kitten on the floor and walks to their parents' bedroom on the opposite side of the salon.

A few minutes pass in silence, and Almy gets up to see what Dani is doing. Just then he appears in the doorway, the quilt from their parents' bed tied around his neck, trailing luxuriously behind him. Almy opens her mouth to scold him, but shuts it again.

He parades past the dining table into the centre of the room, posing here with his fingertips to his chest, gesturing there, looking into the distance – a caricature of Auntie Bizu's grace. He picks up a crayon as he passes by his colouring book, holds it between his fingers and draws a draught as if from a cigarillo. He does not once break character, not even when he starts dancing.

"How about me, Ami, am I being music?" he says, swinging his hips.

Almy knows he is making fun of her, but she cannot stop the tears of laughter long enough to catch him when she gives chase, pushing chairs and knocking over furniture. He dodges her despite the weight of the quilt. Finally, she collapses on the couch, clutching her stomach.

*A*lmy leaves for university the next month, carrying with her Dani's gaiety and her own sense of wonder at the sound of that music. These keep her hopeful after an exhausting day of classes, followed by music lessons with Haik. Learning to play this music, let alone write it, is *not* easy, Almy writes in one of her letters to Dani. She would calculate the time it would take for her letter to arrive, and then call him to talk about it.

In those early days he was more than willing, sharing his latest pursuits in mischief, making her laugh. It is the opposite of the isolation she feels on a campus teeming with militant students. They criticise a government leeching off its people, collecting land tax from peasants who can't sustain their own households. Almy gathers this from her roommates' late night conversations. They boycott classes, stage protests, and throw around language Almy barely understands: 'Revos' and 'Sabos'. The latter is a term that she comes to learn means 'saboteur' and which she is called for want of 'revolutionary spirit'.

Women with picked afros and no make-up come up to her at the library and try to preach about being emancipated.

"I'll emancipate myself, thank you," she says, her tone stone cold.

One afternoon in her second semester, Almy decides to see what all the fuss is about, and follows the rest of the campus population to the main hall. A young man in khaki pants and a safari coat is making a vehement speech to a crowd spilling out the doors. He laments the ruthless bombardment of civilians in Arsi, Bale and Eritrea for their rightful rebellions. He proclaims socialism as the solution to the injustices heaped on the people by Haile Selassie's regime.

Almy looks around as her fellow students cheer with fists in the air. She feels none of their injustice, only an overwhelming sense that she'll be swallowed by their collective anger. She spots her roommates. They wave to her as the crowd breaks out in song, something about Ho Chi Minh and Che Guevara. She pushes her way out and runs to the nearest payphone. Her ears are still ringing as she digs for coins.

"Hello," Muna answers.

"Hi Muna, can you get me Dani?"

"Selam Almy, he's not home, do you want to speak to Ema?"

"That's OK. Ask him to call me, please."

Almy walks the infinite distance to her dorm with her head bowed and her arms crossed. Opening the door, she looks around at the empty room, feeling it might swallow her whole. She jumps up onto her bunk bed and buries her head under the pillow.

Haik's lessons become more demanding. Almy is intimidated, but also relieved for the distraction. She spends more and more time trying to adapt her fingers to the complicated musical phrases; breaking from this and classes only to see Auntie for lunch every other weekend.

"Your brother called for you," Auntie tells her one Sunday, a week before the semester ends. Almy means to call back, but she is reluctant to tell him that she won't be coming home for kiremt. Last they talked, she had promised to take him to the cinema when she got back home. She knows he will be disappointed, but she has already committed to summer classes with Haik.

By her sophomore year, Dani is eleven, and when she does get around to calling home their conversations are brief.

"How's school, Dani?"

"Fine."

"And your friends?"

"Good."

"Have you found any new pets lately?"

"No. Ema wants to talk to you, I have to go do homework."

His curtness throws her off. Almy doesn't want to think about how fast he must be growing. She shrugs it off and bids Ema goodnight.

Almy starts spending whole Sunday afternoon with Bizu. They turn the radio up loud and sip fruity Pimm's cocktails. Sometimes Bizu's friends show up unannounced. If Tegest coaxes her enough, Almy plays them songs on the piano. She still can't write a lick of good music, but it's all the same to them. Almy plays the tunes of the latest hits on the radio and they sing along, making their own words up.

Almy invariably falls asleep on the couch, the anxiety of missing a morning class waking her at first light. She throws her stuff into a bag, runs down the stairs, and takes a seicento to campus.

One morning, Almy rises early enough to walk the whole way back. The crisp morning air tickles her face, the smell of Bizu's perfumed cigarettes still in her hair. A surge of gratitude sends her afloat. She thinks of Dani, how much she wants to tell him about this overwhelming sense that she's leading a double life: one as the doted-upon niece and amateur musician among Bizu's crowd; and the other as an obscure student burying her head in books at the library.

She calls him that evening. Ema picks up. Dani's out playing at the neighbour's. Next time, Ema reports that his voice is breaking.

"Already, at twelve?" Almy is surprised. She asks to talk to him; he says he'll call her back when he finishes what he's doing. He doesn't call. Once again, Almy gets swept into the tide of routine and doesn't hear from either of them for months. Then Ema starts calling her more and more, with no good news to report.

"You will not *believe* what this child has done now." Ema sends him to get groceries, and he shares half the supplies with homeless people on his way home.

"It isn't enough for him that we feed the poor on Sundays. If he cares so much, why doesn't he help me cook for them?"

Apparently that is not Dani's idea of goodwill. The next time Ema calls, it is to complain that the grocer pulled her aside to report that her son talked him into selling bread and butter at a lower price to a group of street children. He appreciates the child's concern, but now his other customers are enraged that he is selling them goods at a higher price. Almy assures her mother it is just puberty.

The year Almy graduates, it becomes clear it's otherwise. Bizu is visiting Dire when she spots Dani holding a "land to the tiller" placard in a street protest. She drags him all the way home by his ear and delivers him to a scandalised Ema. That same month, a band of military men unceremoniously escorts the Emperor from his palace to a prison, abruptly ending the Emperor's forty-four-year rule.

"Are you happy now, kid?" Almy asks over the phone.

"I don't know—" he starts, "but it wasn't supposed to be them." She wonders if he means the likes of her radical college classmates would have been better suited to the job.

In no time, the new military government nationalises all land, supposedly fulfilling its 'land to the tiller' promise.

Dani is fifteen when Muna discovers a pale, dishevelled young man sleeping under a metal sheet behind the new tenants' quarters. Abba questions him at length.

"Barely your age," Abba tells her later, "he was trying to escape to Djibouti through Dire. The kebele is looking for him in connection with forged ID cards."

Abba has him wait until evening to send him on his way. Everyone knows Dani was the one harbouring him. Ema threatens to kill her son with her bare hands before the authorities ever get the chance.

Almy shivers at the news. An image she had recently seen on television comes back to her. It's of Colonel Mengistu smashing bottle after bottle of blood, addressing a crowd, screaming, "Death to the counter-revolutionaries!" A weight heaves on Almy at the thought of not knowing her brother's whereabouts. She calls Abba, and tells him she's coming home.

*O*ne night, seven years after telling Dani she wanted to be music, Almy leaves her bandmate Negatu's basement studio, keen to get home and find her brother. She wants to play him a new song she had composed, one she knows he will appreciate.

There is an understated solemnity to the tune, especially when the brass section plays it: the trombones and washint, a concert of porous vessels for grief to course through. If the Censorship Authority thought their previous records lacked patriotism, they would certainly see this as enemy propaganda.

Almy looks around and realises she is alone on the street. She brings the collar of her coat to her neck and walks closer to the warka trees, seeking cover from invisible eyes. It is not curfew yet, but her neighbours have scuttled home.

She conjures James Brown's 'Get Up' to cheer herself. The song is no longer on the radio, but it is fresh in her mind. The memory of Brown's commanding voice and happy feet is a welcome dare. She spins on her heels and points to an invisible audience, mouthing "thank you for coming out tonight." She half-smiles at the thrill of it. It's a wonder what you can get away with under the cover of darkness.

What she will not escape is her mother's glare when she gets home: "First your brother, now you?" Dani has worn Ema's patience to a thread.

Almy strides along, trying to look harmless. If no one is sitting on the verandah, she will walk around the side of the house and sneak into her room through the window.

That's when she hears it. A woman's voice, at once familiar and alien, splits the air, its tone both demanding and pleading. Almy makes as if to hide, but she's unsure from what. She changes her mind, dashing to the corner to make sure it's not coming from her street.

The streetlights bend mournfully toward the ground. Under their glow, a pick-up truck stands in front of her house, its back tented over by canvas, unmistakably from the kebele. She blinks and squints, her mind failing to register the scene. It is only when she sees Dani's lanky figure flung forward that she knows. A dark figure in military fatigues thunders behind him.

Her mother follows the kebele man out, screaming. He pushes Dani into the darkness under the canvas. Ema is grabbing at the man's uniform. In a fit of impatience, he whacks her in the stomach with the butt of his rifle. She falls to her knees. Almy's own knees threaten to buckle.

She wants to run and save Ema, offer herself in Dani's place: "Take me, please, take me instead. He's only sixteen, he knows nothing." But she remains cemented to the sidewalk.

Ema struggles to get back up on her feet. Almy silences her breath, still unable to move. The man slings his gun around his shoulder, giving the driver orders before jumping into the back under the canvas. Ema clutches at her stomach and hobbles after the truck.

Almy sees Muna come out of the dark. She takes Ema in her arms and has to drag her into the house, screaming at a blood-curdling pitch for her son.

Almy will never remember how she made it into the house that night. While her mother goes from police station to hospital to kebele and then home, Almy remains immobile. She can only sit on the floor of Dani's room, numb, shutters bolted to cover the windows, waiting.

On the fifth day, a thought swims in her mind and she starts to cry.

"Dani, what do you want to be when you grow up?"

Taba

Adelola Ojutiku

I often look back to a day that I didn't think would be significant at the time. It was the first time I heard about taba.

The day was as typical as they come. Mama and I sat outside preparing the evening meal with Mama Jumbo from next door. I picked stones out of beans, Mama chopped the ugwu leaves while Mama Jumbo chattered on. I watched a group of girls nearby as they played one of those clapping games. I knew the song they were chanting.

New money it done come. I buy garri ten kobo. I give Mary to cook am. Mary cook am, it no sweet. I beat Mary, she no cry. I kill Mary, she no die. Which kind Mary be this one?

The lyrics were no surprise to anyone who knew Bonny Island. You could not waste food here and expect to get away with it. The locals had also become immune to death. Foreigners, however, couldn't wait to leave. We joked that Solomon Grundy, who lived his whole life in a week, wouldn't have survived that long if he had visited Bonny Island.

I let myself get distracted by my thoughts so I wouldn't have to listen to the older woman's chatter. But then I heard something that grabbed my attention.

"Ehen, Mama Nimi, have you heard?"

"Mama Jumbo, I haven't heard oo."

"Just this morning, they announced that they're starting a witch hunt for all those men who sleep with other men. They're marching all of them to prison. I hear they already caught so many of them in Abuja."

"So they're only arresting men?" I was surprised at the question; my mother was usually indifferent to gossip.

"Yes now! Women don't do those sorts of things. I don't even like to do it with men. What would make me start doing it with women?"

"Mama Jumbo, I don't agree with you on that. Let me gist you small."

Mama Jumbo was excited that someone was *finally* confiding in her; you had heard the other women call her 'basket mouth' because she could not keep a secret.

My mother went on: "When I was younger, they sent me to this Federal Government Girls College in Ibadan. Sometimes two girls would tie their bedsheets like tents around the bunk and everyone would just shun them and say, o walabetaba, they are under the taba. I even had this girlfriend. We didn't join in taba, but she would write me sweet, sweet letters and sprinkle powder on the paper to give it a scent."

I was shocked that Mama could be with anyone who was not Papa. I thought of the way he would come home every other Friday when he got paid, hiding a black nylon bag behind his back. When he found Mama, he would say "surprise, surprise" and she would shriek like the surprise was not always a small bag of garden eggs. He had been getting them since she once mentioned she liked them. Mama once whispered to me that she had grown tired of the taste, but still she squealed with delight to make him happy. I imagined him getting on his second or third bus on his way home from work trying to figure out how to deal with the relatives that appeared every pay day, while also looking out for the street hawker from whom he would buy Mama's garden eggs. This was what I saw as love – placing another's happiness before yours.

*T*he end of the raining season signalled the beginning of the school year. I was one of the winners of the NLNG scholarship, so I was starting the year at a posh school in Port Harcourt.

It took me a month to realise that fitting in there required labels from clothing outlets that could prove your passport had stamps from at least three different Western countries or a promising boyfriend who could provide these things. Without a passport or the light-skinned curvy body the men here liked, my chances were minimal. I was still in my discovery phase when a senior girl asked me to fetch her friend from one of the other rooms. I went to fulfil my errand, and that was when I saw her.

She reminded me of a mammy water spirit. I had not believed, until then, that it was possible for a person to be that beautiful. No one I had seen on Bonny Island was that beautiful. Not the pinch-nosed white wives of the engineers at NLNG, not even the prostitutes the men paraded when their wives were not around.

I had never considered impeccable beauty before. Hers was a pure one. She had eyes that could tell a story. They danced around when she got excited, fell when she told of a tragedy, and teased until her audience, be they man or woman, felt a sudden wetness between their legs.

She was sitting in the centre of a group of girls. Hearing her speak, I felt the same way I did when I walked into a cloud of perfume. I watched in awe as she controlled her audience. All the girls sought her approval: "Sonia, should I tuck my shirt in or out? Or should I tie it at my belly?" She handled the attention well, careful not to over-compliment anyone so they wouldn't make the mistake of comparing themselves to her.

I listened as she talked about her latest shopping trip to London. Another girl said, "Oh my mum bought me these shoes from that store!" Sonia simply replied, "Hmm, you have to be careful, dear, there are so many fake versions these days." The girl went quiet with shame. She should have known better, really.

As for Sonia, the girl was proud to the marrow. She reminded me of this woman whose car was stuck in traffic; so while her driver remained behind, she walked into Mama's provision store. She sneered as she looked around and then said, "I could reach into my wallet and give you double the worth of everything you have here, but today I'll just have Trebor mints."

I was so lost in my thoughts, I didn't realise she was talking to me.

"And what is this one looking for?"

There was a time when I had skin that could blush; I knew this from the one childhood photo I had, now glued to my wardrobe. At that moment, I felt myself bring back a trait I thought had been destroyed by fifteen harmattans.

"You're just standing there like a zombie." Her comment was followed by laughter from the others.

I couldn't hide my surprise when Sonia woke me up that night to accompany her to the toilet. This was not an unusual request. Very few girls were prepared to brave the toilets alone at night after all the rumours of Lady Koin Koin, a former principal who was murdered during an armed robbery. The story was that one of the robbers had stolen a single shoe of her favourite pair of red heels, and now she haunted boarding schools with the one shoe on while she searched for the stolen one. I didn't believe the rumours. How far could she walk with only one shoe? Really. I was trained to save my fear for practical things.

What was strange was that Sonia had walked all the way from her room downstairs to fetch me. I was sure there were several girls who would have been willing to accompany her, but she chose me; that much was certain.

There was a quarter moon that night, with a few stars. That was enough for me to make out her features. Some skin tones have an inner light. Her milk-tea skin was visible when it wasn't too dark. This wasn't true of the soaked tea-bag colour of my skin. One would think the dark would be impartial to skin.

I listened as she urinated. It was like the tempo of an orchestra. The intense speed with which it started, gradually slowing until all that was left was a faint tinkle similar to the sound of those musical triangles. Once she was finished, she walked ahead, not towards either of our rooms, but towards one of the box rooms.

At that point, I was confused. Maybe she was indeed a mammy water spirit. Still, I followed her in and watched in silence as she retrieved a blanket from a suitcase. She spread it on the floor and motioned for me to sit. I heard the hiss of a match as she lit a kerosene lamp hidden in a corner of the room. The light from the lamp was blue, and it cast a glow on her that made her look even more otherworldly.

Paranoid as I was, I didn't expect it when she took off her shirt. She had the most intricate breasts – round at the base and curving towards pointed, dark nipples. They made me think of all things perfectly shaped. I finally settled on the image of fried puff puffs. I reached for them, unsure of what I was doing, but sure of what I wanted. I nibbled on them as though her breasts really were fried dough crowned with Hershey kisses.

I allowed my mouth to descend, every stroke of my tongue followed by moans that messed with my senses. She had one of those navels that stuck out. I sucked on it for a while before moving further down. I was greeted by a stubble of hair. Her inside was warm and tasted like an overripe orange. It was equally welcoming; it hugged my tongue tight as it got wetter. I made come-here motions on its roof like I owned the place.

I was overwhelmed by a sense of achievement. I had made her come. She rolled around as if in a trance, her grip tightened on my shoulders, her moans became more fevered, and then there was a sudden gush. It was very Moses-like, seducing water from a rock. I stared at the rosary she wore, now settled between her breasts. There was something about the way it looked; the contrast of innocence with desire. That was what I felt for her.

I fingered the rosary. Innocence would have to wait. She moaned again as I trailed kisses down her length. People only become equal when they're overcome by emotion. It's almost impossible to differentiate the groans of the poor from that of the rich. It's even more impossible to tell one's origin from their moans. We only have accents when we create sounds we control.

She jerked away from me. It felt like the separation of Siamese twins.

"You're such a prostitute." My mouth stayed frozen in the position it had been on her body just seconds ago. I could still taste her sweat. In the blur of the moment, I thought I saw her smile.

"I thought you wanted me to." I was fumbling now.

"Oh, I did." She must have sensed my confusion, and shook her head like the subject I couldn't understand was as simple as the difference between boiled and fried eggs. "My mother is a prostitute, too. Even more than you are."

"Sonia…"

She lifted her fist and released a finger to match each point she made. "First, my name is Ladi. It's what I call myself in my head. Second, my mother really is a prostitute. You've seen her, right? Parading herself like she's a big woman, telling people she married a white man when in reality she turned his condom into a sieve so he'd have to give her money for the rest of his life. I don't feel sorry for him either. When we were in London during the holidays, he wouldn't even introduce me to his family. Then one weekend, while they were in France, he took me to their house as if to say 'just so you know who's really important'. It's funny how you think you're rich until you see someone else much richer. It throws you off your balance. That's what their house did to me. And you." She pointed an accusing finger in my direction. "Lest I forget. You're also a prostitute because they are the only people who give pleasure to people who look down on them."

Her expression remained detached the entire time she spoke. Later, I would rank everything she told me by priority, and decide that the insults came in last. This was the paradox of life – the rich were seldom happy. Sonia considered the women in her life to be prostitutes for loving people who would never return their feelings. I understood, at least I thought I did. I had heard other women tell my mother that she was lucky to have a husband who neither beat her, nor chased after other women. Was this her solution to unrequited love? It made no sense that relationships with others had to be based on difference. It was as if self-hatred was the sole purpose of our race.

Still, at that moment, I had to ask. "So what does this mean for us?"

She laughed, mocking me. "Don't you know I have a boyfriend? Osaki."

I nodded. I had indeed heard of her boyfriend.

But why do we need to be labelled because of the way we love? The rooms in our dorm were shared by at least twenty girls. At any time of the day, you could find girls in various phases of nudity. We made comments on each other's bodies, touched our more personal parts just to know how they felt. We often declared love for one another. I had even seen one girl ask a friend to powder her ass, and another ask different girls their opinion on how her pussy smelt. We could do all of this, and only crossed the line into lesbianism if we dared to do these things in private. Then others would taunt you, calling you 'lele' or '37 37'.

I walked back to my room expecting to feel something different, but I didn't. Who would have thought that the day I decided to love a woman, I would walk out still feeling like myself?

*W*e went on meeting in private, mostly using the time to spark pleasure from our bodies. On the night I realised I loved her, she asked if we could just lie there. Soon she was curled up in foetal position, fast asleep. In the awakened silence, I noticed sounds that I hadn't before. There was a dripping from the corner; it had rained the night before. An orchestra of crickets chirped, while a perverted owl somewhere hooted at his discovery of lovers.

I didn't realise I had also fallen asleep till she woke me with her screams.

"What's the time?" She began to jerk and let out another

scream.

"Ladi, calm down. It must have been a nightmare."

She disregarded my words. "Tell me the damn time. I bet it's 3.27am."

I flashed the lantern on the wall clock. It was just a little past midnight.

"God told me," she started to explain. "He told me the other night that *they* are trying to kill me and my father. He said by 3.27am they would try, but I woke up just in time and now we're going to stay up and wait for them." She had the same determined confusion of mad people on the streets.

What prompted all this talk about God? She had never been religious. She only wore rosaries because they were the closest thing to jewellery allowed. And why such an exact time as 3.27am? Why not just wait until 3.30am?

"Ladi." I circled her with my arms and insisted that no one was trying to kill her. When it became obvious that my efforts to soothe her were in vain, I tried something else. I fished out a sheet from my suitcase. There was an opening under one of the shelves. I wrapped my sheet around its legs, turban-style. After a few smoothings, it looked good enough to welcome her into.

"What's that?"

"Come in." I parted the sheet. "It's a taba. We'll be safe here." She crept in and slept without worry. I even noticed a trail of spit making its descent down her face. I thought of how she had the fragility, yet strength, of an egg. She could survive several misfortunes, and only be broken by sudden impacts. I wiped the spit away with my shirt. At that moment, I wanted nothing more than to make the world a crate built solely for her protection. I fell asleep dreaming of magical tabas that transport lovers through oceans and deserts until they find their sanctuaries.

*F*inding love is like walking around on a sunny day without fearing shadows. When the semester came to an end and we had to go home, I felt like something had been dug out of me.

I walked around with a burden that I was sure was heavier than when Atlas was forced to lay the world on his shoulders.

I thought I saw her one morning on my way to fetch water. I rubbed my eyes, sure I was being fooled by the harmattan mist. I opened them and I saw that it was indeed her. The excitement of the moment made me drop my bucket. She was walking towards me with her mother.

When they got close enough, I could tell that her mother was angry. She managed to crush my entire self-esteem with just three glances. "So you're the riff-raff that's trying to contaminate my daughter's life."

Mama came out when she heard the commotion. I wish she had stayed in. I watched her shrink the way she usually did in front of rich people. I was suddenly embarrassed by our unpainted walls and unpaved yard.

Ladi's mother, as if she had not shamed us enough, went on with the insults. "When you grow up in a sty like this, why wouldn't you pick up all manner of perversions? I'm warning you. Stay away from my daughter." She started to walk away, signalling for Ladi to follow her. She was wearing red heels that didn't sink in the rain-drenched soil as she strode on.

Mama finally spoke. "I wish she falls in that koinkoin shoe."

"She won't," I replied. "They never do." I was still shocked. How was Ladi handling it? She hadn't muttered a word the entire time.

As if hearing my thoughts, she turned and walked back towards me. My heart lightened. I started to compose our Juliet and Julianne romance.

She stopped at a distance close enough for me to make out her features, but far enough that I could not reach out to her. Out of nowhere, she started to laugh. I thought the whole thing was staged, a joke, but then a smile spread out across her face. It was a 'now you've learnt your lesson' smile.

How had I missed it? I realised then that she had really smiled that first night when she called me a prostitute. Now, as she walked back to her mother, I wondered: how had I not seen that she was crazy? I should have known. I was under a taba with her. And those feelings will always wind around me.

Who We Were There, Who We Are Now

Nadu Ologoudou

I am expecting to see you.

It is just a few beats short of midnight, and the party is picking up steam on its way from noisy to rowdy. The older guests left, immediately after the hotel waiters rolled out the birthday cake. Before leaving, my father hugged me again.

"I'm so glad you came back."

And I joked that I might have reconsidered if I'd known he would make such a fuss about it. "Or at least waited until my birthday had passed."

He laughed, a little drunk from very, very expensive champagne, and the pride of showing off his prodigal daughter. His body felt smaller in my arms, less solid than I remembered. Tonight I saw the passing of time reflected in the greying hair and shrunken statures of the uncles and aunties – the adults who have grown old while we grew up. It made me fiercely glad that I had returned. Hugging my father, I realised how much I had missed him – not just his presence, but him here, in this country where he belongs, and where I thought I did not, despite my blood, and the bones of my ancestors.

He never asked me why I came back. My father understands

exile, although his own – those two years we never speak about – was forced, and mine self-imposed. He understands that one leaves to survive and comes back when depleted of all the strength it takes to simply exist in a land that was not meant to sustain your kind.

I am depleted.

I came back, but not to you. That was not my move to make. The list of people who could have told you of my return is a long one, and I don't imagine any of them missing this opportunity. You know I am back. And I am expecting to see you tonight.

The lights of the ballroom are dimming now, and the DJ lets loose like he's been waiting for this moment all night, spinning some catchy Ivorian beats with potent ancestral percussions. The song, popular when we were in high school, is now officially old enough to have swung all the way from passé to classic. It acts like a call to battle, shaking off the drowsiness caused by four courses and far too many bottles of wine, drawing the guests out of their chairs.

Laughing, my cousin Ahouefa pulls me into the crowd that is flocking to the dance floor. For a minute, I could swear she is still seventeen, and not a mother of two.

The dance floor, designed with slightly more polite entertainment in mind, is much too tight, and we are all pushed close together. My head is spinning a little, and I take a deep breath, inhaling air that is heavy with perfume, sweat and body heat. My little black dress feels drab against the claret, turquoise or indigo bits of Wax fabric that the other women are wearing, cleverly mixed with silks, organza or chiffon to create a vivid aesthetic that manages to be modern without being Western. The men are comparatively staid: dark trousers, shirts in variations of blue, white and pink – no ties. A sale of their watches and Italian leather shoes would probably raise enough funds to bring drinking water to a village, or three, but none of them are about to apologise for it.

It was at this same hotel that we celebrated your sixteenth birthday – do you remember? It was newer then, recently built to host an international summit of ECOWAS presidents. The plush carpeting is a little the worse for wear after nineteen years of trampling, but very little else has changed. It's the same crowd too, a little older, none the wiser – though we have learned to fake it by now.

A circle has formed around two dancers. Justin, with moves just as smooth as they were eighteen years ago, is throwing down against Kamilou – still the best of rivals. A few steps away, Essenam has kicked off her high heels, along with her public persona as Deputy Minister of Primary Education.

We are the best and the brightest of our generation, the privileged few who followed the footsteps of our folks into politics, business and power. Tonight, I have been welcomed back into the fold, all transgressions forgiven for the moment. I do not fool myself into thinking they have been forgotten.

For now, I am content to float along, letting the rhythm carry me. I am waiting for you. I know you will come. This birthday marks a turning point – we have now been apart longer than we ever were together.

And we were together a very long time. Childhood playmates, thrown together by our parents' friendship.

We never even knew we had a choice.

*W*e are ten. The house is full of women, swarming, their starched kaftans rustling as they hurry past. Voluminous women wrapped in yards of dyed fabric, every gesture punctuated by the clicking of metallic bangles around their wrists. Seductive women whose heady perfumes linger long after they have left the room. Loud women, laughing deep, letting their voices ring across space and fill each corner.

Women coming out of every room, sprawling in every chair, teetering on high heels across the tiled hallway floors. Painted women, wigged women – not always beautiful, but always self-possessed. Bold, confident.

Women in the absence of men.

Their presence has chased us from the living room where we

like to hide behind the sofa and play Ludo; it has driven us from the verandah and our books. Not even your room is safe any more. There are aunties there, aunties everywhere, come to usher a new member into their sorority.

Your cousin Aicha is getting married, and there will be no peace until it is done.

There will be a civil ceremony, a church wedding, but most importantly, the payment of the dowry, which seals the traditional wedding, will occur tomorrow afternoon. Four hundred guests are expected. To accommodate them, several large tents of blue tarp have been erected in the street in front of the house, making traffic impossible for cars or motorbikes. The first trucks of plastic chairs arrived in the morning, and the workers are busy setting them up in neat rows underneath the tarp.

The rear courtyard, near the kitchen, is the hub of activities. Your mother has drummed out her first, second and third circles of friends and relatives to help prepare all the food that will be required. There are heavy cast-iron pots steaming over wood fires, and large baskets full of okra to be minced, potatoes to be peeled, tomatoes to be mashed on large stone slabs. An old transistor radio set on the cement steps by the well is wheezing out popular tunes. Every now and then, one of the women will start singing out loud, soon joined by the others. Aicha, back from her fitting session with the seamstress, is seated among them, eyes lowered as they gently tease her and exchange bawdy anecdotes that us children aren't supposed to hear, let alone understand.

We momentarily become part of the day's entertainment as we cross the yard, looking to escape. You are wearing an old dress that is starting to be just a little too short for you, and your hair has fallen out of the tight knots your mother braided the day before. It's now fanning out like a halo, long and fluffy about your ears.

"Now that's hair worth a queen's dowry," jokes Auntie Sika, running one hand over the crown of your head.

Normally you would have submitted to her touch – you enjoy the attention. But today you pull away. You have been in a bad mood for at least a week, ever since school ended. These facts are not related. You are angry about the wedding. You've always considered Aicha yours, ever since she first came to town to study for university. She shared your room, helped you get dressed in the morning, and spent hours playing with you, never giving the impression she had anything better to do.

Now she's a bride, the first one that you and I have known personally. All the aunties were born married, or at least it feels that way. We have never seen a girl turn into an auntie before – and you are not liking it one bit.

"Why does she have to get married?" You ask your mother, you ask Aicha, you ask me.

"Because all women get married, sooner or later."

"Because I love him."

"Because she is a grown-up."

None of the answers seem to satisfy you. And now Auntie Sika is teasing you as the rest of the women watch.

"Soon it will be your turn."

And you, of course, declare, for all to hear: "I am never getting married."

"Of course you are."

This from Auntie Jacqueline, the only one who is actually your aunt, sister to your mother. She is married to a businessman named Coulibaly, nicknamed Uncle Cool by the older cousins. They live in Ivory Coast and have come down for the wedding. You went to visit them once, and came back with tales of lawn parties and swimming pools, a house that boasted not one, not two, but three formal parlours, and how your cousins took horse-riding lessons.

I like to imagine that Auntie Jacqueline was probably born with her hair done, and her fingernails impeccably manicured and painted coral. It doesn't seem possible that she was once a child with scabbed knees and plaited hair. Her elegance, her grace, never seem to be put on – it's not something she wears for the sake of men, or society.

"We are going to find you a nice, handsome husband," she

says, taking your hand, "and I'm going to wear my prettiest shoes to the wedding, and dance all night."

She spins you around, and you laugh, for the first time in days, and everyone else laughs too.

We both want to be Auntie Jacquie when we grow up. You are starting to suspect it might mean getting married, though.

The women's laughter follows us as we run out of the yard and into the street. It is quiet outside. One pm is nap time for the adults, freedom for the children. There is a vacant, overgrown lot at the end of the street. That's where we find the others, our holiday mates; children from the neighborhood, also out from school – though not our school. The boys are about to start a game of football, and they invite me to join them. Another group, mostly girls, is re-enacting a scene from *Clementine*, the only animated show for children broadcast on national television – with more shrieks and running perhaps than in the original. You immediately demand to play the role of the ten-year-old aviator – and they yield to you.

The games end when siesta does, and the voices of mothers are heard calling for their daughters to come home and help with the chores. We head back too, though no one is missing us – not with the wedding preparations underway.

Hot and sticky with cooled-off sweat, we try to sneak upstairs to your room. As we pass the parlour, however, we see Uncle Cool and Aunt Jacquie. It's just a glimpse, we are almost past before the images fully register: the angry hand gestures, the pushing – the slap.

The sound of that blow echoes in my head as we run upstairs. I can still see Auntie Jacquie stumble, catch herself on the back of the sofa. And again, the sound of the slap. And Auntie Jacquie stumbling. Again and again in my head.

Much later, she comes back down into the courtyard. Her face is impeccably made-up, and she is smiling. She goes up to Aicha, and hugs her hard.

"You are going to be so happy," she says. "So very happy."

That night, you wake up from a nightmare and crawl into my bed, crying. And I hold you, and I tell you that it's all right, that I will marry you when we grow up.

*W*e are sixteen. Meiway's 'Zoblazo', the most popular song that year, is already playing by the time we arrive at the school dance, the music so loud it can be heard down the street as the boys park their mopeds. We are late because you got into an argument with Justin, your boyfriend, over the dress you are wearing. It's a skin-tight jersey number – fashion in the nineties was not kind to us – purchased in Missebo, the second-hand market where clothes discarded in France came to die.

*J*ustin didn't like the dress.

"You like it just fine," you countered. "You just don't like the fact that other boys will see me wearing it."

He made a gesture to convey that this was a distinction without a difference. You refused to change.

"Nina is wearing the exact same thing."

"Nina is not my girlfriend."

There's more he could have said, but he abstained. Justin doesn't exactly dislike me – but I know there are times he would be fine seeing a lot less of me.

The argument continued, far longer than strictly necessary. I worry, sometimes, that you will push him too far, while at the same time understanding that this is exactly what you want to do: drive him to his limits. You remind me of a cat locked in a too-small box, hissing, and spitting, driving itself into a frenzy, struggling against boundaries that just won't budge. It's your luck – and bad luck, perhaps – that Justin has learned exactly when to back off, leaving your anger to consume itself without fuel.

Twinkling coloured lights have been hung from the walls surrounding the school yard, and we immediately join the throng of bodies kicking up dust on the dance floor. You and I dance together, and the magnetic field we generate pulls in the boys.

There are always boys around us, but the boys aren't quite enough.

After fifteen minutes of increasingly catchier, upbeat tunes, the music slows into the smooth, sensual beats of a Caribbean zouk. Couples form.

"Dance with me," you say. And I shake my head, because I know it would be crossing the line. You know it, too. I am not entirely sure what has gotten into you tonight.

Justin intercepts us as we are leaving the dance floor, and pulls you back with him. I continue toward the corner where all our friends are gathered. As I walk past a group of seniors, they catcall, trying to get me to slow down and talk to them. Their leader – Jean-Jacques – detaches himself from his posse.

"Come on, baby, dance with me."

I make light of the request, trying to get away with a smile and a joke. His hand around my wrist tightens, and I know he means business. He wants me to dance with him, and sees no reason why that wanting shouldn't be reason enough for me to give in.

There are a couple of ways to handle such a situation: in the absence of a brother or boyfriend to fight on my behalf, the least troublesome way is to just do what the boy wants.

"You know he has a girlfriend, right?" This from Essie, when I finally disentangle myself from that mess and return to my friends.

"I'm not interested in Jean-Jacques."

She doesn't believe me, because I have been single for nearly three months, and of course I must be searching for a new boyfriend. Never mind the fact that I was the one doing the breaking-up to begin with.

"If I wanted a boyfriend, I could have just stayed with the one I had. Or the one before that."

In the two years since you started dating Justin, I have had three boyfriends. You keep fighting with yours, hoping he will yell at you, hit you, break up with you – do something. I just get bored and move on. It leaves me with a reputation for being difficult, but paradoxically, it's a reputation that seems to make the boys want me even more.

Strange that I would be the one with the reputation for independence, when you are the one who cannot wait to find a way out, always looking for the nearest exit.

It's nearly two am when the night takes a turn for the worse. I've gone into one of the empty classrooms to sit down. Everyone else is dancing, or so it seems. I'm dizzy from the cheap wine Essie has snuck in. All the chairs have been pulled outside for the dance. I'm surprised the room has been left open, but I take advantage. It's dark and cool inside. I go all the way to the teacher's desk in front, and lie down on the hard wooden surface. I close my eyes for a moment.

I don't hear him come in, don't even realise I'm not alone any more until arms close around me and moist lips push against mine. I don't struggle, at first. I'm drunk, mellow, and the kiss is not altogether unpleasant. Being asked my opinion on the matter would have been nice, but I can't be bothered opening my eyes to do anything about it. Only when the kiss deepens, and hands start fumbling with the hem of my dress do I push back, and meet resistance.

"Stop that."

He is not stopping.

"Stop it!"

I can tell he has no intention of listening to me.

I start struggling in earnest, hoping someone will see, someone will hear over the music. He has just pinned me flat onto the table when you come charging into the room. For some reason, you have no shoes, but you are holding a beer bottle. You don't even like beer.

"Leave her alone."

You break the bottle against the wall, and it turns into a weapon.

"Back off and leave her alone."

You are screaming, waving the cutting glass recklessly, and in that moment, there is no controlling you. You are burning with anger, incandescent with fury, and I watch it burst out of you like nuclear energy. You goad Jean-Jacques, willing him to take you on: you want a reason to hurt him, to slash, to cut.

You are angry because he touched me. You are angry because boys are always touching, and wanting, and grabbing, and this attack on me is an attack on you as well.

A crowd has gathered by the door, blocking us all in. Me, crying. Jean-Jacques, cautiously backing off, and you, going at him, pressing, pushing, trying to make contact at any cost. Trying to make him pay.

"Didi!"

I call your name, desperate because I want it to end now. You don't seem to hear. You are locked in your battle with Jean-Jacques. I move forward. You slash at me. I jump back.

"Didi!"

This time, the voice belongs to Justin. He grabs your wrist from behind, and with the other hand he tries to pry open your fingers, force you to release the broken bottle. You fight him, but he is stronger. Jean-Jacques leaves, spewing insults. We don't care.

You are still struggling against Justin, pounding his chest, trying to get loose, but he's got a pretty good hold on you.

"Hush, calm down, Didi, hush."

You are screaming, you are crying, you are trying to kiss him, hit him. He is male, so right now you hate him for it. He is Justin and you love him, in a way. It's an equation you have never managed to balance.

Over your shoulder, his eyes appeal to me. Perhaps for the first time in my life, I don't want to come anywhere near you. You scare me, almost as much as Jean-Jacques did. The Didi mask has fallen, pulled away by Jean-Jacques' actions, and we can see underneath the helplessness turned to despair, the despair turning into rage, hot enough to burn us all.

Still, I step forward. "Hush, doudou."

My hand runs up and down your back, trying to quiet down the great, harsh sobs. We are both trembling, wave after big wave of aftershock. "Hush, doudou."

After an eternity, your breathing seems to even out. You sink against Justin, simultaneously grabbing my hand, pulling me in too, your body caught between his and mine. The three of us remain this way for a long time, embracing, crying, until the DJ plays the last song.

*W*e are eighteen. We have escaped the continent and made it to the Promised Land – Paris. There are five of us, all girls, walking down a street near the Jardin du Luxembourg. We have just walked out of a café. Anne-Sophie is telling a story but I am not really listening, relishing the feel of your hand in mine. All our friends, these days, have names like Anne-Sophie, and Geneviève, or Odile. Although Justin, Essie and most of our high-school friends are here too, we see less and less of them, in favour of the long-legged, stringy-haired French girls we meet in our Poli-Sci classes, or at meetings of the human rights association you have joined. Girls who care nothing that we hold hands in public. In fact, when a man by the bistro calls us 'sales gouines', it's Anne-Sophie who goes after him, hurling insults.

We spend the evening at my place, in Saint-Denis. Through the open window, we can hear, in the distance, cheers from the newly built stadium where they are playing the World Cup. Neither of us is particularly interested in football.

You cook. You have finally learned how.

"Auntie Sika would be so proud. We'll make a good African wife of you yet."

You retaliate by throwing the dishcloth in my face, then kissing me.

We spend the Christmas break hibernating here, reading out loud to each other from books we picked up in the autumn. We discover the sensuality of Colette, and James Baldwin. We allow our bodies to disappear under layers and layers of clothing – jeans, shirts, sweaters, jackets – and wear no makeup.

In the spring, we go to museums during the weekends, or walk along the docks, buying cheap books at the stalls overlooking the Seine.

Now it's summer again. When our parents asked, we both said we preferred staying abroad, working, saving.

"We'll be home next summer."

But that is a lie. We haven't yet figured out a way to be there, and to be ourselves; and until we do, we are staying here. Where we no longer have to pretend.

I am the first one to get up that morning. I go downstairs for croissants – our Sunday morning ritual. At the bottom of the building, waiting on a bus-stop bench, I find Justin.

I'm surprised just how good it feels to see him – I had not even realised I had missed him – missed them all, those friends from back home.

"I'm on my way to the bakery. Walk me there."

It's a slow, companionable walk. We've made our peace with each other, Justin and I, after he finally broke up with you. The two of you are still friends. He and I are working our way toward something that might resemble friendship too. He catches me up on our classmates as we go.

"We miss seeing you guys."

He, of all people, has a pretty good idea why we are keeping to ourselves. The status quo is based on the lie that you and I are just really good friends. I am not sure our friends believe it, but they all need to maintain plausible deniability. That's the only way for them to accept us.

The woman behind the counter at the bakery gives us both that look – the one I have gotten to know since coming to France – the one that tells me nothing has registered beyond the colour of my skin.

We are nearly back to my building before Justin broaches the subject of his visit.

"You need to talk to Didi. She can't continue to run from her parents. She's been avoiding me, but she will listen to you."

I feel like I've walked into a conversation mid-sentence. I hesitate between confessing my ignorance and preserving my pride. Perhaps it is the knowledge of what it must have cost Justin to come here that allows me to drop the mask.

"I don't know what you are talking about, Justin."

He tells me.

You have been lying to me.

Confronted, you say it isn't so much a lie as an omission.

"It feels like a lie."

Your mother is sick and your father desperate to get you home. You have been avoiding them, hiding here.

You don't want to go home.

"Do you really believe they don't know about us? Are you so naïve? Do you think Essie, or Justin, or anyone in the group hasn't told your parents, or mine, that we are together? If I go, there is no way they are letting me come back."

"I don't want you to go. But you *can't* stay away."

"I know that! Don't you think I know that? But not yet. I can't go yet. I can't lose this yet."

But we both know you have already run out of time.

Sleeping with a woman – that was possibly excusable – or at least it could be ignored, glossed over. Not returning home when your mother was sick? There would be no coming back from that particular act. And no forgiving yourself either. The break with your family would be complete. And as much as you pretend you don't care, there is a part of me that isn't sure you are strong enough to endure it.

There is a reason why you have always been able to pass better than me, to skate closer to expectations, when I mostly didn't try. There is a reason you stuck with Justin for nearly five years – hissing and spitting, but never willing to break away. You want to be free, but you don't want to be cut loose. You need the ties, the roots.

That night you sleep on the couch. The ringing of the landline wakes me up. It's my father – on behalf of yours. Despite what you said, I am not sure how much he knows about us – my folks have always been good at not asking questions. It saves me from outright lying, but creates a distance, a gap filled with the things they can never know about me, and all the expectations I will never meet.

"Is Didi with you?"

You are not. The studio is small enough that all it takes is a swift glance to know you have bolted.

It only takes me two days to track you down, though.

It's Anne-Sophie who opens the door when I ring. Wordlessly, she lets me in. Her place is bigger than mine, there is a proper living room. You are sitting on the couch, smoking. The television is on, but I doubt you are actually watching.

"I am not going back."

Those are your first words to me.

"Yes, you are."

This is just a courtesy call. Your brother is over from England, where he is studying, and he has strict orders to see you on a plane.

"I already told him where to find you."

You say you will never forgive me.

"I know."

I am thirty-five. I am home. I have broken the unspoken promise I made to you that morning: that *here* would be yours, and that I would stay *there*.

I broke one morning, under the weight of the frost, the loneliness, the alienation. I slipped on a patch of ice as I ran for the bus, and for the life of me could not get up again. I missed my bus. I missed work. I didn't care. In that moment, I knew I could not take another twenty years – not even another twenty seconds – of Paris. I wanted home. The sticky heat, the bridge-top glimpse of fishermen standing up in their canoes as they cast their nets over the mirrored waters of the lagoon, the shrill voices of the morning girls strolling the street at dawn with that regal stride that came from balancing baskets full of goods on their heads, calling "Hot bread, hot bread" to draw out their first customers. I even missed the gridlock at rush hour, and the zémidjan who have never met a traffic light they didn't run.

Coming home was my move to make. Seeing me has to be your decision. I am waiting for you as I dance. I have been waiting for you all evening, through the cocktails, and the dinner, and the cutting of the cake.

The weight of your hand on my shoulder is not a surprise. Ahouefa, who is dancing next to me, seems to fade away. I will not turn around. I feel your arms closing around my waist. There is so much I want to ask you. So much I know already, through your family and mine: who you married, the names of your children... So much I don't know too. Are you happy? Have you forgiven me? *Are you happy?*

Your arms tighten around me, pulling, and I let go, allowing myself to sink against you, just for a minute. You are here, and the atrophied, hungering part of me that holds everything precious, and sweet, begins to expand, and fill out, gorging on water and sunlight after years of drought and cold.

You are here, and everything that is me settles with a sigh of contentment.

The Geography of Sunflowers

Michelle K. Angwenyi

Something about the geography of that rain, or the lack thereof as it came down in torrents, haunts me to this day. It's been a long while since I thought about that night in 'San Diego', which is what we call that strip of construction sand on the right side of the little pond behind the row of unfinished apartments. It was the day the scapula slid out so smoothly from between the ridges of cooked goat flesh, I nearly vomited.

And when I think of that night, I think of when I first read a poem by Craig Arnold in high school. It was called 'Asunder'. I kept the scrap of paper I wrote it down on, the pencil is fading, but something still breaks inside me every time I read it, and especially as I read it with you, and without you.

Music like the kind my father played in his shop every day after school was playing in the bus as it passed by the soap factory in Industrial Area, where it usually smells like flowers and fragrant chemicals, the same scent I always smelled laying my head on your chest, or burying my face in your flowered shirts when you weren't home.

Now, I cut meat. I cut meat, and I roast it, I grill it, I package it, I hang it. This sounds like brutal, cruel work, but I do it with every delicate intention there is, you should see how gently my fingers move. Gentle as the sunflowers from behind my house I always carry to work with me, gentle as the people who get a free one with their meat, gentle as the people who get a free one just because. I gave one to a group of beautiful children the other day, and their laughter was like the rain, like a cleansing ritual, like the rain that had not come in so long.

Sometimes I want to believe that if my fingers move the right way cutting meat, they could bring forth the rain from the sky. Or moving the right way could be writing, which I try earnestly to do, but I understand it could also be writing without hope of an answer, like in the poem. It could be this, the hopelessness that permeates my days, or it could be that you suddenly weren't there.

Many nights ago, I found myself making a pact with God, my greasy fingers clasped around the rosary you left behind. I was crying like you wouldn't believe. I told Him I would let go, and that He had to understand, He did this to me, that I wanted to live, but that He was forcing me towards death. That night, hopeless, I went to San Diego, and among the chang'aa drunk, sat on the sand with the scapula in my trouser pocket digging into the flesh of my thigh.

The first time I met you, it was in the dark shack where a group of us would meet Friday and Saturday evenings, not to do anything in particular but smoke and laugh, sometimes eat, sometimes drink. When you walked in for the first time, I didn't see your face, but there was something about how you took up the space in the corner you occupied. The way you were not quite folded over, but not quite standing straight either. You asked, through all our noise, very silently, if anyone had a box of matches for your cigarette. Everyone heard you, even as they pretended you did not exist. We did not know what to do, and so there was silence; then someone next to you passed you his matches after a good round of staring at one another.

It had started raining outside, windy all the way down to the soul, there was rhumba playing like always, and you walked out, shadows and all, leaving a trail of smoke behind you. I wondered how your cigarette would stay lit. In the shack, we continued to talk after you left, but your silence remained in that room, between our words. Even when we couldn't hear each other through the noise of the rain, the space you left behind always carried your silence which we were all fearfully aware of.

When I remember San Diego the night I was sitting on the sand with a scapula in my pocket, I really do not know what words or images to remember. San Diego that night was a mystery in that there was a man who was there who I don't think was really there. He came to me, jammed a gun between my shoulder blades. I said, Thank you, God, for remembering my prayers, for remembering my pleas for death. I don't know what he wanted to take from me, but at that moment, before the gun could be fired, I split into various pieces. I spread out over the sand. I was in the sky looking at myself. I was in front of the gun. I was buried under the sand. I saw he held a sunflower in his other hand, but before I could think about any of it, I watched him shoot the piece of me that he could touch, and that piece fell to the ground. My centre.

Then, from the sky, from the sand, from wherever else I was, I rushed back into myself, one body again, except for what had died. The man was running away, jumping over all the drunken men lying on the sands of San Diego, and I followed him, the scapula banging against my thigh. I took it out of my pocket, and caught up with him, and hit him in the back of the head with it. He stumbled and fell down, and then, scrambling to his feet, he looked back at me, with his big scared eyes, *I just wanted to give you a sunflower*, then he continued running into the darkness, leaving his sunflower behind on the ground. I picked up the scapula. That was the night I never thought of you again.

Before all this happened, you were a ghost. The same way the dead goat's flesh would be delivered every Tuesday and Friday, without fail, and without fail, I would wonder where the goat had gone. If there are goat ghosts, they must be asking themselves the same thing: where are they, and if they are still goats. I have never stopped asking myself some of these questions.

I ran out of salt one day. So I started walking in search of it, and I never went back to my shop for the rest of the week. I found some men who were sitting on a part of the road that was close to San Diego, fixing one of those constantly sparking electricity lines. I sat down next to them, and asked them what happens to the sparks when they disappear in the air. I didn't really listen to the answer because they didn't tell me what I wanted to hear: which was that the sparks fell to the ground and turned into salt. Or stayed in the air and turned into ghosts.

I walked back home, still wondering where your ghost was roaming, what you and the goat ghosts were saying about me. It rained that night like something had ended, like everything about the rain had to happen that night without apology, without question. The rain that came down that night must have dissolved all the salt in the earth, extinguished all the cigarettes, and washed out the smell of that Industrial Area soap from the sky.

The next day it was true that nothing was left on the earth, nothing could be smelt or touched or felt: the water had started everything anew. San Diego did not exist any more, and in its place was a thriving colony of little and big tadpoles that would probably not exist by the time the sun as we knew it decided to come out. As for where the world went that night it rained so much, maybe you and the goat ghosts can tell us, but it came back three days later on Tuesday when I got a call from the men who were delivering the meat, but could not find me to sign the delivery sheet. And so I went back, and I found salt right where it always was, like it had never run out.

The next time I met you, it was during the day and you were sitting outside the shack, like a radiance, and I was inside, like a termite afraid of the heat. Thank God I had cut a few of the sunflowers and put them in the cracked green vase next to the shack window, and hadn't given all of them to the children I'd met on the way to work.

I watched you smoke, and noticed you had on a helmet that you had not taken off, so how did I know it was you? And how were you smoking with the helmet covering your mouth? And how did all these events happen as they did, or did time just mix and make you as you were at that moment? You threw the cigarette butt on the ground at your feet. Instead of tobacco fumes, the wind brought in that detergent smell. Then you left before I could register the sound of your motorcycle speeding off down the road.

You came back the next day, and I was sitting outside this time, and I passed you a cigarette from inside my coat pocket, and a sunflower from the vase, both of which you took, and you smiled at me, this time without your helmet. And you passed the cigarette back, half-finished, climbed on your blue motorcycle, and sped away. One day, we talked. A few days later, you were in my room; a few days later, I was in yours. We always smoked, we always shared things as personal as our handwritings with each other. I always brought you sunflowers. You discovered 'Asunder', the only poem I could ever read, the only one that made me feel something, and you also saw everything I had ever tried to write that I hoped might make me feel something again.

I discovered your shelves filled with volumes and volumes of your collections of photographs – from your parents, from your childhood, from newspapers, magazines, even print-outs from the internet. Looking at them was like looking at you from the inside out. There were plenty of photos of motorcycles. Photos of beautiful people on motorcycles. Photos of grand buildings. Photos of people doing things, everyday things, and photos of people doing extraordinary things, like posing up in trees or hugging them, with garlands of bright sunflowers around their necks, which you said you made from the ones your neighbour Zephani Ombati would give you as a child. Here, I remembered Zephani Ombati with you: I put him into my childhood so I could remember him too.

You showed me a photo of your mother. I told you I could not remember having one. I could not remember my childhood as much as I tried; it felt as if I had always been living here and living here and living here, going to school and coming back home to meet my father outside his music shop, and then living here some more. And of course, as all the children and all the children who grew up could never forget, I told you I remembered Zephani Ombati and his sunflowers. You told me you missed your mother and hoped to see her again one day.

Where is she? *She just left.* Is that why you...? *I ride to see if I can see where she went. Can't have gone too far.* I can help you look. *You wouldn't know where to look, but I do. I'm figuring it out, it's taken me all my life. And I'm close to finding out where she is.* At that moment I should have known you would be leaving too, and it didn't take much of a mind, really, to know that you would go and never come back.

After you left, I wanted to kill, so I took pleasure in carving every piece of flesh from the dead goats as they came into my hands, telling myself that this was death I could make sense out of. Unlike the song, science and language of my high-school days, and almost everything that followed after, there was the clarity that came with purposeful death. I really do this for a reason, obscure as it may be, and I continue to have a reason to do this, I told myself.

Thoughts of Zephani Ombati came to me in the days before I went back to your room for the only time after your disappearance. He would plant fields of sunflowers, the only flowers for a great distance, behind our little house, and give them away every day in the streets. I never saw him tending to them there, though, but they could only have been planted by Zephani Ombati. For that name to keep ringing in my head like it was still around, still somewhere, was to say that Zephani hadn't run away, or that there was another one nearby. The thoughts that followed were inevitably of the street boys who would blow kisses through the windows of the bus as it rolled outside town from the bus station, on my way home after school. I smiled at their smiling faces in my memory. Zephani would come out of nowhere, and give them one giant sunflower, the biggest he had. This would make them so happy, and I remember this happiness like the street boys, like a flower, like Zephani.

Eventually, all your poetry became only the first symptom of a greater unrest within. After that, I began to witness you in various stages of mental anguish, beginning with the blank stares, then the endless tears, the long walks to nowhere, the silence – then the screaming. You would scream endlessly into the night, into the days, through the days, and there was nothing we could do to stop it. Finally, one day, it all stopped, and on that day the silence itself was a scream. We never saw you or your motorcycle again.

My father's music continued to play. I learnt how to cut meat. Salt it. Riding the bus through Industrial Area. Smelling the floral soap of your shared atmosphere. Smoking without you. One day, almost three months into being without you, in the depths of my despair, I went to my father's shop. I looked through the window before going in, and saw a gentle yellow swaying of a dress that could only have been your mother, dancing to the music. I had found her, meaning I had found you too, and in the way we ruin things by bringing them to our attention, or bringing ourselves to their attention, I rushed into the room, following your mother's swaying skirts. Swish! And the smell of Industrial Area detergent. Could it be you?

The music was something vague and warm and cold all at the same time – oddly suitable for the moment. The language was definitely saying something about a return; I knew this even if I did not understand the words. A return impossible to return from. Looking back, I now know that they weren't singing about your return to me, but your return to your mother. So I flew into the room, your mother sweeping around and around me, a sunflower in her hair. I spun around too, hoping to see her face, hoping to see yours in there as well. The sound of the music reduced to a soft beating, almost like that of the heart of a bird held in the palms.

A few days before this moment, I had already been aware of the creeping sense that comes before you discover something, or find the answers to big questions, or have big questions discover you.

Your mother turned her radiant head down. My father was crouching at the back of the room, behind a stack of records and cassettes. He raised his head to meet your mother's face and smiled. Then he looked at me standing near the door as he said your name, a big smile on his face – after all this time and searching, you were right here in the room, somewhere underneath our gazes, somewhere behind our eyes, and now moving in the room – if I closed my eyes and imagined quite hard, you would have been as good as standing in front of me, inside me.

Your mother and my father walked over to each other in the trance of the evening light, to hold each other in a long embrace. We had been held together in this strange dance, having come together in the history of time, but staying apart even then, yet always, somehow, in the yellowness, in the music, in the floral abundance of our togetherness, in a place we could find: elusive, transcendental, yet grounded in the earth of killing and eating goats, and grey floods and millions of tadpoles, and of desperate prayers to God, who in His wisdom, is both present, and not, just as you have learnt to be. Your mother and my father, they whispered to each other, almost like I wasn't in the room, and they whispered to me at the same time, and I know what they said to me as they said it to each other, but I can't remember. The room went dark, and I stood outside in the music that continued to play gently from inside.

I refused to go back to your room for three months after you left. After seeing your mother dance, when I could finally go see what you had left behind, I was immediately drawn to the beads hanging out from under your pillow. I lifted it, and saw your rosary nestled among the heads of more than a dozen sunflowers that were growing towards the light that came in from your window. They'd been alive all this time, growing from a soil I couldn't see, their roots going deep down into a place I would never know. Zephani had been there, telling me to pray, signalling me towards God. He'd given you a sunflower before you left, he'd been giving you many sunflowers. And there they were, but you weren't there, of course. Yet I could still smell the floral detergent.

I looked around your room, saw your shelves, their piles and piles of photographs sinking them slowly into the floor. There's a certain holiness to leaving things untouched, to leaving them where they are and letting God deal with them as He deals with things in our absence, or even in our presence where we refuse to see. And eventually I began to see you there, in the pages, in the photographs, walking through them, in them, climbing the trees, smelling the flowers, riding the bikes, dancing with your mother, searching for cigarettes – and then you looked directly at me, with those sharp black eyes, and I couldn't tell if they were seeing or unseeing, but they shone like they'd seen God, and you stretched your hand out into the air between us – and in a flash, a scapula hit me in the back of the head as I fell into a pile of sand near San Diego that was also salt, dissolving, that I had desperately been searching for, and electricity too, and most of all it was sunflowers, and you'd been gone for so long, more than three months, and I started running away, running away, running away from the thought of you, and then, like there was no time in which this had happened, I was walking towards myself, picking up the scapula and going home through a flood that was filled with tadpoles – I was the only one who hadn't seen that it had been raining since you left – and you, my centre, being gone, I continued walking on.

BIOGRAPHIES

AGAZIT ABATE is the daughter of immigrants and storytellers. She was raised in Los Angeles, and writes and lives in Addis Ababa.

HERAN T. ABATE is an Ethiopian storyteller. Her fiction will be published in the upcoming collections *Addis Ababa Noir* and the Caine Prize anthology. She has won an Emmy Award for 'The And', an interactive short film series she co-produced in New York.

ALITHNAYN ABDULKAREEM is a Nigerian writer. Her fiction explores relationships, mental health and queer identity. Her non-fiction covers mostly film/art and development. She has been published by *Transitions*, *Quartz Africa*, *Saraba*, *The Kalahari Review*, *Ozy*, and *The Africa Report*, among others. She works as an international co-ordinator for an education-based NGO in Uganda.

MICHAEL AGUGOM was born in Nigeria. His fiction has been published in *The Cantabrigian Magazine*, *Your Impossible Voice*, *Queer Africa 2: New Stories*, *Hypertext Magazine*, *Capra Review*, *Referential Magazine*, and *Courtship of Wind*. He is a recipient of the 2018 Iceland Writers Retreat Alumni Award.

HARRIET ANENA is a poet and short story writer from Uganda. She is the author of *A Nation in Labour*, a poetry collection. Anena's short stories and poems have appeared or are forthcoming in the Caine Prize anthology, *Jalada Africa*, *New Daughters of Africa*, *Enkare Review*, FEMRITE anthologies, Babishai Niwe poetry anthologies, *Writivism*, and *Sooo Many Stories*, among others. She lives in Kampala, Uganda, where she runs Word Oven.

MICHELLE K. ANGWENYI is a writer from Nairobi, Kenya. She was shortlisted for the 2018 Brunel International African Poetry Prize, and her poetry has been published in *Enkare Review*.

GENNA GARDINI is a writer based in Cape Town. She holds an MA in Theatre-making from UCT and is currently a PhD candidate at Queen Mary University of London. Her debut collection of poems, *Matric Rage*, was published by uHlanga Press in 2015 and received a commendation for the 2016 Ingrid Jonker Prize. She works as a Drama lecturer at CityVarsity and is the poetry editor for *Prufrock*.

INNOCENT CHIZARAM ILO finds time to read, write, tweet, and nurse his fragile ego in between receiving rejections from cat adoption agencies. His works have been published or are forthcoming in *Fireside*, *Reckoning 2*, *A Beautiful Resistance*, *Brittle Paper*, *Strange Horizons*, and elsewhere. He lives in Nigeria and is currently working on working on a novel(la).

CHERRIE KANDIE is a Kenyan writer and a senior at college in the United States of America. She also makes short films and enjoys dancing to Lingala (only in her room).

KHARYS LAUE is a South African writer whose short fiction has appeared in *New Contrast*, *Itch*, and *Pif Magazine*. Her academic work, which focuses on the depiction of race, gender, and animals in South African fiction, has been published by *Scrutiny2* and the *Journal of Literary Studies*. She is an animal-rights activist, and interested in the intersectionality between the human and the animal. She currently lives in South Korea, where she teaches English.

FARAI MUDZINGWA is a writer based in Harare. His fiction has been published in *Enkare Review* and Weaver Press, Writivism and Kwani? anthologies. He has written articles for *This Is Africa*, *The Africa Report*, *Harare News*, *TRT World*, *Contemporary&*, *Africa Is A Country*, NBO Press and *Chimurenga Chronic*.

CHOUROUQ NASRI is an associate professor in the department of English Studies at Mohamed 1 University in Oujda, Morocco. She has authored numerous publications on topics related to literature, media, and visual culture. She recently co-edited *North African Women after the Arab Spring: In the Eye of the Storm* (Palgrave Macmillan, 2017).

SUSAN NEWHAM-BLAKE is a Cape Town-based writer. She is the author of a non-fiction memoir called *Making Finn*. She has worked as an editor and writer, and has been published in *Marie Claire*, *Women's Health*, and numerous other magazines. She is currently employed as the Publishing Director of TPP. Her second book has just been accepted by Penguin for publication in 2019.

ADELOLA OJUTIKU is a Nigerian-Liberian writer based in the United States of America. Her WordPress blog, 'The Africanist Shelf', focuses on the untold stories of Africa and its diaspora, and on remedies for bridging the 'Diaspora Divide'. She is in her final year at the University of Rhode Island, where she advocates for race, gender, and LGBTQ rights.

TOCHUKWU EMMANUEL OKAFOR is a Nigerian writer whose work has appeared in *The Guardian*, *Litro*, Harvard University's *Transition*, *Warscapes*, *Columbia Journal*, and elsewhere. A 2018 Rhodes Scholar finalist, he has been twice nominated for the Short Story Day Africa prize and the Pushcart Prize. His writing has been shortlisted for the 2017 Awele Creative Trust award, the 2016 Problem House Press Short Story Prize, and the 2016 *Southern Pacific Review* Short Story Prize. A two-time recipient of the Festus Iyayi Award for Excellence for Prose/Playwriting, he is currently a 2018 Kathy Fish fellow and writer-in-residence at *SmokeLong Quarterly*.

NADU OLOGOUDOU is a Beninese writer, an avid reader and global nomad who sees home as the place where her books are. Her fiction explores the notions of identity, home, and expectations. She currently lives in Mali, where she works for a humanitarian agency. She is working on her first novel.

MPHO PHALWANE is a fiction and travel writer living in Johannesburg. In between working on her Master's thesis on sustainable African development, she dreams up alternative African futures in her fiction writing. Her favourite place is in her garden, reading, or hiking and dreaming of her next trip to the Drakensberg.

ALEXIS TEYIE is a Kenyan writer. Her poetry is included in the *Jalada* 'Afrofuture(s)' and 'Language' issues, and the *Black Girl Seeks* anthology; her short fiction has been published in Short Story Day Africa's *Water* anthology and GALA's *Queer Africa II* anthology. Her work is also featured in *Omenana, This is Africa*, Writivism, and Anathema's *Spec from the Margins* anthology, among others. Alexis recently co-authored a children's book, *Shortcut,* and a poetry chapbook, *Clay Plates (*Akashic Books, 2018), supported by the African Poetry Book Fund. She is a co-founder and poetry editor of *Enkare Review*.

ÉRIC ESSONO TSIMI is a Cameroonian writer and researcher. He attained a doctorate in humanities from the University of Grenoble-Alpes. His interests include migration, identity, linguistic ethnography, cultural psychology, and the intersections between these. In addition to his academic and artistic fields of work, Éric has expressed his views in media such as *Les Afriques, La Tribune, Le Monde, Slate, Huffington Post*, and *RFI*.

LESTER WALBRUGH lives in South Africa, writes short fiction, and is a member of the editorial team at *Type/Cast*, a literary journal curated from Cape Town. His writing has been published in an anthology spearheaded by South Africa's National Arts Festival, online journals, *The Kalahari Review, Asiancha*, and *ITCH* Magazine.

MICHAEL YEE is a South African writer born in Pretoria. His writing has appeared in the Short.Sharp.Stories anthologies.

NEBILA ABDULMELIK is a photographer, writer and poet from Ethiopia whose work is very much influenced by her pan-African and feminist values. She believes in the power of storytelling as a way of documenting life for the coming generations. Nebila has an MA in African Studies, with an emphasis on Gender and Development, from UCLA. She is currently based in Addis Abada.

HELEN MOFFETT is an author, editor, academic, and activist. She lives in Cape Town and has published university textbooks, numerous academic pieces, a treasury of landscape writings (*Lovely Beyond Any Singing*), a cricket book (with the late Bob Woolmer and Tim Noakes), an animal charity anthology (*Stray*, with Diane Awerbuck), the *Girl Walks In* erotica series (with Paige Nick and Sarah Lotz), two poetry collections (*Strange Fruit* and *Prunings*), a history of Rape Crisis, and a book on conserving water, *101 Water Wise Ways*. She loves collaborations and is passionate about the Short Story Day Africa project.

OTIENO OWINO has been an Assistant Editor at the Kenyan literary publisher Kwani Trust since 2015. At Kwani, he has been part of the editorial teams on the Kwani? Manuscript Project and the *Kwani?* journal. He was the junior editor for *Safe House: Explorations in Creative Nonfiction*, an anthology put together by Commonwealth writers, in which he worked with renowned editor Ellah Wakatama Allfrey. Otieno recently completed an MLit in Publishing Studies at the University of Stirling, UK, as a Commonwealth Scholar. He lives in Nairobi.

ACKNOWLEDGEMENTS

A good writer possesses not only his own spirit but also the spirit of his friends.
– Friedrich Nietzsche

$\mathcal{E}$very publication is the result of a team effort, and none so more than this.

Special thanks to the ID editing team, Helen Moffett, Nebila Abdulmelik and Otiene Owino, whose tireless efforts, keen eyes and dedication helped these twenty-one writers improve their stories and their craft. Also Jason Mykl Snyman and Karina Szczurek, who volunteered to spend many hours proofreading these pages.

Last year, Nick Mulgrew, who has been designing our covers and artwork since we first published *Feast, Famine & Potluck*, stepped down from the Short Story Day Africa Board to continue realising his dream of publishing beautiful poetry as the founder of uHlanga Press. We are grateful for his years of brilliant work and support of our anthologies. He designed the artwork for the call for the 2017 SSDA Prize: ID, and it was translated into the gorgeous cover that binds these pages by Megan Ross. Many thanks to them both for their lending us their skills. Megan is also responsible for the page design and layout.

Thanks to Dan Raymond-Barker and New Internationalist for believing in what we're doing and taking our stories to new readers.

Short Story Day Africa is a project that prides itself in having grown organically in response to the needs of writers on the continent. Over the years, we have identified problems with the reading and judging processes that gave an unfair advantage to previously published writers over new talent. This year we decided to take a new approach to reading the slush pile and to the judging process. As a project that seeks to disrupt preconceived notions of African writing and reclaim a space for African voices to write what they like, it is important to us that raw talent from all over the continent be recognised and nurtured. Therefore, the reading process was adapted in part due to inventive work being missed in past years by volunteer readers accustomed to reading published work, and in part due to the sensitive nature of theme – which called for stories around identity, in particular gender identity and sexual identity. We therefore chose a team of volunteer editors, writers and gender activists accustomed to reading raw work, and briefed them extensively on looking beyond the constraints of 'good English' to the kind of energetic story-telling that makes writing sing. Many thanks to our readers Karina Szczurek, Catherine Shepherd, Jason Mykl Snyman, Helen Moffett, Rahla Xenopolous, Louise Ferreira, Mary Watson, Nick Mulgrew, Rhoda Isaacs, Louise Ferreira – and particularly to Efemia Chela, who read over one hundred of the stories that were entered.

A new, more democratic approach was taken for the judging process, too. Grateful thanks are due to the Short Story Day Africa Board, which now includes the tireless Lizzy Attree, and *The Johannesburg Review of Books* (with special thanks to JRB's Jennifer Malec). Their careful reading of the stories and the new scoring system gave us a shortlist of nine exceptional stories – in the past, we have had six. The reading process and judging, as always, was blind, and stories were judged on merit alone. However, experience has taught us that a meritocracy can only work if the playing field is even (or has at least some of the worst bumps flattened out). Last year, we experimented with sending the stories for judging after one round of editing, and this year, judging took place after the editing process had been finalised, giving emerging writers an opportunity to compete as equals with those who have more publishing experience. The results speak for themselves, and something that is particularly gratifying is the youthful profile of both the longlist and the shortlist. In fifty years' time, as the world grumbles "Not another writer from Africa! Give the rest of us a chance!" every time the Nobel Prize for Literature is announced, we will smile from whatever realm we inhabit.

The team at Short Story Day Africa recognises that we have had the privilege of working in a country that has a vibrant publishing industry and literary landscape. The history of the African continent means that not all our compatriots have similar access to spaces where they can develop their craft. With the small resources at our disposal, we work hard to share the skills we have developed. However, without the assistance of organisations with similar aims, our arms would not be as long.

We cannot give enough thanks to the Miles Morland Foundation. Their generous funding assistance allows us to continue our work in developing writers and creating a platform for their voices. Their support has been invaluable in a time when funding for the project is dwindling. Thank you Miles, Michela and Mathilda for continuing to believe in us.

In partnership with Goethe-Institut, we ran eight ID Flow Workshops across the continent, in Addis Ababa, Cape Town, Johannesburg, Kigali, Lagos, Nairobi, Windhoek and Yaoundé. We are eternally grateful to the participating institutes and their liaisons: Julia Sattler, Yonas Tarekegn, Yonatan Girma, Nicole Meyer, Katharina Hey, Safurat Balogun, Eliphas Nyamogo, Detlef Pfeifer, Paulina Hamukwaya and Uwe Jung for their enthusiasm, and for providing materials and refreshments to keep the writers going during the long and arduous hours of the ID Flow Workshops.

Thanks also to my co-facilitators, who took the materials I designed and ran the workshops I could not with superb energy, each bringing their own wisdom and writing experience to the work: Agazit Guramayle, Efemia Chela, Louise Umutoni, Dami Ajayi, Anne Moraa, Sharon Kasanda and Dzekashu MacViban.

Thanks especially to Brigitte Doellgast and Stefanie Kastner, the Goethe-Institut's former and current Head of Library & Information Services, Sub-Saharan Africa, for being so open to our ideas.

Many thanks to the Cape Town Public Library and the Kigali Public Library, who gave us space to host the ID Flow Workshops in their cities.

Two years ago, I was asked by a writer who wished to become a professional editor if she could edit the *Migrations* anthology. As Short Story Day Africa's editing process was designed as a means to transfer skills to writers, it was not possible to have someone with no experience edit the work. However, her request planted the seed of an idea in my head, one that I bounced off Helen Moffett: to create an editing mentorship and extend the development work we do with the anthology to editors as well as writers. Helen's enthusiastic response spurred me on to approach our very first sponsor, Worldreader. As was the case last year, this year's editing team was part of a mentorship programme made possible with the generous support of Worldreader. I'd especially like to thank our Worldreader liaisons, Nancy Brown and Roberta Campassi, for their continued and enthusiastic support that has allowed us to grow that seed into fruit. Both Editing Fellows from last year now work professionally for both publishers and journals (and do fine work developing the talents of young and novice African writers), and we wish the same for the *ID* Editing Fellows.

And so the African literary landscape and industry grows, one hand helping another.

For an organisation that runs on volunteers and donations, I am eternally grateful to anyone who looks into their wallet and finds spare cash to assist us in continuing the work. Thank you Diane Awerbuck, Fiona Snyckers, Caryn Gootkin, Sarah Lotz, Kristien Potgieter, Jo-Ann Thesen and Nick Wood for your generosity.

I am grateful to the members of our board, who continue to work enthusiastically on all aspects of the project, for nothing more than the love of the African short story and their fellow writers: Helen Moffett, Isla Haddow-Flood, Karina Szczurek, Mary Watson, Jason Mykl Snyman, Lizzy Attree and Rahla Xenopoulos. It is thanks to their enthusiasm that the project continues to run in these dire financial times. We are also indebted to Efemia Chela and Catherine Shepherd for their hard work, ideas and effort.

The number of people willing to lend a hand grows every year and I am, as always, amazed at the generosity of spirit in the African writing community and those who support it.

If I have left anyone out, I apologise.

Hence, to all the writers and readers of African fiction: thank you.

Rachel Zadok
Short Story Day Africa

DONATE TO
SHORT STORY DAY AFRICA

Please support African writers, editors, and publishers.
Scan this qr code on SnapScan to donate. Every cent counts.

To donate through PayPal, please visit

shortstorydayafrica.org/donate

Caine Prize 2018

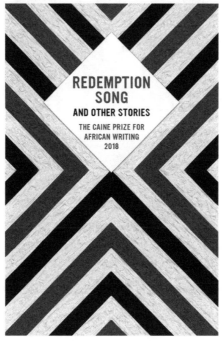

A boy dreams of escape to America from his troubled life in a slum on the Lagos lagoon... A woman discovers that a strange creature has taken up residence inside her vagina... Armed robbers announce their intention of visiting Abati Close, throwing all the residents into confusion... Meri is not like the other street kids – there has always been something different about her... The real story of Solomon Grundy, born on a Monday, involving an Ifá priestess-to-be, doomed romance and a breach in the fabric of time...

The authors shortlisted for the 2018 Caine Prize are joined by 12 writers who took part in the Caine Prize Writers' Workshop, where they each produced a special story for this volume.

Price: UK £8.99
ISBN 978-1-78026-461-5

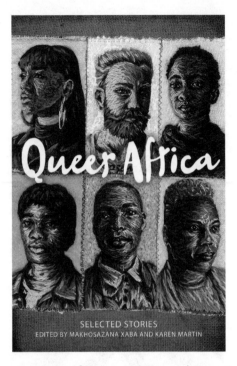

SELECTED STORIES
EDITED BY MAKHOSAZANA XABA AND KAREN MARTIN

In recent years some African governments have attempted to clamp down on sexual diversity. But Queer Africa will not be silenced, as this groundbreaking collection of stories from across the continent makes clear.

'Queer Africans exist in every stratum of society – even if some political leaders say we don't... This sterling collection contains exquisite writing that again and again has the ring of truth. It is a wonderful treat.'   Chiké Frankie Edozien

'In this timely collection, writers from across the African continent tell their stories of living, loving and longing. Here is fiction that is at times transgressive, at times gentle and tender, at times indignant – but always acknowledging the very human desire to find a place of solace, acceptance and love.'

Ellah Wakatama Allfrey

Price: UK £8.99, US $14.95
ISBN 978-1-78026-463-9